The Case of Kitty Ogilvie

By the same author

ELEANORA DUSE

MY GRAND ENEMY

THE
CASE OF
KITTY
OGILVIE.

A NOVEL

BY JEAN STUBBS

 Walker and Company • New York

First published in the United States of America in 1971 by the Walker Publishing Company, Inc.

Published simultaneously in Canada by Fitzhenry & Whiteside Limited, Toronto.

ISBN: 0-8027-0356-9

Library of Congress Catalog Card Number: 74-161103

Printed in the United States of America from type set in the United Kingdom.

This book is largely based on the meticulous researches compiled by the late Theodora Benson over several years.

When, by arrangement with the legatee of her copyrights, I came to go through her notes, I was fascinated by the mind that had collected and worked on them. Often, as I dug further into the case and asked questions, I found them already answered. I hope that this book will be worthy of its originator.

A percentage of the proceeds will go to one of her favourite charities, the People's Dispensary for Sick Animals.

The book would have been dedicated to Theodora Benson, but a dedication was found among her papers, and it was thought she would prefer this to stand. Theodora Benson would have dedicated her book to:

> DAVID TEMPLE BERNARD
> who was its begetter and who
> died in his fortieth year on
> the ninth of February, 1958.

> '*Still are thy pleasant voices, thy nightingales, awake:*
> *For Death, he taketh all away, but them he cannot take.*'

I should like to thank Dr Carson Ritchie, M.A., for all his help and advice with historical detail and background, and his readiness to be consulted on the slightest matter. Without him, the trial could not have been reconstructed.

J. S.

Contents

A Bride for Eastmiln

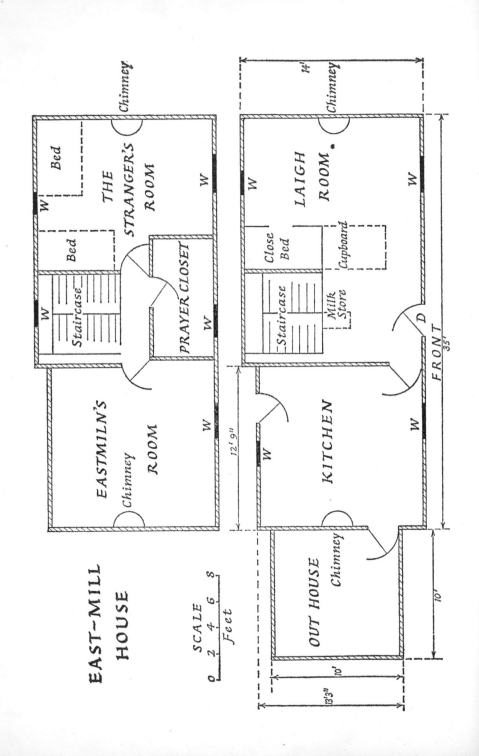

EAST~MILL HOUSE

SCALE

0 2 4 6 8
Feet

EASTMILN'S ROOM
Chimney
W

Staircase
W
Bed

THE STRANGER'S ROOM
Bed
W
Chimney
W

PRAYER CLOSET
W

LAIGH ROOM.
W
Close Bed
Milk Store
Staircase
Cupboard
W
Chimney
14¹

KITCHEN
W
W
D
FRONT
35¹
12¹ 9″

OUT HOUSE
Chimney
10¹
10′
13′3″

I

The marriage contract between Thomas Ogilvie, laird of East Mill, and Katherine Nairne, daughter of the late Sir Thomas Nairne, was signed at Glenkilry on 29 January 1765. As they penned their signatures – his a little cramped and ailing, hers dashing and careless – they might just as well have set their names at the foot of a death warrant. But, though Kitty's family was not over-pleased at her choice of husband, they admitted that he was well-born and kind; and she seemed so radiant, clinging to his arm and laughing into his face, that they conceded all could go well.

He was the husband she thought she longed for: a father–lover who would combine tenderness with passion. And she was more than he had dared dream of, even when he was young and brave and fought in his father's regiment for the Prince in the Rebellion of the '45.

So Thomas and Kitty graced the celebrations, and smiled, each wrapped in a different illusion. And then set out on that brief wedding journey which was to bring them to the house at East Mill, and disaster.

The two horses stepped out briskly over the frozen ground, in the bitter cold of an early February day. Their riders were diminutive figures in a vast white landscape: the man wrapped in his faded plaid, the girl in her glowing scarlet cloak and hood. Though the winter of 1765 had not been a severe one, winter was evident, etching the vistas of the Grampian rim, freezing the bracken into a fantasy of stiff lace, powdering the gaunt trees. On the ridge a stag lifted his head and sniffed the wind, remaining motionless

11

for a few moments before turning easily away. And before them the Glen of Isla cut deeply into the hills, its scattering of inns and kirk and cottages and farmhouses the only life in this immense and silent grandeur.

Thomas Ogilvie reined in his horse and cleared his throat. A man of forty, pinched by the weather, conscious of the differences in age and temperament, he sought for words to encourage his bride. She, reining obediently beside him, pushed back her hood and looked eagerly at the glen below.

'It'll not be long until we're home,' said Thomas, at length.

Poor words from a treasure-house of feeling, but she had enough spirit and loquacity for both of them. Already she was laughing and pointing to a rabbit, which leaped almost under the hooves of her husband's roan, and skittered to shelter.

'Are you cold, Katie?' Thomas asked shyly.

She was speaking and laughing at once, hopping from one thought to the next so that it made him dizzy to follow her. He listened in wonder, watching the bright face and glossy black curls, until she stopped to take breath.

'My mother will be ready for us,' said Thomas, picking on one sentence which suggested his bride was hungry. 'There'll be a grand meal at East Mill.'

She pulled up her hood and flicked the reins on her horse's neck.

'I'll race you, Thomas!' she cried, and was off before he could caution her, careering down into the glen over frozen hummocks and under laden boughs which discharged their contents on her shoulders. He was not possessed of a great imagination but love sharpens all the senses, and for a moment he pictured her flung down into the snow, lying in her mantle which was the colour of blood. So, clicking his tongue at her impetuous descent, he followed faster than he

12

should have done, and arrived at her side in a flurry of fear and anger. But, even as he opened his mouth to scold her, she leaned across his saddle and kissed him full on the lips to silence him.

'Behave yourself, woman!' he cried, without conviction.

'But I want to get there!'

'We'll soon be home,' he said patiently, 'but no galloping, mind. This is a drove road, not a turnpike.'

The chilly fields spread and stretched and climbed, marked by rough stone dykes. Glenisla was narrow country, with no more than half a mile of arable ground on either side of the water, and as they rode towards East Mill the few trees grew sparser: two firs huddled against the cold, a larch, a silver birch, a clump of stunted bushes.

'My father's family are great tree planters,' said Kitty, momentarily forlorn at the memory of the Nairne parkland, of the beeches about Dunsinnan House and those planted along the Lady's Walk twenty years before.

'Trees take all the goodness from the soil,' said Thomas. 'We live harder here.'

He had no need to tell her that. In summer, no doubt, the Angus braes would blow purple and yellow with heather and gorse; haystacks be tawny in the tawny fields; the blue lines of the Sidlaws to the south, the purple wall of the Grampians to the east, would loom protectively. But in the grip of winter Glenisla was a desolation of rock and snow and swollen river.

They crossed the ford in silence, their horses' feet throwing up sprays of water which hung in drops on the hem of Kitty's skirt. Thomas pointed out the kirk and manse standing squarely on their left, spurred his roan along the last stretch of frosted ground and cried, 'Welcome home, Mrs Ogilvie!'

The courtyard at East Mill House was formed by a granary and byre on one side and a stable and barn on the other. In the middle of the yard the fowls on the midden nursed their broods, and between the cobbles stumps of nettle and dock promised a fine harvest in the Spring. The house itself was low, white harled at the front and grey stone at the back, with a chimney pricking from each end. The sturdy door was set between two small windows. Five more windows stared from the thick walls on the floor above. With the total disregard for view, prevalent at that time, the farm had been built in a hollow. One little window at the rear looked out on to the Freuchies, but the rest were confronted by a bare hillside with no special beauty to commend it. And in its claustrophobic setting East Mill bore a remote and private air.

Following her new husband more slowly now, the girl said to herself, 'There is painted paper on the walls of my mother's dining room.'

He did not hear her, clattering excitedly into the yard, jumping from his horse with the agility of a man half his age, shouting that they had arrived. And as the house became alive with welcome he came to lift her carefully down, putting back her hood with his own hands that they might see her. She clung to his arm, trembling, for their marriage was but four days old, and she not yet twenty.

They pressed forward to greet her: Lady Eastmiln very gracious in her present poverty, Thomas's plain raw-boned sister Martha who was to be married herself soon, and a long sunburned young man in his early twenties – who swung her up in his arms without ceremony and kissed her soundly on both cheeks.

For a moment, half-sick with strangeness, she wondered how to take this familiarity. Then as they all laughed and scolded him, and she stared into his smiling face, she was back in an instant at Dunsinnan House where frolic was paramount. He swung her up again and she squealed with pleasure and pretended fright.

14

'Set her down, Patrick, you great fool!' cried Lady Eastmiln, but her tone was indulgent and Kitty recognised a favourite.

She came to earth with a flourish of red heels, and leaned against her bridegroom to recover breath. Tenderly, as though she might break in his hands, Thomas took off her cloak and pushed her forward to make her obeisance.

'Ma'am,' said Kitty, dropping a deep curtsey to Lady Eastmiln. 'Miss Ogilvie,' another curtsey.

She acknowledged with a smile and an inclination the bobs of Lizzie Sturrock and Annie Sampson the maids. And they, in their short coarse plaid gowns and dirty bare feet, were agape at her beauty. Then she turned to Patrick and said, 'I believe I have met this gentleman before?' in her best manner, eyelids half-closed, fingers fashionably extended for him to kiss.

They roared again, enjoying her teasing, and she laughed with them and tossed her curls and showed her excellent teeth, mistress of the situation. While Patrick Ogilvie, late-lieutenant of the 89th Foot, made a fine bow as he stooped over her hand.

'We are in straitened circumstances, Katherine,' said Lady Eastmiln, 'owing to our allegiance in the '45 to the King across the water. An allegiance of which we are proud,' she added, 'despite the fact that my son Patrick has worn King George's uniform for five years and served him abroad.'

Her eyebrows lifted, indicating that life was hard, opportunities few and principles often expendable.

'Give me a rushlight, Lizzie,' she commanded, turning to the taller of the two servants. 'I shall show Mrs Ogilvie to her room myself. And Thomas,' as sternly as though he were a boy instead of the laird, 'take off that damp plaid or you'll catch your death. Patrick, give Thomas a dram. Come, Katherine, Lizzie has lit a fire for you.'

The smell of peat in the parlour hearth was sweet and close. Lady Eastmiln switched up her shabby skirts and held the light high, preceding Kitty up the wooden stairs. The laird's bedroom, known grandly as the West Room, had been swept in honour of her coming, and fresh rushes lad down. The great bed, in which Lady Eastmiln had borne five sons and a daughter, took up one quarter of the space. Otherwise there was a heavy clothes chest, an oval table with a piece broken from one leaf and two old rush chairs.

Lady Eastmiln set down the light and drew the curtains at both windows.

'It will not be difficult to find your way about the house,' she said with some irony. 'On the other side of the staircase is the Strangers Room where my son Patrick sleeps. On the landing is the laird's private prayer chamber, but we find it more useful to keep the meal and beef there, and to use it as a storeroom. And we are none of us kirk-crowders, so the laird might say what prayers he has on his knees at the bedside. Below this room is the parlour which you have already seen, where Martha and I sleep. And beneath Patrick's room is the kitchen where the maids have a box bed.'

In Dunsinnan House, thought Kitty, we have a Powder Room and a Rose Room and a dining room and my mother's sitting room, as well as the bedchambers. But she only smiled nervously at the upright old woman who watched her. And then was suddenly laughing and chatting about the cold wedding in her sister Bethia's home at Glenkilry, and the colder journey here, and the night they had spent with the Shaws of Little Forthar, and the two with her friends the Farquharsons of Lintrallen, of a gown she had forgotten to pack, and Thomas's shabby plaiden jacket which she abhorred.

Lady Eastmiln listened and faintly smiled, losing the drift of this changeable nonsense.

16

'You must speak up and speak slower for me, child,' she said, as Kitty drew breath. 'I get deafer every day and I can't tell the half of your clatter. Thomas's jacket, did you say? He must not leave that off, miss, nor his body-belt!'

Kitty made a private face into her little travelling portmanteau, and wondered whether it might be possible to wear her silk gown for supper.

'The laird,' said Lady Eastmiln, pressing her point, 'is delicate in health and no longer a young man. He suffered an ulcerous fever six years ago and must keep his body warm lest he catch a chill. Do you hear me, child?'

But Kitty was drawing out the gifts Lady Nairne had instructed her to bestow, and pressed little luxuries of preserved fruits, of English pickles and Catch-up sauce upon her new mother-in-law.

'I can see,' said Lady Eastmiln, looking askance at these strange bottles and jars, 'that we shall have some gaiety in the house, at least. There's been a sorry lack of it these twenty years. I leave you to warm yourself. Supper is ready when you care to come down.'

'If I could have some water, ma'am, to wash my hands and face, I should be vastly obliged,' said Kitty.

'Water?' said Lady Eastmiln, puzzled. 'But it is not Sunday, Katherine.'

'I should like to refresh myself after the journey,' said Kitty apologetically, who had been brought up unfashionably clean.

'Well, you may have the water,' said Lady Eastmiln. 'The water is no trouble, but I do not know what we shall put it in. Would a porridge plate suit your purpose? Or Lizzie could bring in the calf's drinking bowl.'

'A porridge plate would suit admirably, ma'am.'

'Very well,' said Lady Eastmiln, very dignified. 'But if I were you I should take care, Katherine. So much washing, and in the winter months, can do you an injury.'

17

'I am obliged to you, ma'am,' said Kitty. 'I shall be down directly.'

Lady Eastmiln paused by the door, curious as to the white soap produced from Kitty's portmanteau.

'You must have got that from Edinburgh,' she said, becoming even more stately. 'I have heard it is a penny the ounce. For ourselves, when we wash at all, we find plain oatmeal serves us.' Another thought occurred to her. 'East Mill is considered a very fine house for these parts,' she said, conscious of unspoken criticism. 'And we do not go short of food or firing as many do. Though I have never tasted an English pickle.'

She emphasised the 'English' to make Kitty aware that they were honest folk who wanted no foreign heresies on their table. But the pretty face and smiling mouth softened her next remark.

'You will do very well, child,' she said, 'and no doubt supply us with amusement, which we sorely lack – or did, until my son Patrick was invalided home. Now *he* is a merry fellow, and can play the fiddle and sing as well as any I ever heard. And though I am old now, and life has been hard, I was once as young as you.'

Alone in the room Kitty shook out her one silk flowered gown and searched the bare walls for a looking-glass.

'There'll be no looking-glasses at East Mill,' her mother had said, and in a burst of generosity had let her take her own, which Kitty now removed from the protection of two cotton shifts.

The image in the glass pleased her intensely, and she thought of all the pretty compliments Pieter van Dukker had paid her when he painted her portrait four years ago. The fine arts were not greatly encouraged in Scotland, which was still a poor country after the ravages of Prince Charlie's holocaust, but the Nairnes were fashionable folk and encouraged the young Dutchman – who had travelled

18

from London to Edinburgh and was quite the rage – to broach the wilds of Dunsinnan. So he had travelled somewhat painfully along the wretched roads, with his man jogging behind him, laden with canvas and colours and frames.

Courtship mingled with the sittings, and Pieter van Dukker had gone so far as to ask Sir William Nairne, Kitty's uncle, for her hand in marriage. He was paid his ten pounds and told to go about his business, and Kitty had cried for two days.

'For his hair was as smooth and yellow as butter,' she said to herself, remembering, 'and though he was a big man he walked very light. Poof!' she cried, sending this old ghost into the shadows, 'I was a child of sixteen, and did not know my own mind!'

But she had known her mind about Thomas, though the family were bitterly against her choice.

'You may as well take a vow of poverty and chastity as take Thomas Ogilvie,' her mother had said. 'He was no great hand with the lassies that ever I heard, and his family live in the mud with their sheep – which was all King George ever left them!'

'Oh, divil burst them!' cried Kitty, jubilant with her newly married state.

So she thanked Lizzie for the slopping porridge plate of cold water, and coaxed help from her with regard to the silk gown – which Lizzie smoothed in amazement. And, as a final adornment, Kitty fastened about her neck an amber drop which Thomas had bought her, when William Craig the chapman called at Glenkilry. She was ready to dazzle the entire world, let alone three poor Ogilvies with a farm swinging about their necks.

The food was abundant, but indifferently cooked and worse served. Kitty wiped a grease smear surreptitiously

19

from her pewter plate before a portion of rabbit, smothered with onions, was slapped upon it. They ate together: Thomas in his high-backed chair, Lady Eastmiln and Martha on one side, Patrick and Kitty on the other, the servants sitting with their backs to their betters, on stools at the foot. Dishes were set on the table all at once: a thick barley broth, a sheep's head still bearing tufts of singed wool, eggs in the shell, the smothered rabbit and a tansy baked in honour of the occasion.

The table-cloth had been woven locally and bore signs of the mid-day meal, and when Kitty saw the maids dip into the platters with their horn spoons, and observed that Patrick and Lady Eastmiln shared the same fork, she was glad that her mother had provided her with her own cutlery. Though by the time the silver knife, fork and spoon had been passed admiringly round the diners she wished there was a basin handy, in which she could wash them. Her table napkin seemed indifferently clean, but Lady Eastmiln interpreted her look another way.

'We have a fine stock of linen put aside,' she said grandly, 'but I'm not so foolish as to use it. Why I have cloths that I brought with me on my marriage that have never so much as been spread.' And she bent to her food with an air of satisfaction.

In my mother's house, thought Kitty, we have the Edinburgh weave in patterns of lavender knot and burdseye. And my uncle's linen comes from Holland and Bethia has Dunfermline damask.

'Martha has baked the tansy,' said Lady Eastmiln, and Martha blushed and ducked her head.

'Martha having caught a husband,' said Patrick, 'is determined to keep him by lining his stomach well!'

He saw that his sister was uncertain of the compliment, and immediately softened it.

'For beauty fades and youth vanishes,' he said, half-

20

serious, half-fanciful, 'but the wife who keeps a good table is a jewel in her husband's bonnet!'

Martha laughed and blushed again, and hid her hands in the folds of her grey skirt, seeming suddenly large and red and awkward.

'You are to marry Mr Andrew Stewart of Alyth, I believe?' said Kitty, to keep the conversation alive, for it had lain heavily upon them so far.

Martha nodded and smiled shyly.

'Has the cat got your tongue, miss?' Lady Eastmiln demanded, spooning tansy on to Kitty's dirty plate. 'Tell your new sister Katherine the day!'

'Friday, March the twenty-second, Katherine. God willing.'

'And then there'll be but one in my bed,' said Lady Eastmiln, practical.

'Aye, indeed,' said Patrick, 'for Martha will be in Andrew Stewart's bed – God willing!'

'Hold your tongue,' cried Lady Eastmiln, in the sharp tone that was still indulgent. 'You put your sister to shame, and Katherine is but newly a bride. You are not carousing with your fellow-officers now, sir!'

The ale was plentiful, and two bottles of claret had been set near Thomas, though only one glass to drink the wine stood at his elbow.

'Then let us drink to long nights and happy days,' cried Patrick, filling the solitary glass and passing it round for the toast.

Kitty slid a look at Thomas, but he was eating steadily, either not listening, or forgetting the fiasco of his wedding night when a nervous stomach warred with desire and won. She hoped that married life would become more satisfactory, and sighed, and caught Patrick's glance. He winked, and she blushed.

'Why, what's all this?' he cried incredulously. 'Here are

all the lassies ducking their chins and turning the colour of boiled beets at the mention of long nights.'

Lizzie Sturrock and Annie Sampson were convulsed, and Lady Eastmiln warned them that if they could not behave more seemly they must finish their meal in the kitchen.

'Eat your pudding, sir, and be silent! Katherine, what do you think to Martha's tansy?'

'It is exceedingly good, ma'am.'

'Tell your sister Katherine how you make it, Martha!'

Obediently, Martha said, 'Of eggs and cream and sugar, well-beaten, and flavoured with rose-water and the juice of tansy herbs, and the whole baked in butter.'

Katherine smiled, and removed a cow hair from her pudding. The conversation floundered again, but Lady Nairne had trained her three daughters to sustain it at all costs.

'Why, what a heap of weddings you have in your family, ma'am,' Kitty said. 'Your youngest son, Alexander, was married but a fortnight since!'

The comment brought Thomas's head up from his tansy with a jerk. Lady Eastmiln set down her spoon and Martha stared at an ale-stain on the cloth.

'I beg your pardon, ma'am,' said Kitty, dashed. 'I had forgot the wedding did not please you.'

'Oh, but my mother was delighted,' said Patrick drily, 'on top of his medical fees at Edinburgh, and his debts to the ale-house, Alexander has done her the honour of bringing a porter's daughter into the family.'

'I daresay the slut was with child by him,' said Lady Eastmiln.

'That is no excuse for making a match,' said Thomas sternly. 'He must have got many a porter's daughter in trouble before now.'

'Her name is Ann Rattray,' Martha whispered across to Kitty, but Lady Eastmiln's ears were sharp enough to catch that indiscretion.

'Her name is of no consequence,' she said coldly, 'since she will not be received in my house, though they married twenty times. My youngest son, Alexander, is a scandalous fellow, Katherine. He was apprenticed at fifteen to Dr Murray of Edinburgh, but has passed no examination that I am aware of. His talent is the ability to call every tavern drab in the city by her first name. The subject is now closed. Will you have more pudding?'

'No thank you, ma'am. I have had sufficient.'

'We must entertain Katherine,' said Lady Eastmiln in a different voice, for the girl was pretty and well-bred and had brought a fine dowry with her. 'Thomas tells us tales of a merry household at Dunsinnan and another at Glenkilry and we must not let you be dull here. Patrick, give us a tune or two on your violin.'

'Yes, Patrick,' said Thomas, 'and while the women clear away – a word in your ear, brother.'

As they mounted the stairs he slipped an arm about Patrick's shoulders.

'She's very young,' he said in a low voice, for every spoken word could be heard through the unplastered walls. 'I'm twice her age, and her family were against the match. I understand why,' he added quickly. 'She could have done better for herself by far. But she wanted me, brother, she was not forced. They let her have her way in the end, for she is the youngest daughter and the favourite . . .'

They stopped on the small landing and looked at each other; Patrick holding the candle higher to see his brother's face.

'So what do you ask of me, Thomas, aside from my heartiest good wishes?'

The laird clenched both hands and put them to his breast in an unusual display of feeling.

'I have a slow tongue and a slow head, brother. What I

feel for her I cannot say. Keep her happy for me, while you are here. She will settle in a month or so, a year or so. You know how it is. Women change when their bairns come. But she is only a bairn herself, and strange to us. Amuse her for me.'

Only Thomas in his innocence could have asked that. Only Patrick's light heart and head would have accepted the request.

'She'll be as safe with me as an egg in a duck's belly,' he said earnestly. And then gaiety came uppermost and he laid a hand on his brother's sleeve. 'You could not have asked this of Alexander!' he observed mischievously.

'Oh – aye,' said Thomas wryly, understanding him. 'I wouldn't trust that corbie to give me the time of day!'

II

The city of Edinburgh towered within its walls, ten and twelve stories high along the mile of street from Holyrood to the Castle, and branches of wynds and closes housed its people cheek by jowl. The narrow lanes and projecting gables brought neighbours near enough to 'heng oot the windy' and exchange news. And below them ran the great gutters full of filth and refuse in which pigs rooted for scraps. But the city, though dirty and malodorous, with its evening stench of urine and excrement paralleled by the stink of burning brown paper supposed to deodorise it, was nevertheless oddly beautiful. And its roistering social life, passed in taverns and oyster cellars and clubs, in dances and assemblies and concerts, and in the bright slaughter of the cock-pits, added to its charms. Only the previous year a theatre had at last been licensed. And for thirty years the first circulating library had flourished in one of the shops in the Luckenbooths. Gentlemen enjoyed archery and golf and raced their horses on the sands of Leith. And ladies held small tea-parties in their drawing rooms if they had them, and in their bedrooms if they were cramped for space.

But the taverns supplied both accommodation and refreshment, business and pleasure. In these dingy rooms clients, lawyers and advocates discussed their cases over a mutchkin stoup of sherry: tradesmen and customers wet a bargain with ale: the Lord Provost drank his guests under the table with French wine: the blades toasted their mistresses in punch and brandy: the porters drank the beverage which possibly took its name from them: and all who could afford it became merry or fuddled on whisky.

This was an age where a man was judged according to his capacity for liquor, an age where any excuse was good for a glass, an age where the host was accounted poor in hospitality if his fellow-drinkers could walk home. And into this age and this city Alexander Ogilvie had been dispatched at fifteen, to be apprenticed to Dr Murray for five years, and gain a degree at the Edinburgh University Faculty of Medicine. As the youngest son of a small estate he could expect nothing that his own wits and industry did not obtain for him. As a late child, arriving unexpectedly in his mother's middle-age, he had not been welcome. His temperament and her obduracy estranged them one from the other; and his violent demands for notice, since love was not available, cut him off from the rest of the family. So Lady Eastmiln did her duty by giving him an education, and made sure that the education took place a good way off. Thomas had brought him, kindly and paternally – for there was twenty years between them – in 1760. And there he left him, to live for three years with Dr Murray, and then to sink or swim with the other students until he should be qualified.

Even nature had not been on Alexander's side, for he stood a head shorter than his other brothers and swarthy as a gipsy, with thick black brows that met tempestuously over his nose. But he was a strong and handsome lad in a fierce way, and possessed of a spirit as wild as his appearance. His friends and family nick-named him the *corbie*, the carrion crow, finding in his purposeful waiting and black visage something akin to the bird which feasts on another's downfall.

That February evening in 1765, the corbie sat in Luckie Middlemass's tavern in Cowgate. And the girl squealing in his lap was neither his bride Ann Rattray nor his steady mistress Anne Clarke. She had indeed only just made his acquaintance, being new to her work and scarcely fourteen; had passed by with a platter of raw oysters and been pulled

26

suddenly on to the knees of this gentleman who made free with her gown. He was already drunk and likely to be drunker, and she struggled in genuine fear for her safety. For had they not brought the oyster wenches in to dance the other night, and taken them on the floor like animals? So she slapped his dark cheeks and pulled his dark hair and screamed aloud for her mammy.

'Put the bairn down, Alex,' said a dry voice.

Miraculously he did, and the girl bobbed a curtsey to her rescuer and began to retrieve the fallen oysters as fast as she could, and wipe them on her skirt.

'I had forgot,' said Alexander Ogilvie, 'that you frequented these kinds of places, Miss Clarke. But then, I took you *out* of a brothel a year ago, didn't I?'

She did not answer, mopping porter from the seat of the chair with her handkerchief. Then she sat composedly in her decent grey gown and decent black cloak and bonnet, like some decent little governess seeking an interview with her employer.

'We've not spoken since my wedding night, have we, Annie?' he said, and began to laugh. 'Ah! that was a braw wedding, Annie. The bride commended herself to my graces by dancing on the table until she fell among the pintpots – and may she miscarry in consequence! – and the bride's father first offered to break my head if I ever laid a hand on his daughter, and then knocked down his good wife to set me an example. You should have come, Annie. You should have come to drink our health.'

'I was not asked, as you well know,' said Anne Clarke ironically. 'Nor was I told that you intended to marry her – I'd thought you were lifting her skirts, not losing your senses!'

'Aye. Well. We thought it best you shouldn't be troubled, Annie, since you were sharing my lodgings at the time – and might have prevented it.'

27

She looked at him contemptuously, at the black hair falling in his eyes, at his stained clothes and dirty linen.

'I *should* have prevented it,' she observed. 'You did not have to marry the slut. There are two or three that could have filled her belly, besides yourself. But given a fool and a gentleman, and one that could make their daughter a doctor's wife, the Rattrays chose *you* to sire the bastard!'

'What does it matter?' he said idly. 'I can go to the devil all the faster.'

'How did they get you to agree? Did Rattray threaten you?'

He nodded.

'You should have told me,' she said, musing over possibilities now past. 'But instead you come bursting into our room with a drunken rabble behind you, and tell me you have stood up before the minister – and I can take my leave. With your bride grinning, and the guests laughing, and your precious father-in-law offering me shelter!'

He shrugged uncomfortably, and glanced slyly from under his lids. It had been the only time he saw her vulnerable. The remembrance frightened and exhilarated him.

'Did Rattray put you up to *that*, too?' she asked fiercely.

He frowned, pretending to wipe a drop of liquor from his shirt front.

'Did Rattray say to you, "*Let's have a wee bit of sport with your whore, Alex. Fair exchange is no hardship. Your drab for my lassie – and here's a dram of it!*" – did he say that?'

'It was only in fun, Annie,' said Alexander. 'We were pissing drunk. And how could I have a wife and a mistress in one room? Rattray helped me out – and, after you'd fetched him a slap that staggered him, you went off as peaceable as if it were your own choice.'

'I am not lodging with the Rattrays out of choice,' said Anne coldly, 'but out of necessity. Where else could I go, but back to a bawdy house?'

He sniggered, and then lowered his eyes at the expression on her face.

'And how do you pay for your lodging, Annie?' he asked slyly.

'How I pay is my business, not yours, but between us we have adopted a fine family. The father a hog, the mother a rabbit, and the daughter a bitch. Well, I shall think of something. In the meantime,' she continued, and her tone was lightly conversational, 'your family has cut you off, declining to claim kinship with the brat of an Edinburgh porter!'

'Who told you that?'

'William Craig the chapman, who plies his wares between here and the country surrounding East Mill.'

'You have not come to advise me of my ill and ungrateful return for your services in bed and at board?'

'To what purpose?' said Anne Clarke. 'You will be glad of me very soon. I look to your comfort and good fortune, and am a better mistress than any doxie that spread her legs in Edinburgh.'

'That's true, that's true. Annie, you are the only wench I ever knew who could hold her tongue and keep her head.'

He raised his tankard of porter to her and drank, the drops falling from his chin to the breast of his scuffed velvet coat.

'And I come with news of other weddings,' said Anne. 'The Ogilvies have taken to coupling with a vengeance, it seems. The laird, your brother Thomas, has taken one bonnie Katie Nairne to wife. And your sister Martha is at last to be married to Andrew Stewart of Alyth.'

The news reached him, even through the quantity of porter, and all he could say was, 'Who told you?'

'William Craig the chapman. Who else?'

He rubbed his eyes as though to bring fresh light on this

new turn of events.

'As to Martha – I am glad of it. For she has been under my damned mother's hand all these years, and waited for him to speak. But as to Thomas – you say she is bonnie? Who is she? Where did he find this bonnie bird that would lie with such an ailing stick as himself?'

'Katherine Nairne has brought a dowry with her of five thousand pounds Scots. But that was not the inducement. She is young, she is pretty, and she comes of good breeding stock. Two sisters, two brothers, all healthy. And her sister Bethia, who married George Spalding of Glenkilry, presents her husband with a bairn a year – and each bairn as sound as a nut.'

He sat down his tankard and flung himself back in his chair, glowering at her.

'You are a bearer of ill tidings, Annie. I thought the malaria might have carried Patrick off, and Thomas dropped dead with a chill on the belly!'

'Yes,' said Anne. 'I know you hoped for that, and I told you many times that only the weak *hope* for something to happen. The strong *make* it happen.'

'Unmake his wedding, then!' Alexander cried. 'For if you do not there'll be half a dozen fat brats between me and the estate!'

'I have been thinking,' said Anne, apparently at random, 'that it would be well in me to pay my respects to your mother. To smooth the way towards a reconciliation with your family.'

'They'll not speak to me again, because of the Rattray jade.'

'But she will speak to *me*, Alex. I am her dead sister's child, and your cousin.'

He laughed out loud.

'Shall you tell my mother that you worked in a brothel, first as one of the taupies and – after your bloom had faded

– as one of the madams? Shall you regale her with tales of Auld Reekie?'

Her colour did not alter. She became, if anything, a shade more demure.

'I shall explain that after my own parents died I was thrown unhappily upon a world that does not welcome virtue. That my life was hard and my principles preserved at the cost of poverty and loneliness. That her despised son Alexander, under whose dirty waistcoat lies a good heart, showed me both kindness and friendship – and treated me as well as though I was his own sister. Will that do?'

He flung back his head and slapped his thighs, laughing until he coughed, and coughing until he was wordless.

'You talk too much and think too little, Alex. I never utter a word nor write a line that has no bearing on the course I have set myself. I hold my tongue and put reins on my pride. I watch and plan and wait. You know that. How could you have lived without my management? And who else, after your treacherous foolery with Ann Rattray, would have come to this tavern and spoken like a true friend?'

He shuffled his feet: a handsome, reckless lad of nineteen.

'There is a weakness in the men of your family,' said Anne relentlessly. 'Your father threw in his lot with Prince Charlie, instead of finding out which way the wind blew. And even when his friends helped him from Edinburgh jail he had to fall and break his neck! Your eldest brother, discovering that life after the '45 was not to his liking, hanged himself in a sheep-cote. And there is another fool for you – he fails to hang himself the first time because the rope stretches! Does he thank God on his knees for a second chance? No. With the mark of the rope still raw on his neck he digs a trench beneath his feet – and hangs himself for good on the next try!'

31

'That's enough, woman. I need another tankard. Hey, you, wench. Fetch me another.'

'I have not yet finished,' said Anne. 'I am not speaking to you out of malice or amusement. I am setting my finger on a weakness that I wish you to recognise, and to avoid. Look at Thomas, an old maid riddled with stomach ulcers and under his mother's thumb! Look at Patrick, the dare-devil, mother's favourite child! Oh, such a fine laddie, off to serve in India at fifteen with King George's soldiers – that same King George who imprisoned his father and impoverished his family, as it happens. And all goes so well. Patrick is brave and well-liked and ready to be promoted as Captain. And then, of a sudden, he is not healthy and must be invalided home. His mother, glad to have him at her skirts again, says he is simply wanting a little rest, a little change. Fiddlesticks, say I! He is there for good, crippled with malaria, his commission resigned, no means of earning any other living, and only his wits and his fiddle-playing to compensate for his keep.

'Look at *you*! Do you work to take a degree and make a profession for yourself? No. But you will scramble some sort of knowledge together from your Dr Murray, so you *could* practise outside Edinburgh or Glasgow. And will you, Dr Ogilvie, find yourself a practice? No. You will frequent the taverns and oyster cellars, looking – I suspect – for some woman who will keep you and sleep with you and think for you. Well, you have found her.' She touched her breast. And for the first time, had he looked up from the wet table, he would have seen how much he meant to her. 'I am everything you need,' Anne continued. 'I even understand that a lad who is barely twenty will tire, from time to time, of a woman who is thirty-two. I do not mind if you lift a stray petticoat now and again. But what *do* you do? You *marry*, you *marry*, a porter's daughter who can only be a drag on the pair of us!'

He said wretchedly, his bombast leaked away, 'I knew you would make a pother, Annie!'

She said, 'I have never once raised my voice, and never shall. If it is the fine company that disturbs you let me set your mind at rest! All about us think I am your decent wife, pleading with you to come home to the bairns. One last word, Alex, you need all the money that can be got from that estate. You are not the laird, so cannot inherit. You are not Patrick, your mother's favourite, so cannot wheedle money from Thomas through her. You have only one hope of return and that is through me.'

'And what can *you* do?'

'I can find out what is happening, and turn it to your advantage.'

'How?' he said, slurring the word. 'How?'

She lifted her shoulders and spread her hands in a rapid, graceful gesture, and laughed for the first time that evening.

'What a child you are,' she said fondly. 'How should I know until I get there? And now,' she took money from her purse, though there was little enough in it. 'I'll pay the reckoning, and you must go home.'

He scratched himself fretfully. The pints of porter and Anne's frankness had taken the man away and left the boy behind.

'I think that damned jade has brought bugs to my bed,' he complained.

'I do not doubt it.'

'I want to go home with you, Annie,' he complained, and would have laid his head on her breasts if he could have stood up.

'Very well,' said Anne, who had expected this. 'Then we must get rid of your cutty queen and send her about her business.'

'But if her father threatens?'

'I know every rat-hole in Auld Reekie,' said Anne com-

33

posedly, helping him to his feet. 'So we will turn your lady wife out, and scotch the bugs with oil. And if her father thinks to bite us I shall tell him that there are bigger rats in Edinburgh than Rattray – and one of them might tear his throat!'

III

The laird had been up two hours, and taken his 'morning' of ale and visited his stables and fields, before Kitty came yawning down the stairs in her red and white calico bedgown. She noted with distaste that the table-cloth had not been changed, and showed unmistakable signs of last night's banquet. But there was porridge with milk, and a wooden platter of barley bannocks, butter scattered with cow hairs, a jar of honey, and mutton collops for the men. Thomas said grace and sat down to his breakfast, resplendent in his bonnet. Patrick was not yet up, and Lady Eastmiln explained his late rising as being in consequence of his health.

So Kitty drank a dish of tea and ate a little porridge and spread a bannock with honey. And afterwards, when she had dressed and set her gown to rights and curled her hair, she had nothing to do but sit and look at the bare hillock in front of East Mill House. Lady Eastmiln gave the orders, Martha saw that they were carried out, and the two maids kept the great iron pot over the kitchen fire filled with water – when it was not simmering with beef or broth – and beat the barley at the knocking-stone, and slithered the pewter and wooden plates and earthenware jars through a bowl of water, and kept the fires smoking with peat, and shuffled wet cloths over the floor with their bare feet and sprinkled it with sand.

'Have you no needlework I can do, ma'am?' Kitty asked, as a last resort.

But Lady Eastmiln preferred to keep her mending to herself.

'Knit yourself a pair of thread stockings, child,' she suggested.

'I have above a dozen pairs in my trunk, ma'am, bought at the hosier's shop.'

'Do not the Edinburgh ladies knit their stockings and gloves even at the tea-table?' demanded her mother-in-law, with some scorn.

'Not for these many years, that I have heard, ma'am.'

'Then talk with Martha, Katherine.'

But Martha, though admiring and anxious to be pleasant, never began a conversation and had difficulty in sustaining it. And when they had discussed her approaching wedding she lapsed into awkward smiling silences. And Lady Eastmiln's own way of passing the time was to dwell on Patrick's health.

'The weather is poor,' she said, 'or you could take a turn in the garden. Though there is nothing to be seen there at the moment. In the summer it is very fine, with hollyhocks and pinks and columbines. And we grow sweet herbs for medicine and the kitchen.'

'I do not mind the weather, ma'am. Martha, would you not like to walk a little way with me on the braes?'

Martha shook her head and busied herself with a torn shirt.

A great crash from the store-room brought Kitty to her feet, but it was only a rat – Lizzie explained – that had gnawed the rope holding a cheese to the rafter, and the cheese had fallen down. So she sat again and studied her hands.

'Although we are somewhat pressed for space,' said Lady Eastmiln graciously, 'the hospitality of the Ogilvies has never been in question. We have always kept the Strangers Room, in which my son Patrick sleeps. And indeed, if a gentleman should need to pass the night here he could take the other bed.'

Kitty stopped biting her curls.

'But where will Kate Campbell sleep when *she* comes, ma'am?' she asked.

'Kate Campbell? Kate Campbell?'

'My sister Bethia promised you, ma'am, that she would send a washerwoman out of her own service, to help with the extra washing. Pray ma'am, where shall poor Kate Campbell sleep?'

The old lady frowned, Martha flushed, the honour of the family hospitality at stake.

'Why, that is very easy,' said Lady Eastmiln slowly, thinking. 'She shall sleep with Lizzie in the kitchen box bed, and Annie Sampson shall have a shake-down in the byre.'

But Kitty was bored and could not resist naughtiness.

'What if a *lady* should seek shelter, ma'am?' she asked demurely.

'A lady?' cried Lady Eastmiln, bewildered. 'What lady, pray?'

'Why, any lady, ma'am.'

Martha looked at her mother, and the old woman looked back, both in deadly earnestness.

'She would share with Martha and me,' said Lady Eastmiln, forfeiting what little comfort she enjoyed in the parlour's press bed – which was scarcely four feet wide.

Kitty's spurt of laughter passed unnoticed, for a creaking and groaning overhead announced that the Lieutenant was rising at last.

Lady Eastmiln knocked on the hearth with a poker, though her words could have been heard in the kitchen anyway.

'Tea for the Captain!' she called.

'Why, ma'am, I thought he was a Lieutenant!' said Kitty, keeping a straight face.

'He should have been promoted in another month or so,' said Lady Eastmiln with dignity, 'and so between us we call him the "Captain", Katherine.'

Kitty jumped to her feet, and laughing at the foot of the stairs, cried, 'Will you not come down, Captain, and take a dish of tea?'

'I fear not, Mrs Ogilvie,' said Patrick's voice, audible to everyone in the parlour. 'I am in a pretty poor way, and would beg you to bring it up!'

'Lizzie will take his tea,' said Lady Eastmiln, thinking of the proprieties.

But Kitty, still laughing, snatched the bowl from Lizzie's hands and ran up the stairs. The two women, open-mouthed, heard an exclamation, a resounding slap, a shriek of pretended horror. Then Kitty was back again, cheeks pink, eyes bright, in a turmoil of explanations.

'I slopped the dish down his shirt front!' she cried, between bursts of laughter, 'and he was fit to die!'

'And I fetched Mrs Ogilvie a clap across the backside!' Patrick shouted.

In another moment he had joined them, a plaid slung over his nightshirt and the empty bowl in his hand.

'Here, Lizzie,' he said, 'give me another, for not a drop of this has wet my gullet.'

'Come, sir,' said his mother, uncertain of these fooleries, 'whatever will your brother say if you make light of his wife?'

'Madam, I am but doing what my brother ordered. He said that Mrs Ogilvie was not to be dull, and that I should take care of her. Now, madam, I have made Katherine merry, and I have mended her manners – my brother will clasp my hand when he hears of it!'

His impudence and Kitty's helpless giggles made them all laugh.

'He is a rogue,' said Lady Eastmiln fondly, 'and Katherine is a child. What harm should there be in a little sport?'

'But my brother should not drink tea with us in his night-shirt,' said Martha, disturbed.

'Get your clothes on, sir,' cried Lady Eastmiln. 'And then you shall have your tea. Lizzie we shall all have tea, and a finger of shortcake with it. Why, we were all sitting like broody fowls until my son came down. Hurry, sir, if you please!'

'I wanted to go for a walk, Captain,' said Kitty childishly, smiling up into his face.

'Then you shall walk with me, Mrs Ogilvie,' he replied, 'and we shall see who tires first!'

He made a sweeping bow to the company and disappeared, the plaid trailing behind him. And Kitty, kneeling on the press bed, rapped her knuckles at a flock of finches, feeding on the garden wall. She was humming a little tune to herself that she had often sung at home when she lived with her mother.

'The Captain is still abed, Mr Gillock,' said Lady Eastmiln, 'but you may take no notice of him. Perhaps if he hears you fitting the locks and brass-work on his chest of drawers he will rouse himself!'

John Gillock was a sober young craftsman in his twenties with a fresh face and a pair of good blue eyes. He walked as softly as he could up the stairs, tiptoed past the alcove bed where Patrick sprawled asleep, and began his work, whistling quietly as he took out the drawers. A creak at the door made him turn. He nodded courteously at the new Mrs Ogilvie, who smiled back and twisted her curls, and peeped over the back of the bed.

Seeing that Patrick did not stir she cried in a loud voice, 'John, are you begun?'

'Aye, Mrs Ogilvie,' he replied, and indicated that the Captain should not be disturbed.

But Kitty was of a different frame of mind, and thumped the bed wilfully.

'What, are you not up yet?' she cried, and dodged and laughed as Patrick tried to catch her wrists.

'Here, look what I have brought you,' she continued, and sat on the edge of the bed, to John Gillock's stern amazement, and flourished a piece of sweet bread under Patrick's nose.

He snatched at the bread and she pulled it away again.

'It is fresh from the market,' she said, tearing it in half and offering him a share. 'And you must give me some for my trouble in carrying it upstairs. Will you have a bit, John?'

'I thank you, Mrs Ogilvie,' said John soberly, 'but I have had my porridge and want nothing,' and he busied himself with his task.

'*I* shall use those drawers,' said Kitty, swinging her foot and eating and laughing, 'for I have nothing in our room that locks.'

'You will keep to your own furniture, Mrs Ogilvie,' said Patrick, grinning. 'These are for me.'

'But you will let me have *one* drawer at least – for the sweet bread and my company – will you not?' she demanded, her pretty head on one side.

'We shall see whether you deserve it.'

'I deserve anything in the world, do I not, John?' cried Kitty, drawing the carpenter into their conversation.

'I do not know, Mrs Ogilvie,' he replied stiffly.

She turned again to Patrick and laid her hand on his bare chest.

'Lady Eastmiln keeps telling us how delicate you are,' she said, off on another tack, 'and yet you are not poor, but pretty fat. Come you must get up and entertain me! Thomas ordered that, you know, and we are dull downstairs.'

'The bride of a full fortnight is dull already, John,' said Patrick gaily. 'What shall we do about that?'

'I do not know, Captain Ogilvie,' said John in a low voice, very busy with the locks.

'Well I am going now,' said Kitty, shaking the crumbs from her lap. 'So make haste, Captain.'

As she turned towards the door Patrick gave a great whoop and kicked up the bedclothes. And John Gillock, scandalised, saw that he was naked. He looked quickly at Kitty to see if she had observed, but she was tossing her curls unperturbed.

Over her shoulder she cried, 'Ah! You daft dog!' and ran down the stairs.

The wright went on with his work, tutting under his breath and shaking his head.

'Will you not walk with us, Martha?' Kitty asked prettily.

'I am poor company,' said Martha, bending her head over her sewing, 'and have much to do before the wedding.'

'But I like us *all* to walk!' cried Kitty, feeling that more companions made for more amusement.

'I think I should stay with my mother, Katherine.'

'Yes, stay with me, child, and let them paddle through the rain together. They are very merry,' she observed, with satisfaction, as the door closed.

Martha bit off a thread.

'They are also very free with one another,' she said tentatively.

'That is their nature,' said Lady Eastmiln, dismissing the subject. 'But you and I are quieter, so we shall stay indoors.'

'Why are you putting up your hood?' Patrick asked.

'So that my hair should not get wet, you daft creature!' said Kitty.

He pushed the hood back and placed both brown hands on her head.

'Now it will stay dry!' he said, smiling at her.

She ducked away, laughing, and he chased her until they were both breathless.

'See,' she cried, shaking the drops from her curls, 'see what you have done with your nonsense!'

He pretended to polish the rain from her hair with the sleeve of his wet coat, and she pushed him away, giggling.

'Behave yourself, you great fool. You forget I am a married woman.'

'I remember,' he said, taking her hand. 'I remember every day that you are my brother's wife – and every night. And I envy Thomas.'

'Envy is a sin,' she said, colouring, withdrawing.

'The Ogilvies were never kirk-crowders,' said Patrick easily. 'I wouldn't know a sin if I met one in the glen!'

'I wish the Spring would come, and the rain stop,' said Kitty at random, breaking off a spray of alder.

'I wish many more things than that.'

She peeped into his young brown face and tickled his nose with the Twig.

'Come,' said Patrick, seizing the sprig, 'you shall pay me for your impudence, Mrs Ogilvie.'

They tugged. Green and resilient, the alder held, and Kitty was pulled against his chest, protesting heartily.

'A forfeit!' cried Patrick.

Forfeits, played at Dunsinnan House: shrieks and laughter and stolen kisses and long confidences afterwards about the handsomeness of this and that young man, with Anne and Bethia her sisters. Kitty stood on tiptoe and joyfully kissed his nose. Still he held her. In the silence that fell between them they stared at each other. Then he bent his head and kissed her full on the mouth.

At the far side of the stream David Rattray, who lived in

the neighbourhood, watched them until they sauntered away hand in hand.

From his house in Glenkilry, George Spalding wrote to his mother-in-law, Lady Nairne, enclosing a copy of Kitty's contract of marriage and begging her to make legal provision for her daughter without loss of time.

> East Miln was threatning a Decay some time ago and I do not think him in a good way just now, his friends seems to reflect much on us as we did such gentile things for Her . . .

He added a note about his wife Bethia, who had recently given birth and was having trouble with her milk. Then signed himself her Ladyship's Most Obedient, etc. George Spalding.

Scanning the letter for a second time before he sealed it, he regretted that Kitty had been introduced to Thomas Ogilvie under his roof. But with Kitty so close to her sister and Eastmiln an old friend – what could one do?

On 18 February Kate Campbell arrived at East Mill House, having begged a pillion ride from a man who was passing through Glenisla. Her reception was something of a failure, since she spoke little English and had less intelligence. But Kitty danced to her rescue in a flurry of explanation and introduction.

'Poor Kate,' cried Kitty,' she does not talk much, but she washes linen like a Hollander, don't you, Kate? And as she and I are both Katherine by name you must call her Kate, so that we shall not be confused. For what would I do if you asked me to wash the sheets? And what would Kate think if the Captain asked her to walk with him? Now,

43

Kate, you are to sleep in the kitchen with Lizzie Sturrock here, but you won't mind that I dare say. For Kate,' she explained to the company, 'has come from Ireland where they are exceedingly poor, and fortunate to eat a baked potato for their suppers. And Kate, you will find no fault with the food here, for Lady Eastmiln keeps a good table. So come, Kate, and fetch your bundle with you. And she shall have a bowl of broth, shall she not, ma'am, after her journey? And Lizzie shall fry her a sour cake, and there is some bread pudding left from yesterday.'

'Give the wench ale,' said Lady Eastmiln sensibly, 'and hush your clatter, child, for she is quite bewildered.'

Kate Campbell smiled vacantly.

'Can you tell what Mrs Ogilvie is saying about you?' Lady Eastmiln questioned imperiously.

'No, ma'am,' said Kate, and was startled by the burst of laughter that followed.

'Here, lassie,' said Patrick, 'listen to none of them and warm yourself with this. It is a raw morning.'

And he offered her a dram which she tossed off at once, coughing and smiling at the sharp hot taste. Then wiped her mouth with the corner of her shawl and waited for further orders.

'Come, Kate,' said Kitty busily, 'and I shall see that you are settled. And Annie, here is tuppence for you, because you must sleep in the byre. And tell me, Kate, how is my sister Mrs Spalding, and the new baby? Tell me. And tell me how you came. Did my sister give you any message for me?'

Lady Eastmiln shook her head as they went through to the kitchen, with Kitty asking questions faster than they could be answered, let alone comprehended.

'What a rattle that child is!' she said. 'It is a good thing I am deaf or my head would ache as much as her tongue should!'

44

Thomas sat contentedly enough at the head of his table, eating his hare collops and pease pudding. Martha was miles away in a dream of marriage, when her house would be her own, her bed belong to her husband, and years of servility to her mother be over and gone. And Lady Eastmiln asked shrewd questions about the management of the farm, and complained that Thomas had left off his plaiden jacket again, and remarked that Patrick's health seemed much improved.

Kitty, returning, insisted on sharing Patrick's dinner, which she said was better than her own, and made him choke on his collops. So that Kate Campbell was astonished at her mistress's frivolous behaviour and her eyes grew round.

'Mrs Ogilvie,' said Thomas formally, for he would only call her Kitty or Katie in private, 'I have received a letter from your uncle regarding your settlement.'

'From my Uncle William? Did he say anything about Frisk?'

'Frisk?' Thomas repeated, at sea in an instant, for he could think of only one thing at once.

'My mother's little dog. Oh, he is such a romp is Frisk,' said Kitty, turning to Lady Eastmiln. 'He is a cocker spaniel, very smooth of coat, with the brightest eyes you ever saw. And though he was my mother's pet he loved me better than anyone, and every morning he would wake me by putting his cold nose on my cheek. And once . . .'

'Child, child,' said Lady Eastmiln, raising her hand, 'your husband is trying to say something of importance. We can talk of Frisk later.'

'Your family consider,' said Thomas, as temporary silence was restored, 'that in the event of my death you should be possessed of an income from my estate – and that is only right.'

Lady Eastmiln leaned forward, one hand to her ear.

'How much do they suggest?' she asked.

'One thousand Scots merks a year.'

He and she were at one, considering the fairness of the suggestion. Then Lady Eastmiln signalled Lizzie to remove the plates.

'I think you should go to Dunsinnan, my son,' she said, 'and deal with this matter at once.'

'And I will come too, Thomas,' said Kitty, excited at the prospect of a jaunt, 'for I have not seen my mother since we were married.'

'You had best stay here, Katherine,' said her mother-in-law, putting one hand over hers. 'Your husband will want to talk of business undistracted.'

She lifted her eyebrows at Patrick, who responded immediately.

'You must not leave me forlorn, Mrs Ogilvie,' he cried, and shook out his handkerchief and applied it to his eyes.

The visit was forgotten as she seized his handkerchief from him, and dropped it to the floor, giggling.

Across them Lady Eastmiln said, 'You had best go before the end of the month, Thomas. There is a great deal to do about the farm in March. And Katherine will be safe with us.'

He nodded. Kitty, conscious that she had lost a treat without a struggle, looked up, sobered.

'Well, you will take messages from me,' she said, 'and perhaps we can all go there together next time.' And then beseechingly, as they rose from the table, the matter settled, she said, 'But did my Uncle William say *nothing* of Frisk?'

IV

Kate Campbell at twenty-seven years of age had worked hard all her life, and now she took on house-work and bed-making as well as washing. Her long silences and few words and her simplicity tended to make people discount her presence. So she possibly saw and heard more than either Lizzie or Annie, and kept her own counsel. Coming from Bethia Spalding's household, and admiring Kitty, she regarded herself as set apart from the Ogilvie family, as being someone special to the new bride; and consequently planned to keep her mistress company when the laird went to Dunsinnan.

'You will not be dull without me,' said Thomas, wrapping himself very carefully against the cold. 'Patrick will keep you cheerful.'

He noticed an unusual languor about her as she fiddled with his stirrup.

'I have got all your messages,' he said, at a loss. He remembered something. 'I shall take particular account of Frisk,' he added kindly.

Her chin shook, tears trembled on her lashes.

'I shall be back in a few days,' he said.

Then looking about him to make sure that no one observed them, he stopped to kiss her cheek. She tried to laugh, but brushed her hand across her eyes.

'Are you not well, Katie?'

'I am very well.'

'Then here is Patrick with his fiddle to make you merry. Come, brother,' he said, and motioning Patrick closer he whispered, 'I think she may miss me, so be fond of her for my sake.'

Patrick nodded, bringing the fiddle up under his chin and drawing the bow across the strings in a resounding chord as Thomas's horse trotted sedately off for Dunsinnan.

'We can see him go along the road for quite a while,' said Patrick, as she kept her back to him. He held out his hand, 'Come, Mrs Ogilvie, and you and I and the fiddle shall see him on his way.'

They ran to the top of the hillock, and while Kitty sat on a rock and watched her husband go, Patrick played a lament – in a mixture of tenderness and fun.

'Are you coming home, Mrs Ogilvie?' he asked, when the drove road was empty. 'There's a wind blowing up to remind us that March is on its way. And I think an hour's tales of India by the fireside is better than the shivers outdoors. Come, and I will tell you how a mermaid sang to me once, off the shores of Asia!'

'Is Asia in India, then?' she asked in a small voice.

He roared again. 'Why Mrs Ogilvie, did they not teach you the use of globes? What a goose-cap you are!'

She turned to him, the tears coming thick and fast, and sobbed aloud.

'Will you miss Thomas so much?' he asked, astonished.

'Oh, it is not that,' cried Kitty. 'It is not that!'

And she clutched him, fiddle and all, and wept like a child.

'Then what ails you, Kitty?' he asked, stroking her hair and holding her to his shoulder.

'I miss Dunsinnan so,' she cried. 'I miss Frisk, and the beech trees, and the rose garden, and the little things I took every day for granted. I miss my mother.' She doubled her fists against his chest and beat at him, sobbing. 'I miss my mother. I want my mother. I miss my mother.'

He held her close, soothing her with endearments and caresses, while she cried herself out.

48

Supper was a silent meal, though Patrick attempted to enliven the evening by telling them of the lady who wore beauty patches when her husband took her to visit a Rajah. And the Rajah was so saddened by her obvious disfigurement that he sent for his own physician to try to cure her. But Lady Eastmiln, being tired, missed half what was said, and Martha was too timid to laugh by herself, and Kitty did not listen.

Unnoticed, Kate Campbell served her mistress with the choicest pieces of fowl and drowned them in egg sauce; and nodded her head in sympathy and understanding as Kitty touched hardly any of it. She was ready with a lighted tallow candle when her mistress excused herself, and ushered her up the stairs importantly. She would have liked to express what she so deeply felt, but contented herself by saying, 'Whisha, whisha' as she helped Kitty to undress. Then she hurried downstairs to bring up her own mattress full of straw ticking, and her two ragged blankets.

'What's this?' said Kitty, as the servant began to spread her bedding before the bedroom hearth.

'I be fine wid you,' said Kate Campbell, nodding and smiling. 'Fine wid you, mistress.'

'Take those things downstairs again,' Kitty cried. 'I want to be alone. I want to be by myself.'

Kate Campbell stood there crestfallen, her poor blankets dribbling down over her arms and on to the rushes that covered the floor.

'The laird's awa' and I be fine wid you,' she explained, bewildered.

'I don't *care*!' Kitty said relentlessly. 'I don't care *who's* away. I want to be alone. I want you to go downstairs.'

For fully a minute Kate Campbell stood there, her broad red face perplexed, tears slowly filling her round blue eyes. Then she took in the meaning of the command, clumsily gathered up her bedding and began to make her way back to the kitchen box bed, in the bitterness of rejection.

Behind her, unmindful of the hurt she had dealt, Kitty buried her face in the chaff pillow and wept. The fire, which Kate Campbell had thought would warm and comfort both mistress and servant, flickered on the bare walls and over the dark beams across the ceiling. Kitty heard Patrick mount the stairs lightly and turn into his room. She heard the bed-time conversation between Lady Eastmiln and Martha as they undressed and creaked into the parlour press bed. She heard Annie Sampson grumble her way to the byre, which was cold and draughty. She heard Lizzie Sturrock question Kate, and Kate mumble a reply. She heard the rats scutter in the storeroom and the owl hoot in the cold. She heard the rain beat on the slate roof and spit down the chimney and hiss on the flames. Then she blew out her candle, noticing a light through the cracks in the floorboards.

'Are you not yet to bed, Kate?' she cried.

The voice of Kate Campbell, thick and inarticulate, replied humbly, 'No' yet, mistress!' And then, fearful of further reprimand. 'I'll gang soon.'

Kitty thought of her mother's room with the carved reliefs round the fireplace, of the plaster frieze of vine leaves, of her sisters gossiping over their embroidery when they were all at home together, of Frisk's cold nose and bright black eyes. She thought of the men who had courted her, and wondered whether any of them would have made a better husband than Thomas. The personable James Campbell, whom Bethia had invited to Glenkilry to meet her, and could chatter almost as amiably as Patrick. A half dozen young bucks with fewer years and more money. And her butter-headed Dutchman, who secretly kissed her ringlets as he placed them more becomingly on her neck. But how was any girl to know that an older man would lack experience of women, or that he wore an ugly flannel belt

50

under his clothes to keep the chill off a weak stomach? How could one know that his love for her would be less than the love of old habits? How had she come to mistake dull silence for quiet wisdom? And why, above all, did new people and new places change for the worse as one grew used to them?

A noise in Patrick's room roused her, and she sat up in bed listening. Muttering and stumbling like a man in a nightmare, he made his way across the landing and clutched the bedpost to support his shaking limbs.

'What is it?' she whispered, curious and fearful at once.

'I have the ague upon me, Mrs Ogilvie. Can I warm myself by your fire?'

She indicated that he should, and watched him, fascinated. Fully dressed, he crouched over the flames until she smelled his coat scorching, and shivered and jerked convulsively.

'Is this the illness that brought you home?' Kitty whispered.

He nodded, almost burning himself in the effort to keep warm. Then turned to her bed, flung back the covers and climbed in.

'Oh, fie! Fie!' cried Kitty in horror, then giggled and clapped her hands to her mouth.

In a moment or so she bent over him, and saw he was not aware of her, so stuck a bolster between them for the sake of decorum and tucked the blankets around him. Still he jerked and mumbled, and she watched over him with an interest that became tenderness. Gently she traced the strong cheekbones and square jaw, stroked his curly head, and observed again that his chest was not white and frail like Thomas's but broad and brown. She patted it childishly.

'Why you are as shaggy as a dancing bear!' she whispered, and smiled as his eyes opened.

51

He managed a wink, in spite of his troubles, and placed one sunburned hand on the bolster that lay between them. She covered it with her own.

'Good night, dancing bear!' Kitty whispered, comforted. 'Good night, Mrs Ogilvie.'

Long before his shivering subsided she had fallen asleep.

But awake and staring in the kitchen lay Kate Campbell, in a trance that bordered on superstitious terror. She had heard the doors open and the footsteps across her mistress's room; heard the shriek of 'Oh, fie! Fie!' and the creaking of the laird's bed; and she crossed herself, and said a few Christian prayers and added a few pagan spells, to keep her safe. Until the small hours of the morning she pondered, and tried to put her ponderings into intelligible English, and wondered whether she should tell somebody, and if so whom, and how?

At sunrise Patrick was up before anyone, begging a bowl of hot tea, slapping Lizzie's haunches, chucking Annie under the chin, putting his arm round Kate's shoulders. But she moved away from him, scandalised and afraid, thinking him the devil in disguise, and yet ventured a reproof.

'Ye're o'er free wid the lady.'

'Why, Kate, my bonnie wench,' said Patrick, standing in his nightshirt with the plaid trailing to the brick floor, 'the laird bade me be fond of her, and keep her cheerful while he was away, and so I do.' He sipped his tea. 'There's no harm in it.'

She would not respond to his good humour, and when he had gone outside she begged a word with Lady Eastmiln. That old woman, keeping up appearances even in the discomfort of having to dress in a hurry so that breakfast could be laid, was more than usually stately.

'Speak up!' she commanded. 'Speak up, girl!'

Kate's careful phrases fled before the tone. From the depths of her jumbled mind she could hook up only one word, 'Frighted'.

'Frightened? Frightened of what? What frightens her, Lizzie?'

Lizzie thought it might be the owls hooting at night. Kate Campbell shook her head and twisted her hands in her skirt.

'Frightened of *me*?' Lady Eastmiln questioned, with some humour.

A shake of the head. The flat face crimsoned, the rough hands twisted and twisted at the skirt, as though words could be wrested from it.

'Of what, then?'

'Frighted. Frighted,' said Kate Campbell, caught in her own incantation. 'Frighted. Frighted.'

Lizzie came officiously to her rescue.

'She has the Sight, my lady. Maybe she sees a death in the house.'

But Kate only said, 'Frighted. Frighted.' and shook her head, until she was roundly scolded and sent upstairs with a bowl of tea for her mistress.

Kitty was still abed, and announced that in view of the cold morning she would stay there. She spoke gaily to her servant, but offered no explanation or apology for the night before seeing no need of either. Though Kate hung about and hinted as best she could; and hoped for a word or look of personal affection, which would have bound her tongue for ever. When she found none her face stiffened, became closed and secretive. So far she had not spoken to Lizzie Sturrock, though Lizzie had mentioned strange sounds in the laird's room. Now, feeling herself put aside, her loyalty ignored, her love rejected, she dropped her championship of Kitty. Downstairs she clattered, no longer outside but a part of the kitchen gossip. And when she had confirmed Lizzie's suspicions, and indicated to the gaping Annie that too much was afoot between Mrs Ogilvie and the Captain, she motioned them to follow her upstairs.

So far they had let her make the beds unaided, but now they came bustling to help her.

Not a wrinkle disturbed the covers of the alcove bed. And Kate looked expressively at her fellow-servants across the smooth pillows, and turned down the corners of her mouth, and turned up her eyes in silent condemnation. Suddenly allies, they whispered and shook their heads together. And then Lizzie hissed into the tight little circle, her face a caricature of scandal, 'Incest. Incest.'

They drew apart, the word hot and sweet on their tongues. And, in their three minds, Patrick and Kitty curled like scraps of burning paper in the flames of hell.

V

The Turnpike Act of 1751 had greatly improved travelling conditions in Scotland, and the forty mile turnpike road between Edinburgh and Perth was said to be the finest in Britain. So Anne Clarke had come like a lady by chaise to Queensferry, crossed the water between South and North Queensferry, taken Inverkeithing, Maryburgh and Kinross in her stride, and arrived at Perth to stay overnight. Beyond Perth the Brechin road ran to Coupar Angus and on to Meigle for a bone-shaking eighteen miles, and then went on without her. For at Meigle she took refreshment, and walked a weary mile on foot to the Boat of Bardmony. The failing light of a winter afternoon, combined with a rising mist, made an obscurity of both persons and place, so that she saw the River Isla as grey smoke, and the approaching boat loomed like Charon's ferry through the fog.

Only one passenger was aboard: a tall, stoop-shouldered man, wrapped in an old plaid. He glanced at her as he stepped ashore, waiting for his horse to join him, and then courteously helped her to her seat. She thanked him graciously, seeming not to notice him more than good manners warranted. But in the boat, left to her own thoughts and the quiet lap of water against the wood, she scrutinised his face from memory, finding pain in the heavy lines from nose to mouth, and sickness in the pinched features.

'That gentleman has trouble with his liver or his stomach,' she said to herself.

On the far side of the Isla no transport could be found. The day had waned and all honest folk were at their firesides. A steady drizzle soaked her mantle and seeped through her shoes as she trudged the last two miles to Alyth, carrying her valise. Now she looked every year of her age, and felt it, and as she came into the town she hastened to smooth her straying hair and shake her cloak and dress into some semblance of respectability. Her soft, well-spoken tones gained her admittance at a private house; and she was careful to pay for her supper and lodging in advance, so that they should not think she came a-begging. And even as she entered she perceived that her hostess had two weaknesses: a small son and an unusually immaculate parlour. So Anne Clarke bent to speak to the child and pat his silky head, and then to exclaim, with sincerity, at the scrubbed perfection. Long since she had learned the value of a complimentary tongue and a pleasing manner; and before she stepped upstairs with her tallow candle she had gained a pillion ride to Glenisla, for the following day.

Refreshed and rested, with her shoes dried by the fire and the worst of travel stains removed from her cloak and gown, she set out on the first of March in good heart. The drove road was rough and the weather inclement, and fifteen long hard miles were engraved in her bones when she slipped down from the pillion at the Kirktown, and asked the way to East Mill. From the bottom of her purse she counted out sixpence for the man who had brought her, and he touched his bonnet respectfully before striding into Fergie Ferguson's for ale.

Near the end of both money and strength, she tackled the last half-mile; forming phrases of introduction in her head while the mud sucked her shoes and dabbled her stockings and skirts. As the long low walls of East Mill came into view she paused for breath and removed a clog of earth from her foot. Then resolutely made her way to the front of the house and knocked on the door.

The latch was raised by Martha, who stood in mute astonishment, and Anne immediately placed her as a good-

56

natured fool who must be the daughter.

'Miss Ogilvie?' she said easily. 'I am Anne Clarke, your cousin, come to visit you.'

Martha held the door open and called loudly to the family who sat at their mid-day meal in squalid abundance.

'It is a cousin by the name of Miss Anne Clarke.'

Solitary and self-possessed, Anne looked at the parlourful of surprised faces, labelling them in her mind. Pretty Kitty, Captain Patrick, three lumps of serving girls, and Lady Eastmiln herself. As they stared, she set down her valise, put one hand to her mouth, seemed to recollect her behaviour, and hurried forward to the old lady.

'Why, ma'am,' she cried, and there were tears in her eyes, 'you are the image of my dear mother, your sister that departed this life ten years since. I am rejoiced to meet you.'

'My sister? That married Allan Clarke?'

'Both departed this life, my dear aunt, to my everlasting grief.'

'Well, you are very welcome, Miss Clarke,' said Lady Eastmiln. 'Lizzie, take Miss Clarke's mantle and set another place.'

In an instant Kitty had offered her a room as a temporary tiring place – a thought that would never have occurred to any Ogilvie.

'I had heard, Mrs Ogilvie, that you were bonnic,' said Anne, with a brilliant smile that made her appear much younger, 'and I see the reports are well-founded. You are also most perceptive, and kind, and I thank you. I should like to appear less of a scarecrow before I eat.'

'Then come with me, Miss Clarke,' cried Kitty, and was ordering a porridge plate to be filled with hot water, and a dish of tea, and running up the stairs before anyone could speak.

Anne dropped a reverent curtsey to Lady Eastmiln, a

civil curtsey to Patrick and Martha, and followed the excited Kitty decorously.

'Now I have been praying for pleasant company,' Kitty cried, offering her looking-glass and tucking up her curls before handing it to Anne.

'Are you so dull, then, Mrs Ogilvie?' Anne asked, smiling.

'Oh, the laird is away – though he is not very talkative – and the Captain is a great romp, and everyone else is pretty well and comfortable. But I long for a new face!'

She came close to Anne, who was looking for a clean fichu in her valise.

'In my mother's house at Dunsinnan,' said Kitty, 'there was new company almost every day.'

She saw comprehension and pity in the clear grey eyes.

'And so you are homesick?' Anne said gently.

'Oh no,' Kitty cried proudly, with a toss of her head, but turned away to the window and looked on the bare hillock at the front of the house. 'No, Miss Clarke. I am very merry.'

'I have been homesick and heartsick in my time,' said Anne. 'It is the saddest thing in all the world until one learns to be alone.'

'I could never be alone!' cried Kitty, horrified.

'You never will be,' said Anne, setting her hair to rights, 'for you are young and pretty and have some fortune. When I was heartsick I was merely young.'

Kitty inspected her curiously.

'But you have great elegance, Miss Clarke, and are so clever I am sure.'

Kate Campbell blundered up the stairs with hot water, interrupting their conversation. And Anne observed the heavy set of the mouth, the jealous eyes, and the surly emphasis with which the servant set down the porridge plate.

'This is Kate Campbell,' said Kitty, 'who has little English, but she does very well. She comes from my sister Bethia's house.'

'Then you are both new here together,' said Anne pleasantly, and saw Kate Campbell's face lighten. 'Your mistress will be glad of you, Kate.'

'Fine,' said Kate, reddening as she struggled for words. 'Fine wid me.'

'Of course she is,' said Anne smoothly.

'I would – sleep – there,' said Kate, marvellously encouraged, and made a motion towards the floor in front of the bedroom hearth. 'The laird's awa, mistress,' she explained. 'The laird's awa.'

'Is he indeed. I had hoped to meet him.'

'I would – sleep – there.'

'Oh, go away, do, Kate!' said her mistress impatiently. 'I sleep very well alone.'

Something wrong, thought Anne, noting Kate's return to sullen silence.

Aloud, she said, 'Thank you, Kate. You and I will do very well together.' And saw the woman's pleasure come again, out of all proportion to the remark. So she smiled, and repeated it.

The press bed proved to be too small for the three of them, and in view of Thomas's imminent return, Martha was farmed out to the Shaws of Little Forthar, and Anne's presence became a welcome one. She knew too much about men to find the Captain a problem, and struck a delicate balance between friendship and familiarity with him, from the beginning. She was reverently affectionate towards Lady Eastmiln, prepared to listen to her anecdotes for hours, and to find her imperious tongue a delight. With Martha she was tactful and kind, with Kitty a confidante of sisterly quality. The servants she treated according to their natures: encouraging poor Kate's stumbling English, enjoying Lizzie's sharpness, and pronouncing young Annie Sampson a good girl for sleeping in the byre.

The domestic arrangements were rough enough to bring a wrinkle to her brows, but the wrinkle remained a private comment between herself and herself. Outwardly she praised the Ogilvie's generous table, and saw that the food was better prepared and cleaner served. She commended the Captain's smart appearance, and sewed new ruffles to replace his torn ones. She praised the house as a fine establishment, for all its smallness, and discovered a better place for everything but the fixtures. Smiling, she inspected the kitchen, and put a broom in Annie's red hands. Unobtrusively she tidied clothes and shoes into chests.

'You are a good girl,' said Lady Eastmiln, as Anne set a stool beneath her feet.

'And you, ma'am, are a good mother,' said Anne easily. 'As good a mother as mine ever was, God rest her soul. Shall we sew first, ma'am, or take a dish of tea?'

'We shall take a dish of tea,' said Lady Eastmiln, well-pleased, 'and a finger of shortcake. You will find it in the basket on the side-table, where it is kept filled. For my son Thomas so relishes shortcake that he eats it with his "morning" of ale, or else with his first dish of tea. Though we never shake enough sugar on it for *him*, and he always puts a little more. He has a sweet tooth, but I think so much sugar cannot be good for his health. Where are the children?' she asked indulgently.

'Dancing on the brae like two small bairns!' said Anne, peering through the parlour window and waving to them.

Martha frowned over her needlework.

'My daughter thinks the Captain and Katherine are too free,' said Lady Eastmiln, 'but she was always an awkward girl with the gentlemen, were you not Martha? Had Andrew Stewart not spoken for her at the last she would have been here until she died. But they knew each other from childhood, so are used to one another. And I find that love fades but habit is strongest.'

This view of her charms and matrimonial prospects brought Martha to a crimson and tearful state in a moment. But before Lady Eastmiln could scold, Anne moved in kindly.

'Mr Stewart is an honest gentleman with a good reputation in Alyth, I am told. So Miss Ogilvie has chosen well for herself, and will find much happiness in such a bond of love and fellowship. May I suggest, Miss Ogilvie, that you sew a ruffle or two upon that nightgown?'

Martha stared at the voluminous white tent she was sewing, and seemed uncertain of such fripperies.

'A ruffle about the neck and sleeves, and another on the hem,' said Anne, coaxing the blighted femininity in Martha's breast, 'will be most becoming.'

'Give her that gown, child,' commanded Lady Eastmiln, 'for you look like nothing at all with your plain skirts and straight bodices. Miss Clarke has some taste, I can see, though her own dress is hardly new.'

'Hardly new at all, ma'am,' said Anne. 'I have not been so fortunate in my family as Miss Ogilvie. Now this linen is very fine. I compliment you. Did you buy it of the chapman? It does not look to be made locally. A tuck here, and another there, you see, and I will sew the ruffles for it myself if you wish.'

'Oh yes,' said Martha, suddenly smiling. 'That is most pretty, Miss Clarke.'

'And here is the tea,' said Anne, gently relinquishing the nightgown, 'and the shortcake on the side-table, I see. Everything in its place. You run a very proper household, ma'am.'

'Discipline,' said Lady Eastmiln, raising the bowl to her lips. 'But my eyes and ears are not what they were, Miss Clarke.'

Nor were they, for she had missed a blob of grease on the rim of the bowl, which Anne removed with her handkerchief before it could float across the tea.

'Seeing and hearing more than any of us,' said Anne, 'you can *afford* a little less sharpness, I feel ma'am.'

'My children have never said any of these things to me,' said Lady Eastmiln, 'but you are very genteel, Miss Clarke. The Ogilvies, except for my son the Captain, were never sweet in the tongue. But he, you will have noticed, can turn a very pretty compliment.'

'I think he is your favourite, ma'am,' said Anne lightly.

'He was born so late, you see. There was fifteen years between himself and poor William.' She ignored the birth of Martha, squarely between the two sons. 'He came like a blessing into my middle years,' she said.

Her fingers trembled over the shortbread, and a little scattering of sugar fell into her lap.

'I had my first two sons in two years. James and Thomas. William came three years after. But they were always wild fellows, and the Ogilvies are not much for the kirk, so one Sunday they set the cows loose among the minister's crops! Why, what a fuss he made!' She lifted her hands and raised her eyes to witness his lack of humour. 'But he was a bonnie scoundrel, and not fit for his cloth, so they sent him packing.'

'He preached the sermon not long after,' Martha reminded her.

'You were but a bairn that could not wipe her own nose,' said Lady Eastmiln sharply, 'so how could *you* remember?'

'I do not remember, mother, I was told. Did you hear of that sermon, Miss Clarke? The Reverend Mitchell cursed our family, and said that if the Ogilvie men died in their beds God did not speak through him.'

'Aye, aye,' said Lady Eastmiln grandly. 'And why *should* God speak through a whisky-sodden, wench-spoiling old cask like Mitchell, miss?'

'But four years after,' Martha pursued, 'my father fell on the south side of the Castle Rock, making his escape in a net slung from an iron hook. And died on the instant, of a fractured skull. And seven years later my brother James hanged himself in the sheep-cote.'

'Well, well, miss! Your brother Thomas is alive and well, and looks to sons of his own, I hope.'

'But William died, crushed between two ships. And Thomas is but sickly,' said Martha, relentless for once, 'and Patrick has been invalided home . . .'

'Aye, aye. But Patrick was not born when the minister spoke – so there flies your mystery out of the window, miss!'

'And nor was your youngest son, Alexander,' said Anne, like silk.

A silence fell upon them.

'You know of my son, then?'

'Why, yes, ma'am. I have waited these three days, endeavouring to puzzle out how to tell you the purpose of my visit. But I see you are too quick for me, so I must come to the point and beg your sense of justice to bear with me.'

'Speak up! Speak up, Miss Clarke!'

'I kept house for my father and my brother when my mother, your dear sister, died. And we were very well together. Then my father died and my brother married, and there was neither home nor money for me. I will not be tedious, ma'am,' said Anne with difficulty, some real and some assumed, 'but it is not easy for a virtuous girl to find employment. Rest assured, ma'am, I have not brought shame upon my mother's upbringing, but I worked as a servant in one and another place.' She indicated her neat grey dress and immaculate fichu. 'I learned fine sewing, ma'am, and kept my honour and my dignity, but little else. About a year ago your son Alexander came across me, when

I was chambermaid at a small inn in Edinburgh, and by chance we found that we were cousins. Whereupon he said I should not stay there, for the good name of the family, and my own sake.'

Lady Eastmiln stared at her long and shrewdly.

'And what relationship did you enjoy with my son Alexander?' she asked.

'Look well upon me, ma'am,' said Anne, holding her gaze. 'I am no beauty, as you can see, and my years number thirty-two. Your son is wild, I grant you, but he is scarcely twenty and a handsome lad. Our relationship was not a lewd one, rather we were like brother and sister, and the sister like to a mother.'

'And since he has never found his allowance sufficient,' said Lady Eastmiln, 'what employment did he find you?'

'I took in fine sewing for various of his acquaintance in Edinburgh, such as the wife of his tutor Dr Murray. I valued his championship, and discovered a good heart beneath his wildness. In your name, ma'am, I saw to his linen and his comfort.'

'There has been little love between myself and Alexander, Miss Clarke. So do not seek to flatter me, girl, or to make pretences. Let us be honest, if we are nothing else.'

'I have indeed been honest with you, ma'am,' said Anne proudly. 'Do you imagine it was easy to expose my poverty and degradation to you? All I say is that your son Alexander showed me a Christian charity that none other extended – save yourself and your family these few days.'

'Well, well. What then, miss?'

'He is as proud as yourself, ma'am, and has not your experience. He confided in me his grief that you had cast him off since his marriage.'

'Ah yes!' said Lady Eastmiln, spying a sitting duck among the reeds of explanation. 'That marriage! And if you were as close as you say, what were *you* about, miss, to let him marry such a hussy?'

'I was not told, ma'am,' Anne said truthfully. 'I was sewing in my room when your son came in with his bride, and said they had stood up before the minister. Her family is very sly, ma'am, and had trapped your son properly, so that even his friends did not know until it was over!'

'What explanation did he offer you?'

'None, ma'am, except that of misguided honour.'

'You mean that he had got her with child?'

Anne inclined her head.

'What then?'

'Ma'am, you will scarcely believe this,' said Anne, knowing the value of a half-truth, 'but I felt it my duty to be near him lest he need my help. So I gave up my poor room and found lodgings with Ann Rattray's parents.'

'The *porter* and his wife?' Lady Eastmiln inquired, with slighting emphasis.

'Just so, ma'am. They are rough folk, but kindly enough. But I could not get to see your son, for his wife barred the door against me, and he was ashamed. But in less than a fortnight he was back at the tavern again, and there I found him one evening, sincerely repentant.'

'But drunk, no doubt.'

'Aye, indeed ma'am. But drinking because, like any foolish lad, he had done his family an injury and did not know how to set it or himself right. I talked with him, and I was not kind, ma'am. I spoke out as you would have done. And in the end he begged me to come here on his behalf, and went home to send his bride about her business. She is no longer there, ma'am. And that is what I have come here to tell you.'

'This tea is cold,' said Lady Eastmiln pettishly. 'Take it away. You have wasted your time, Miss Clarke.'

'Then I heartily beg your pardon, and will take my leave. And I thank you a thousand times for your hospitality.'

In silence she removed the tea and set the parlour to rights. She let them see that though she was endeavouring to hide her tears they *would* fall.

'I have no objection to *your* presence, Miss Clarke,' said Lady Eastmiln, at length. 'You have been most agreeable. I had hoped you would stay for Martha's wedding.'

'That I should like above all things, ma'am,' said Anne, almost inaudibly, 'but my mission is over, and however much I treasure this glimpse of a good and tranquil life it is not for me.'

Lady Eastmiln tapped her stick irritably on the brick floor.

'Come,' she said. 'You are my sister's child, and she and I were very well together. You have made yourself useful to us and we are neither uncharitable nor inhospitable. You may stay on your own account.'

Anne shook her head, unable to speak.

'I command it!' cried Lady Eastmiln, in a fine tantrum. 'And I will not be disobeyed, miss! Martha, tell your cousin that we wish her to stay as long as she pleases. Why, good God, girl, *you* are leaving me, *she* can stay, can she not?'

Mindful of the kindness Anne had shown, and the promised ruffles for her nightgown, Martha added her pleas.

'You are very good. You are too good,' cried Anne. 'I have had no home in a great while. These hands and this heart are yours for the asking, as long as you care to have me. And when you do not, then say so, ma'am, and I will go. For I have learned these long years to earn my bread, and can do so again.'

She knelt at Lady Eastmiln's feet and covered the old hands with tears and kisses.

'Forgive me, ma'am. I have not your powers of commanding my weaknesses. If I could retire to Mrs Ogilvie's room for a while I shall collect myself.'

'Do, child,' said Lady Eastmiln graciously, 'and let us hear no more of your going. I shall tell the laird that I wish it.'

'Then how can he refuse?' said Anne, and hurried away, as though overcome.

But, upstairs, she dried her cheeks and sauntered to the window to watch Patrick chasing Kitty on the hillock, and smiled.

Lady Eastmiln, enjoying her position of benefactor – a rare occurrence these days – took it upon herself to inform Kitty and Patrick of her intention to befriend Miss Clarke, and recounted Anne's sad history. They were delighted, for Anne encouraged them in their nonsense and acted as an indulgent chaperone. Also, her evident attachment to Lady Eastmiln absolved them from possibly tedious attentions when the placid Martha had gone.

So on the afternoon of 7 March they all three ventured out to discover signs of Spring in Glenisla. And once or twice Kitty put her arms round Patrick's neck and kissed him, and looked roguishly at Anne.

'Are you not going to scold me, as Martha does?' she cried.

Anne shook her head. 'I am of Lady Eastmiln's mind,' she said easily, 'and say – let the children play!'

But she had already gleaned the gossip of Patrick's night prowl from the servants, while scolding them roundly for repeating such wicked rubbish, and she watched her charges narrowly.

Now what good would it do, she pondered, if the laird was to be cuckolded by his brother? Miss Kitty might be packed off home, but while he might not marry again as long as she lived, supposing the girl was with child? And would the Ogilvies risk even the open scandal of a separation? The old woman is shrewd enough to smooth anything over, and once Kitty produced an heir they would cling to it whoever had been the father. All in the family. All in the family. Still, everyone likes *me*, so that is a good beginning.

The weather was fickle, and they drew the shabby curtains that evening to shut out the dark and the rain. And they were merry by the fireside because Patrick brought out his violin and played some of Mr Handel's airs, and some old Scottish melodies, and sang duets with Kitty. And Lady Eastmiln reminisced on past glories, and Martha dreamed a wedding, and Anne praised and listened and saw that everyone was comfortable.

The door almost blew open at nine o'clock, and a tall stoop-shouldered man blew in with it, shaking the rain from his streaming plaid. A shriek from Kitty brought them all to their feet.

'Oh, you are back, you are back!' she cried, full of pleasure at the surprise. 'And have you brought me a message from my mother, and did you see sweet Frisk, and was . . . ?'

'Be quiet, you goose-cap!' Lady Eastmiln said amiably. 'Lizzie! Annie! Kate! The laird is home again. Look to his horse, and warm a brick for his bed, and set the table.'

'Welcome home, Thomas!' cried Patrick, laying down his fiddle and holding out his hand, smiling. 'You may have your bride – she clacks all day like a flock of hens! Let me pour you a meridian of brandy to keep out the cold.'

'Thomas,' said Martha, anxious to commend herself, 'I am glad you are back, for it's but a fortnight to my wedding.'

Anne Clarke recognised the worn face and courteous manner, even as his eyes questioned her presence, and she saw that he knew her again.

'Why, sir,' she cried, 'we have met before, at the Boat of Bardmony, and I did not know you then or I would have spoken.'

'This is your cousin, Anne Clarke,' said Lady Eastmiln,

68

in her new dignity as protectress. 'She is my late sister's daughter, and is to stay with us here.'

Thomas disengaged Kitty's arms from about his neck and welcomed Miss Clarke to the hospitality of his roof, but he seemed disturbed. Perhaps it was the thought of yet another person to be reckoned with, yet another wrinkle in the monk's habit he had enjoyed for so many years. Or perhaps, looking into Miss Clarke's cool grey eyes, he felt a twinge of fear that was almost superstitious.

But he shook off his instinctive reaction, let them fuss with his boots and plaid, and sat in his big carved chair before the fire to warm himself, a laird at ease in his private kingdom.

VI

The horseman galloped as though the devil himself were at his heels, his coat skirts muddied, his thigh boots splashed with mire. He was well away with whisky, the only warmth that could reach his bones on such a ride in such weather, and as he urged his hireling horse along the road to Alyth he sang to keep himself company.

> *The corpse lay stripped and naked,*
> *He said to Doctor Munroe,*
> *'Oh cut me open gently*
> *and cut me open slow.'*

Fifteen years had lain between William and Patrick, he reflected, interrupted only by a daughter who showed signs of neither spirit nor beauty. Fifteen years and a final blessing. And Lady Eastmiln had held her head higher than ever with this last late son, born twenty years after her marriage, and the handsomest and gayest boy of them all. His presence had comforted her in the dark days of the '45, while her husband busied himself raising money and men for the Prince, took her three elder sons with him as Ensigns in his regiment, and skirled off to war without a backward glance. And Lady Eastmiln had feared and watched and waited, along with thousands of other women, until they clattered home, lathered to the hocks, for a respite between campaigns. And in that respite the laird had taken his aging wife into his arms again, and conceived yet another child.

The lady held her head as high as before, and thanked

God for a fifth son – a second daughter would have been the ultimate disaster – and named him Alexander. But though the boy seemed healthy he was as black as a crow, short-bodied and self-willed. Sensing a spirit as indomitable as her own, weary with this latest and unwelcome birth, she set herself out to break him into submission, since the men were away and could not help her. He resisted her; at first in bewilderment, then in fear, finally in fury. His temper became as black as his hair. A child of the Rebellion, he fought his own childish campaign against his mother.

By 1747, the estate neglected, her husband imprisoned for treason, her eldest sons trailing home from France under the Indemnity Act, Lady Eastmiln had made an enemy of her baby, and he had made an enemy of the puzzling world.

A huddle of sombre houses through the drizzle marked the advent of Alyth, and interrupted the rider's train of reflection. He spurred his horse and sang into the driving rain.

> *Feed your hungry students*
> *Gathered row on row,*
> *Carve them up the gibbet meat*
> *That dangled on a tow.*

None of them could deal with the boy, and none apart from Martha – he remembered – tried to reach him. Even she, patient with everyone, accepting the fact that a son could do as he pleased and a daughter must hold her tongue, found him an unpredictable companion. He would not be driven and he could not be led. His mother had cried that the Reverend Mitchell should have seen *this* devil, as Alexander chased the sheep over the fields with whoops of contempt, made Thomas's horse start so that the laird nearly fell from his saddle, and broke the last of her delft ware.

Sullenly Alexander had watched her make a favourite of Patrick, and pondered on the differences between them. Perhaps, he thought, she preferred Patrick because his hair was brown and curly instead of lank and black. Perhaps if he, Alexander, learned to play the fiddle, to tease and laugh and be impudent, his mother would love him. So he took the violin into the barn, lost his temper at the unearthly sounds that tortured the air, and broke it across his knee in a rage. He pulled Martha's locks to make her giggle, and she screamed with pain. He laughed at the wrong things for the wrong reasons, and instead of Patrick's chuckle heard a raucous cry of derision that brought his mother's hands to her ears. He attempted to be witty, and his wit scalped them. And everything was wrong, terribly irretrievably wrong. So he hid in the byre and held himself lest his heart break, and could not weep because of the pain in his chest.

It's up and down the ladder
To the dance on air below,
And it's new beef for dinner –
The feast of Doctor Munroe.

Then Patrick, whose father had died and whose brothers had fought for Prince Charlie, enlisted at fifteen in the 89th Foot under Major Hector Munro's command. For the first time in his life Alexander saw his mother cry.

'Oh, my son, my son, to stand before me in King George's uniform!' she said, as Patrick saluted.

And Alexander waited to hear her pronounce his brother no Ogilvie, and to banish him from the house. But after a while she dried her eyes, and patted his chubby cheeks and his scarlet sleeves, and spoke of buying a commission for him, and stroked his curly head.

'Times change,' she said at length, 'and we must change with them – or break. And what have any of my sons to look to, if they do not make their own way?'

So even spiritual treason could be excused, and Patrick spoke of the places he would see, to comfort her; and marched off, with a flourish of drums and a proud face, to broach strange lands and hear strange tongues and meet strange people. And Patrick was a hero.

But how could they rid themselves of Alexander? He refused King George's uniform, saying it was the colour of spilled blood. Thomas refused to have him on the farm, and the entire neighbourhood wanted him anywhere but at their own doorstep. So in the end they told him he had a fine head for learning, and dispatched him to Edinburgh to learn to be a sawbones.

'You might become a ship's surgeon,' said Lady Eastmiln, attempting kindness.

But he knew that the kindness overlaid a hope that he might sail away for good, and leave them in peace.

> *Wash it down with liquor*
> *And let the whisky flow,*
> *There's plenty round the gobbets*
> *You pickled long ago.*

'Now here's a dark face on a dark night,' said the landlord of *The Creel* in Alyth. 'Stable his horse, Tom, while your mistress sets the table! Welcome, sir. Why, sir, is it not Dr Ogilvie of East Mill?'

'Himself and no other,' said Alexander easily, and came slowly from his horse because he was tired.

'You have ridden a fair way, Dr Ogilvie. Your poor jade can scarcely draw breath. Tom, give her a good rub down, and a warm drink and bran mash, laddie. Come your ways in, Dr Ogilvie. You are very welcome. You could take a dram, I'm thinking?'

'I could take three or four. Fetch me the bottle, Master

Murray, and the bottle and I will consult together. You have a good fire.'

He drank a glass straight down and poured another. Then, wet and muddied as he was, he turned out again into the yard and went to the stables. Young Tom looked up almost in fear at the dark sturdy man with his gipsy face and black forelock.

'I'm come to see to my horse,' said Alexander abruptly.

'She's gae weary, master,' Tom mumbled, angered beyond caution. 'She's mud on the hocks, master.'

The mare stood, head hanging, flecks of foam on her mouth, but did not start as Alexander drew near. Then unexpectedly he caressed her neck so lovingly that Tom was amazed.

'I'll curry her myself,' said Alexander. 'Show me where everything is, boy, and get about your business.'

The lad shrugged and obeyed. But hesitating at the stable door, the saddle over his shoulder, he watched Alexander examining the mare's hooves and legs, and heard him talking softly.

'Whisha, whisha,' he was saying. 'I've ridden you hard, my beauty, but I wish you no ill.'

He groomed and watered her, and she ceased to tremble. And as she fed he stood by, stroking her haunches and talking to her in his strange whimsical manner. And when she had done she turned her head and nuzzled him, eyes dark and gentle.

'You're o'er fond of her, I'm thinking,' said Tom, won round. 'How long have you owned her, master?'

'She's not my horse,' said Alexander calmly. 'She's a hireling. But that's no fault of hers or mine.'

He came over and leaned on the door jamb, looking down at the freckled stable lad with some irony.

'You're thinking I'm a fool to make such a splother over a hired mare, are you not?' he said, amused. 'Well, let me

74

tell you this, laddie. She's carried me from Edinburgh without so much as a murmur. She's ridden her heart out for me, and it's an honest heart, laddie. And after all that she gets but a few kind words and her supper, and yet she thanks me for it and would carry me again – to the world's end, if need be, and to the end of her strength. Tell me, laddie, what human being would do the same?'

'I don't know, master,' Tom muttered, his wits astray at this odd philosophy. 'I know nothing, master.'

'Then remember that,' said Alexander, once more withdrawn. 'You'll get better service and purer love from one poor beast than your own mother would give you. There's wisdom for you – and in case wisdom isn't enough, here's a penny for being sorry for her!'

And he strode back across the yard to his bottle of whisky.

'Now, Master Murray,' he said. 'You can chalk up my score to my brother, the laird, who will pay you when he next comes to Alyth. And as he is paying, and you will enjoy my company until late tomorrow, we'll make a merry stay of it. So tell your good wife to put a pair of fowls to roast, and stick her salt beef back in the storehouse where it belongs. And while I'm waiting I'll have a platter of buttered bannocks to go with the whisky.'

He threw himself full length on the settle and propped his legs on the chimney-piece, staring into the flames.

'You'll be come to Miss Ogilvie's wedding, I'm thinking,' said Mistress Murray, as she set the dog turning the spit.

'I am, Mistress.'

'Mr Stewart is an honest gentleman.'

Alexander did not answer, brooding over the whisky.

'And has a fine business in Alyth,' she pursued. 'And I have heard that the wedding is to be a bonnie one, with bagpipes bringing in the day, and pipers following both

75

bride and groom on their morning calls, and two dinners – one for Mr Stewart's friends and one for Miss Ogilvie's . . .'

'And the laddies firing pistols,' said Alexander in dour humour, 'and the entire occasion bearing the appearance of a military march rather than a tender mating!'

'Aye, aye,' said Mistress Murray, uncertain of his meaning. 'And the fiddlers in the house and the pipers in the fields, and dancing both indoors and out.'

Alexander turned slowly round to face her, and smiled deliberately into her good-natured face.

'Well, Mistress, that is as it should be. For Andrew Stewart has been a bachelor long enough, and my sister is in her twenty-eighth year, and we are all well pleased that they have got off at last!'

Misliking his smile, and fearing other sarcasms, the landlady gave the dog a final clout to keep it moving the spit, and left him to his bottle and the fire and his own dark thoughts.

'Yon's a right black corbie!' she whispered to her husband.

'Aye,' he said, fingering his beard, 'and I'm no sure they're expecting him to the wedding. But that's none of our business. Never come between an Ogilvie and his purpose, they say in Glenisla. And even the minister cursed them!'

Alexander had drunk only enough to keep himself warm, and ridden slowly and set out late the next day, so that he would arrive after dark. For, Anne had counselled him in Edinburgh, even a black sheep will not be turned shelterless into the night. 'So come softly,' she had said, 'and come soberly, and try to keep a civil tongue in your head. It may be that I can win your mother over, and then I shall send an express to tell you you are wanted. Otherwise I dare not

76

write to you for fear of exposure. We must seem friends, but not lovers, and not accomplices. And if you do not hear from me, then come nevertheless, eight or ten days after me, as though you could not bear to miss your sister's wedding. And I shall see that all is as well as it can be.'

'Why, she is as good a jade as yourself,' Alexander said to his mare, who trotted steadily along the drove road, fed and rested as she had not been since they left Edinburgh. 'And I only promised her a new gown when I became the laird!' Alexander added.

He stopped a little way from the house at East Mill, his heart hammering in terror and anticipation, and he hated them for making him afraid. Slowly he rode towards the lighted windows, hearing Patrick's blasted fiddle playing, hearing voices raised in laughter and singing would would cease at his entry.

'As though I carried the blight!' he said bitterly.

One voice at least was raised in welcome. From the barn a collie ran, in hysterical delight, and leaped about his legs as he dismounted.

'Why, Rabbie,' cried Alexander, 'you have not forgotten me!'

He squatted to fondle the silky ruff and pricked ears, and hold the warm muzzle to his cheek. Excited, the collie ran a little way ahead, and then ran back, urging him on. And Alexander followed reluctantly, leading his mare, and tying her reins to the garden gate. Alone, he was wholly vulnerable, his mouth softened, his eyes bright. For a moment he stood before the door, wondering what it must be like to be Patrick; imagining the joy that would surge through the house as he came on them like a blessing. Reality wiped the smile from his face. Roughly he brought down the latch and flung back the door, and the company turned towards him, voices and smiles dying, and the fiddle trailing to silence.

Weather-stained and thigh-booted, his plaid dabbled

with dirt, his hair hanging dankly over his forehead, Alexander surveyed them.

'Bring out the fatted calf, Lady Eastmiln,' he cried, 'for your prodigal son has come home!'

VII

Good humour vanished with Alexander's arrival. Lady Eastmiln became more perverse with Martha – the only member of the family, apart from the dog, to show any affection in Alexander's presence. Thomas, while declining to show his displeasure in matters of food and lodging, made it plain that his youngest brother was no longer welcome. Patrick attempted to keep out of his way, and answered sharply or off-handedly when driven to it. The servants took their tone from their employers. Kitty began by being playful, and stopped abruptly when Alexander showed he knew a trick or two with flirtatious lassies. And Anne Clarke, watchful and diplomatic as always, smoothed over this conversation and that remark, with little effect.

On an impulse, Kitty and Thomas and Patrick decided to ride over to the Spaldings in Glenkilry. Their departure was slightly hysterical with relief, though Alexander had been in the house less than four days. So they rode swiftly into the weak March sunshine, leaving the old, the timid and the servile to cope with his black humours.

In Kitty's mind they were returning to one of the two places she still thought of as home, and East Mill House became a mere stepping stone of the past, something to be put behind her. She had always possessed the gift of forgetting what was disagreeable, and now she forgot the Ogilvies for a while. Instead of a married woman visiting her married sister, in company with her husband and brother-in-law, she was transformed back to pretty Kitty Nairne riding with two cavaliers towards a loving and indulgent family.

Patrick, sharing her ability to enjoy the present and see no further than his nose, or as far as tomorrow, joined in her hilarity. They raced each other along the road, and cantered back to Thomas crying that he was a slow-coach. But he, wrapped in his own problems, paid no heed to them.

He was struggling with an apprehension that had been called up by something deeper than Alexander's profligacy. He was afraid of Anne Clarke. Until her coming his family had been predictable in their behaviour. Without hope or fear of change, it had seemed to Thomas that they would remain in their usual jigsaw of autocracy, irresponsibility, timidity or hatred until death scattered the pieces one by one. But this small, soft-spoken, grey-eyed woman wrought differences in days. Lady Eastmiln listened to her, acted on her suggestions. Patrick thought her a good-natured wench and succumbed to her flattery. Martha was showing signs of a miniature rebellion, which would fortunately be doused or absorbed by her coming marriage. Kitty had confided more to her than she ever did to him. And Alexander was planning something. His unpleasantness carried a threat.

'Katie!' Thomas called, and obediently she reined in beside him, her cheeks brilliant with exercise. 'Kitty, what do you think of Anne Clarke?'

She thought a great deal of her, and said so in a tumble of half-finished sentences.

'So kind, so understanding. I feel I could tell her anything.'

'Well, do not tell her too much,' Thomas counselled, disturbed.

She made a face, and cantered back to Patrick. That morning Anne had told her, in the most tactful way, that she should watch her husband's health, and she recollected the circumstances with some pique.

'For though he is old enough to be your father,' Anne had

said, smiling, 'and though not every pretty girl would think him gallant, nevertheless he is an honest gentleman. And we poor women must do what we can with the husbands it has pleased God to give us. Why, I should think myself very fortunate in your place.'

Kitty was not subtle enough to trace the sting in the words, only to feel it; and as she frowned uncertainly, Anne put a hand on hers and delivered the *coup de grâce*.

'See that he does not ride too far, too long,' she had said, in sisterly entreaty. 'I have some little knowledge of medical matters, both by experience and through listening to Dr Ogilvie, and I think your husband somewhat sickly. The laird would do well to wear a warmer coat.'

She raised her voice slightly on the last sentence, and Lady Eastmiln caught the drift of her advice.

'Why, I have told Katherine time and time again that he should wear his plaiden jacket, and that good body belt. And indeed, before he married, he used to wear a striped woollen night cap on his breast that kept him warm. But she will not have it, and he listens to *her*. He listens to *her*.'

Kitty had stood amazed at the querulous note, for so far her word – however frivolous – had been law.

'It is an old ugly jacket, ma'am,' cried Kitty in a temper, 'and makes him ugly, too.'

'You think too much of looks, miss, and not enough of what is sensible and right. If you spent less time on your toilet and more on your husband's health I should be a contented woman!'

Into the promised fray slid Anne, hands outstretched to both parties.

'Why, ma'am. Why, Mrs Ogilvie. What is this?' she asked, laughing. 'High words before breakfast? Never quarrel on an empty stomach, I beg, for you can quarrel better after food!'

They laughed with her, but an uneasiness remained, and each remembered that the other had spoken over-frankly. And Anne, gently chiding Lizzie for eavesdropping on her betters, had carried a little smile on her lips for quite half an hour afterwards.

At Glenkilry, Kitty looked from her tired husband to hearty George Spalding, and compared them to Thomas's detriment. And as Bethia led her away to see the new baby Kitty asked almost fretfully if Thomas was not greatly improved in health.

'He seems well enough,' said Bethia, still uncomfortable because Kitty had met him under their roof, 'but he is very quiet and a little pale.'

'Oh, that is all a nonsense!' Kitty cried, and stared at the baby without seeing it. 'One would think, from the way everybody carries on, that I had married an invalid. He is but a few years older than your own husband – I would have you know!'

But she was beginning to see herself as a laughing stock, and could not bear it, so romped with Patrick. And when Thomas complained that his stomach hurt him, and George Spalding kindly mixed a glass of hot ale and whisky with a scrape of nutmeg, Kitty laughed until the tears stood in her eyes. His stomach continued to plague him, and the antics of Kitty and Patrick embarrassed their hosts. So the visit, which should have been a welcome interlude, became a weariness, and they prepared to return sooner than they had intended. But before they went Bethia took it upon herself to administer a salutary scolding.

'You are too free with the Captain,' she began. 'I wonder that your husband says nothing – mine would send him packing, and give me a slap into the bargain. You are too careless entirely, Kitty. Careless of your husband's health and feelings, and of your reputation.'

Seeing the girl's mouth tremble, remembering what a

gay lass she had been and what a child she still was, Bethia patted her cheek.

'Do not misunderstand me, Kitty. We wish you so very well. We *know* you, but others do not. What passes as harmless fun in the family may seem scandalous elsewhere. Look to your husband, who seems neither as strong nor as happy as he should be!'

A child called, a servant asked for instructions, a multiple small domestic cares laid claim to Bethia. But when she had gone from the room, Kitty stamped her foot and folded her arms, and stared out of the window: as bleak as a little girl who has asked for a doll and been given a sampler to work.

'Oh – divil burst the Ogilvies!' she cried, ashamed and sorry for herself. 'I wish to God I was free again!'

George Spalding also had his say, with Thomas, and received the customary excuse of Patrick's keeping Kitty merry with a lift of the eyebrows.

'God love us, Thomas,' George remarked with some humour, 'if any brother of mine made so free with *my* wife's waist I should throw him over the barn! Get her with child, man, and get her settled. She's too flimsy by half for a married woman! This situation suits as ill as a demi-pique saddle on a draught ox!'

Thomas mumbled and smiled into his dram, deeply hurt and doubly helpless, since Kitty had shown signs of disliking his tepid embraces already.

'Well, well,' said George good-naturedly, 'it is not for me to meddle, but we love you both and would see you happy, with a quiverful of bairns like our own.' And taking Patrick aside he spoke to him cautiously but shrewdly. 'A fine set-up man like yourself must find time hanging on his hands at East Mill,' he said. 'Is there no chance of your re-enlisting? And, if not, there must be a dozen ways of using an experienced soldier. Why, man, you do not want to sit by your brother's fire and eat his bread for ever! How do you think of employing yourself?'

Patrick said he did not know.

'You are but two and twenty,' said George, puzzled at his apathy. 'You cannot think of spending the rest of your days idle?'

Patrick said, with a laugh and a shrug, that he enjoyed but poor health and might not live long.

'Nonsense, man. Why, you will wake up one of these fine mornings and long for a horse between your knees and a foreign coast, surely? It must be a weary business sitting with the womenfolk, drinking slops, after the life you have led!'

But Patrick had not taken such a close hard look at his future before, and was discomposed. So the three of them set out for Glenisla in three separate dudgeons, and arrived to find the Ogilvie household at odds with itself, and added to the confusion. Had it not been for the tact and kindness of Miss Clarke, as Lady Eastmiln herself said, the evening might have ended in bloodshed.

VIII

'Will you walk with me on the braes, Miss Clarke?' said Alexander. 'For my mother and sister have a wedding in their heads, the children play hide and seek, the laird works for us all, and no one but the dog cares for my company.'

Anne hesitated, and looked at Lady Eastmiln.

'Walk with my son, Miss Clarke,' said the matriarch, 'if you will be so kind. And a moment with you, miss.' Here she pulled Anne down to whispering distance. 'Get him gone, miss. Get him gone. He is malcontent and a scapegrace. The laird will have none of him, and no more shall I. Get him gone, Miss Clarke, if you please.'

'But not until the wedding is over, surely, ma'am?'

'He may not stay a day after! We have been at odds since he arrived, and might have come to blows, too, but for your good self.'

'Well, ma'am, I shall think of something, Dr Ogilvie,' she cried, 'I am at your service for a half hour or so.'

Together they strolled, careful to maintain the appearance of mere friendship: he scowling and hacking at the heather, she taking his arm.

'You were a fool to think it would work, Annie,' he said at length, but not unkindly.

'I am no fool at all,' she replied. 'I have kept my mouth closed and my eyes and ears open, and this is only the beginning. You have played *your* part badly, for certain. But never mind. Alex, you will have to go back and leave me here, and when it is time to come I shall send a message for you by William Craig the chapman.'

Suddenly wretched at the thought of his shabby lodgings

off the Dumbie-dykes, and the attentions of his bride – who nightly hammered on his door and screamed abuse – he began to argue and to grumble.

'Listen to me, Alex,' she said, restraining him, 'what do you expect to wring from them beyond a grudging board and lodging? I can get more for you. Why, the whole house is but a pack of cards ready to tumble. Your mother trusts me, the Captain and Mistress Kitty are longing to fall in bed together, and the laird is an ailing man. The servants are already talking of incest, and may soon talk of murder.'

He stopped and faced her.

'Aye, aye,' said Anne lightly. 'I do not waste my time, Dr Ogilvie. Mistress Kitty returned from Glenkilry with a face as black as your hair, and spoke to me of giving a dose to her husband.'

'Are you sure? She? That goose-cap will say anything, and forget it a minute after. She did not mean a word of it.'

'I do not care whether she meant it or not,' said Anne. 'She *said* it to me, after the visit. I did not take her seriously, of course. But she will say it often in the next few weeks, until I begin to wonder whether it is true. And then she will embroider her statement by telling me she purposes to buy poison – either from Mr Robertson of Perth or Mistress Eagle of the seed shop in Edinburgh, both of whom have supplied her with medicines from time to time. Then I shall warn her that if she does such a thing she will be brought to an untimely end. She may ask me if I can procure poison for her secretly, and in joke I shall say I can – but never do so. And at the last, Alex, she will be driven to persuade the Captain to find some.'

'This is moonshine!' he shouted. 'Are you out of your wits, woman?'

'No, indeed, Dr Ogilvie. There are more purposes than one for procuring poison. Wild dogs may be spoiling the game, and need to be put down. There may be too many rats in the storeroom or the barn. But poison will be in that house, and Mistress Kitty and the Captain are very thick, and she talks too freely for her own good. So,' said Anne, turning again for home, 'should anything happen to the laird, should he – for instance – suffer another ulcerous attack which proved fatal, I will send for you.'

He took her hand and swung it to and fro, thinking. Then he clapped his own upon it and laughed.

'And what will you be doing, Annie, while all these plots bubble about your head?'

'I shall be full of concern for all parties,' she said lightly. 'I shall warn Kitty against her foolishness, which will make her obdurate. I shall take Lady Eastmiln into my confidence at the right moment, and she will warn the laird – so that he will know whom to suspect, and whom to blame, when he is stricken. I shall prevent the servants from gossiping, saying that this is not right – and they will see that I am anxious to keep matters dark, and gossip all the more. And when the laird is taken ill I shall nurse him, and do all I can.'

'He does not care for you, Annie.'

'No,' she said, with a little grimace, for she had her share of vanity, 'but in the end he will be glad of me, and estranged from all the others, save my good aunt – who trusts me.'

'And suppose Mistress Kitty is pregnant before the laird takes a chill? Suppose, in a gush of fatherly foolishness, he forgives her and banishes the Captain, and all are as merry as larks in a pie?'

'If she does become pregnant,' said Anne, 'the laird will be given to suspect the Captain of doing his work for him – and *there's* a pretty pickle!'

He looked at her in astonishment; at the light grey eyes and the smooth coil of brown hair, at the neat grey dress and white fichu, and the dark decent cloak and hood.

'Well, by God, Annie,' he said appreciatively, 'if I did not know what you were I should call you a tidy little spinster!'

He glanced about him, but the braes were inhabited by nothing but heather.

'Annie,' he said persuasively, 'it's been a while since that last night in Edinburgh together. And that slut Rattray never knew one end of a man from the other!'

'No, Alex,' she said, and put one hand lightly over his mouth.

'For God's sake, woman, are you made of granite? I've lain in the Captain's room and you have lain with my mother in the parlour – and both of us wide awake and staring at the ceiling, I swear. Just this once, Annie. There's nobody coming.'

'Are you mad?' she said quietly. 'Would you risk all for a tumble? We can wait until we are at our ease in East Mill House. And what will you do about your wife when you are the laird of Eastmiln?'

He brooded and shrugged.

'If you can make way for me as laird,' he said slowly, 'I don't doubt you can make way for yourself as lady.'

She smiled and turned about.

'It is time we were going home again, Dr Ogilvie,' she said, pulling up her hood against the wind. 'And remember I have persuaded you to return to Edinburgh after the wedding.'

IX

Weighing his position in Glenisla against his pocket, and feeling that everyone would like to congratulate his sister on her marriage, Thomas had decided on a 'penny wedding'. In former times each neighbour had contributed one penny Scots, but money was in short supply and the present charge of one shilling could only be a barrier to their attendance. So for some days gifts of meal and ale and kain hens had been left at East Mill House, and the servants sat up at nights plucking and dressing the fowls and making preparations. And the beggars from miles about passed the word that there would be free food and drink at East Mill.

Kitty, greatly excited by the coming celebration, insisted on observing all the old customs, and personally instituted the bridal eve ceremony of foot-washing, though her own wedding had been grander and more decorous. So the farmhouse was full of giggling girls, scrambling to seize the wedding ring from its pail of water before washing Martha's feet. And higher than any of them rose Kitty's own laugh, as she attempted to persuade Martha to have her feet stained with henna and her eyebrows with antimony.

With an eye to the possible tantrums of weather, Anne Clarke saw that the barn and grannary were swept to save guests from a wetting. Tallow candles, usually burned in miserly proportions – early bed being a great saver of fuel – were used by the dozen, and no one thought of sleep before midnight.

The morning of 22 March 1765 dawned cold and fine, and the household rose at five o'clock. Anne and Kitty, taking over the laird's bedroom, commanded the calves' bucket full of hot water, and prepared to dress the bride.

Kitty had presented Martha with a box of fashionable wash balls, at the personal cost of four shillings Scots and many instructions to the chapman. Their mixture of white lead and flour and powdered rice, of starch and orris root was said to cleanse the complexion and impart a soft and natural bloom. But when Martha held on to the bedpost and her breath, while they laced her stays, she emerged so flushed that Anne declared her to be pink enough. They had washed her hair in a decoction of young birch tree buds, and released each brown and shining curl from its swaddle of calico strips. And Martha, in a clean white cambric shift, drew on a pair of white thread stockings and fastened her new blue silk garters.

'My shoes will soak through in an instant,' cried Martha, of the flimsy slippers, 'and they were six shillings the pair!'

'You are not married every day,' said Kitty, 'and I have heard that the King of England's daughters wear out a pair like these every week. Here is a sachet of herbs for your bodice. Now hold your head steady while we drop the gown over your hair!'

Very carefully, their tongues between their teeth, their whole beings concentrated on the final effect, they settled the crimson velvet petticoat and cherry silk hoop.

'Is my mother not dressed yet?' Martha asked, concerned that she took precedence, even on her wedding day.

'Lizzie Sturrock is with her,' said Kitty, 'and will do very well.'

They escorted Martha down the stairs with some pride, and found Lady Eastmiln very fine in a blue silk gown that smelled of the black pepper used to preserve it from moths.

'Turn round, miss,' Lady Eastmiln commanded, and tapped her stick for emphasis. 'You look very well, very well indeed, Martha. Why, miss, you are almost pretty.'

Martha, overcome by the compliment, stood stiff and

90

breathless in her elegance.

'Sit her down and wrap a sheet about her,' said Lady Eastmiln, as though Martha were a valuable parcel. 'She must not slop tea on her skirts. Kate Campbell, be quick with the bed-making, and tell the Captain and the Doctor they must get up and dress now. Have the men set tables in the barn, Miss Clarke?'

'Yes, ma'am.'

'Be a good girl, will you, and see that all is proper? For Katherine and Martha are too fine to risk their gowns, and I am too old.'

'Yes, ma'am.'

'Do I recognise that dress, Miss Clarke?'

'Indeed you do, ma'am, for Mrs Ogilvie gave it to me yesterday. Without her,' said Anne graciously, 'I should have cut but a plain figure.'

'You look very well in it, Miss Clarke. A pity you have not more money, for your taste is excellent. Lizzie, make tea for us – and tell the laird that his room is empty now, should he wish to change.'

A skirl of bagpipes announced that the festivities had begun. One by one the Ogilvie men gathered in the parlour, splendid in velvet coats and lace cravats and ruffles and buckles, which had emerged from a chest in the garret.

'What smarts you are!' cried Lady Eastmiln, proud of her progeny.

'The fiddlers are come, ma'am,' said Anne. 'Shall I give them a draught of ale before they begin?'

'Aye, and moisten the pipers' throats, too. For they must keep playing and they get very dry. And here is Mr Stewart in a bright blue coat – is that a Dunblane blue, Mr Stewart? And silver buckles on his shoes. Mercy me, what a spectacle!'

The Reverend Masson conducted the service with a sense of irony, since the Ogilvies only attended church when they were to be married, christened or buried. But he paid a compliment to the bride, shook hands with the groom, and drank his dram down with the rest of them like a good soul.

Then Thomas stepped forward with a great bowl of ale and drank their healths, and Kitty broke an oatcake over the bride's head and joined in the scramble for lucky fragments. Owing to cramped space and general inconvenience they had passed over the custom of untying every knot in the bride and groom's clothing before the service, so Martha was spared uneasiness and the necessity of being tied up again immediately afterwards.

Under Anne's excellent management the servants had produced a feast of gargantuan proportions. The trestle tables were heavy with cold roast and boiled meats, with fowl and game, with puddings of every kind, with pickled salmon and calves' feet jellies. And in the centre of each table sat a great syllabub, rich with cream and wine, perfect in shape, which had cost more tears and time and trouble than all the rest put together. Barrels of ale were broached, bottles of whisky and claret were opened, and a haunch of venison turned on the spit.

The bride and groom sat quietly together, but now and then they exchanged a smile, and once he took her hand and squeezed it respectfully. They would rarely see each other so fine again. This was their day and they regarded it with reverence and some wonder.

The laird moved among his guests, clapping this man on the shoulder, making his bow to that lady, urging all to eat and drink as much as they could hold. And the beggars gave him a special cheer, which he acknowledged courteously. Patrick joined the fiddlers, and played so gaily that they allowed him a performance of his own, and everyone applauded. Alexander, for once, behaved himself, lulled by a family gathering that accepted him as a part of itself.

Lady Eastmiln was lost on a tide of reminiscence. Anne saw that glasses were passed round and plates replenished. And Kitty, let loose in a world she wholly comprehended, flirted with every man who approached, to their mutual delight.

As the afternoon drew on, and some of the proceedings became less decorous, Kitty and Anne took Martha upstairs and helped her to change for the ride to Alyth. The three women talked softly and easily as they made ready for the departure.

'The roads are not bad,' said Kitty. 'You will be at your home before nightfall, Martha.'

Martha's plain face was rapt.

'Why, I am Mrs Stewart, now!' she cried, and they all laughed. 'Miss Clarke,' she continued, 'you have been more than kind. My brother is most generous, and my mother likes everything to be fitting, but it is you who have made my wedding a fine and happy one, and I thank you from the bottom of my heart.'

'You are a good woman, Mrs Stewart,' said Anne slowly. 'I was glad to be of use.' And she held out her hand, which Martha shook earnestly.

Kitty stood, her pretty head held to one side, twisting a nosegay of Spring flowers which Patrick had gathered for her. Martha turned, and hugged and kissed her.

'I beg your pardon, Katherine, if I have ever seemed unkind,' she said, flushing, 'I am a dull creature and do not always understand.'

Kitty wept and clung about her neck, and cried that she could not be unkind if she tried, had never been dull, and possessed all the understanding in the world.

Martha adjusted her mantle.

'I shall expect you both at Alyth,' she said, with a new confidence in herself. 'I hope to see you both often, and we shall be very merry.'

Andrew Stewart helped his bride on to her horse with

great gallantry, made his obeisance to the ladies and shook hands with the gentlemen. Then he swung into his saddle and flicked the reins.

'Come, Mrs Stewart,' he said, 'we must be at Alyth before nightfall.'

United for once, the Ogilvies saw them as far as the drove road, and watched in silence as the two horses and their riders trotted peacefully out of sight. Behind them the wedding feast threatened to spill over into the following day, but that was to be expected; and there would be dozens of aching heads at breakfast, and a clutch of beggars to be driven off, and possibly a virtue or so lost in the haze of drinking and dancing. But Martha and Andrew Stewart would enjoy a goose-feather bed and a long night.

'Why, she has done the best of any of us,' said Alexander wryly. 'I have been told that the meek shall inherit the earth, and by God, it appears to be no more than the truth!'

Lady Eastmiln, suddenly tired and old, said peevishly that she must sit down and take a dish of tea or she would die. Kitty pulled Patrick back into the roistering guests. And the laird reminded his youngest brother that they were making an early start for Dunsinnan, and would accompany him part of the way to Edinburgh.

'Well, miss,' said Lady Eastmiln to Anne, as she was helped into the house. 'I have never seen such a countenance on you before. What ails you, child? Did all not go well enough for you?'

'Why, ma'am,' said Anne, disposed for once to be honest. 'I was but thinking that if all good beginnings made good endings life would be very well. Only it is not so.'

'We must take what comes,' said Lady Eastmiln, lifting the chin that had confronted so many humiliations and disasters. 'The minister urges people to be *good*, Miss Clarke, but I have always urged them to be *brave*. Clear that

94

drunken fellow out of my chair, if you please, Miss Clarke!
I *will* sit by my own hearth though it *is* my daughter's
wedding!'

She sipped her tea, and demanded a dash of whisky in it
and more sugar. And they sat by the fire together, making
quite a private little group, though the party roared on
around and behind them.

'The minister tells us that pride is a vice,' said Lady
Eastmiln, 'but I say not. Miss Clarke, *I* will tell you, I have
sat a hundred times with only pride and courage to sustain
me. It is pride that keeps my head high, and my back
straight. And courage that enables me to sit and bear
trouble. And I fear I shall need both, even now, at the end
of my days.'

Their kinship was evident in the high nose and cheekbones and the stubborn chin, and in some set of countenance which promised endurance.

'Miss Clarke, they call me an arrogant woman, and they
are right. They say I have not much feeling for my children, and I acknowledge that I have been harsh with them.
But I tell you, Miss Clarke, that I am neither heartless nor
unfeeling. I am only a woman who has found living a hard
business, and is resolved – whatever the cost – not to be
broken by it.'

A Death for Eastmiln

X

Their week's holiday at Dunsinnan, in spite of Frisk's hysteria, did not come up to Kitty's expectations. Her behaviour with the Captain had trickled through from Glenkilry via Bethia's letter; and the frolics which had brought indulgent laughter in her single days now drew frowns and scoldings. She sat on a footstool at her mother's feet and yawned over her embroidery.

'Why, you have been married scarcely two months,' commented Lady Nairne, 'and pay more attention to the dog than to your husband!'

'But Frisk is more fun,' said Kitty candidly.

The smile she sought was not forthcoming.

'Think shame on yourself for saying such a thing, miss!'

'But you yourself said that the laird was elderly, and looked like my father.'

Lady Nairne bit off a silk thread and regarded her daughter severely.

'I said what had to be said, and yet you would not be told, miss. And now Mr Ogilvie is your husband you must do your duty by him – and one of those duties is to refrain from discussing his appearance and nature with anyone else.'

'Oh, Lor',' said Kitty diminished. 'Can I not confide in *you*, then, that the house at East Mill is small and crowded and somewhat dirty?'

'It is your own house. See that your husband builds another room or so on to it, and make your servants keep it clean.'

'But it is *not* my house. It belongs to Lady Eastmiln. She

99

and Miss Clarke do all between them. And besides,' she ran on, 'they were to build an outhouse that would serve as a kitchen, and then the kitchen could be a dining room, but it is only half-finished and already falling down again! Oh, Frisk! Naughty Frisk! Look, he has torn my sampler!'

'It is your own fault for brandishing it beneath his nose. Let him be, miss, let him be. You look pale,' she added. 'Can you be with child already?'

'I hope not,' said Kitty, 'for the poor little thing would have nowhere to lay its head. Oh, mamma, I am not well. I am not well!'

'I see you are not. Come, dry your eyes, and tell me what ails you.'

'I think it is the food,' said Kitty frankly, wiping her eyes with the torn sampler. 'We eat well, but we eat so coarse. I have not so much as seen an orange, and I am costive, and cannot sleep at night.'

'You must take salts, then, to make you regular, and a drop or two of laudanum to make you sleep. There is no harm in that, provided you do not make it a habit. And ask for a little fruit now and again, and a salad, instead of so much porridge and pudding. You must look to your own comforts, miss, since no one else can look out for you.'

Kitty could not see Frisk clearly for the tears in her eyes.

'You are a married woman,' said Lady Nairne inexorably, 'and marriage brings a woman many hardships, but that is natural. Now, run and wash your face, and we shall have dinner directly. You will not die of grief. I did not!'

'Oh, I should like to be nineteen for ever, and stay at home with you, and flirt with the gentlemen, and never, never be married!' Kitty sobbed. 'For we used to be so merry, mamma, you and I, and now you are no better than the rest with me! And the Captain is my only friend, and they say I must not have him so. And oh – Frisk, Frisk, I love you more than anyone else in the world!'

The spaniel barked in sympathy, clutched to her bodice, and whimpered and wriggled as her tears watered his smooth coat.

So they trailed home again, to find Anne Clarke established as a permanent housekeeper, and Lady Eastmiln ready to find fault, and Kate Campbell watching sullenly.

'I cannot do with Kate Campbell,' Kitty cried, after supper, irritated by that hang-dog countenance which seemed to reproach and judge her at every turn.

'Why? What has poor Kate done?' Thomas inquired good-naturedly, 'save make her red hands redder by getting my shirts to perfection!'

'I will not have her spying on me.'

'Well, *I* have not seen her spying, miss,' said Lady Eastmiln reasonably. 'And if she did what good would it do her, for she cannot speak of it? All I get is a mouth full of gibberish when I ask her the least thing.'

'Oh, but she *does* spy, mother,' said Patrick. 'She is always tip-toeing in when I lie abed, and peering round the door in the mornings. And whenever Mrs Ogilive and I so much as walk in the garden – there is Kate Campbell a-gaping.'

And he mimicked the stolid staring face to such perfection that even Lady Eastmiln smiled, and called him a fool.

'She is devoted to you, Kitty,' said Thomas, with unusual perception, 'and you make too light of her. If you were as comfortable with her as Miss Clarke is you would find her a loyal personal servant.'

'I had not thought,' said Kitty, considering. The idea of a loyal personal servant in a house where everyone paid deference to the laird and his mother appealed to her. 'I shall give her one of my old gowns,' she said, 'and make up my differences with her.'

Anne Clarke reflected that if Kate Campbell was to

change sides she would have lost an ally and gained an enemy.

'She is a good girl,' said Anne quietly, 'and I would not for worlds speak a word against her, but she is very simple. For that reason I would not call her dishonest, since I think she does not distinguish between what is hers and what is not. And after all, Mrs Ogilvie, what does it matter if she takes a ribbon or two? I have known worse servants in my time. Far worse.'

Her voice, soft and unemphatic, annoyed Thomas.

'I have heard nothing of her stealing,' he said abruptly.

'I did not say she *stole*, Mr Ogilvie, if you will excuse my correction. I said she did not always distinguish what was hers by right.'

'I never knew she was a thief,' cried Kitty, disturbed. 'An eavesdropper, perhaps, though most servants are spies and gossips – but never a thief.'

'What are you all mumbling about?' cried Lady East-miln. 'Speak up, speak up! I must know what is going on in my son's house.'

'We must keep our voices down for the moment, ma'am,' said Anne, speaking confidentially in her ear, 'but I shall tell you the drift of our conversation when we are alone.'

'Well, *I* have missed no object of any value, for one,' said Patrick.

'Nor I,' said Thomas, rising, displeased. 'Nor do I expect to. I have nothing against Kate Campbell.'

'Why, what is there against Kate Campbell?' asked Lady Eastmiln, catching the name. 'She is a good poor girl, is she not?'

'Aye, ma'am,' said Anne, raising her voice. 'And I have never known a better for washing the linen.'

And she smiled at Kate, who blundered in to set the dishes. Her eyes rested for a moment on the thick waist and spreading hips.

102

'Why, Kate!' she said gaily. 'East Mill suits you rarely. 'You grow fatter every day!'

Kate Campbell fumbled the plates, reddened, attempted to speak, and blundered out again in a panic.

'Has she been with your sister at Glenkilry very long, Mrs Ogilvie?' asked Anne smoothly.

Kitty ceased to curl Patrick's hair round her fingers, and thought.

'She came about November, Miss Clarke, if I remember rightly.'

'And before then?' Lady Eastmiln interrupted, for her eyes missed nothing, though her ears sometimes confused her.

'She had been with a Mr Rattray of Dalrullion, for I saw her papers, and he said that she was a good girl – but that he was about to be married, and his wife would bring her own servants.'

'*About* to be married?' said Lady Eastmiln. 'Were there many servants in the house? Had he a mother or a sister living with him?'

'Why no, ma'am. He was a bachelor gentleman, and Kate Campbell did all for him.'

'Aye, so I was thinking.'

Kitty's mouth dropped open. Thomas frowned. Patrick threw back his head and laughed. But Anne Clarke's charitable smile remained.

'Was she ever sick at your sister's house?' Lady Eastmiln persisted.

'You will excuse me, mother,' said Thomas, 'but this conversation was none of my begetting and I mislike it. I have work to do about the farm.'

'Aye, ma'am,' said Kitty, heedless of her husband, 'she was very often sick, at first, but did the washing even so – though she felt poorly. And then about Christmas she was better and has not complained since.'

'Six or seven months with child,' said Lady Eastmiln, her arithmetic completed.

'You would not dismiss her, ma'am,' cried Anne. 'She needs employment more than ever now. And you, Mr Ogilvie, you would not be so unkind!'

But Kitty was childishly concerned with the honour of her family, and Kate had annoyed her.

'I am no preacher, Miss Clarke,' she said spiritedly, 'but I cannot bear with *all* Kate Campbell's faults. If I so much as miss a ribbon – off she goes!'

'She is but a simple-minded girl, ma'am,' Anne pleaded, turning to Lady Eastmiln, 'and means no harm.'

'Aye, aye. But we cannot have a thief *and* a bastard under our roof. Let her be for a while, and I shall think about it.'

Thomas thought about Kate Campbell, too, and that afternoon, when James Millam's wife threw a pair of stout shoes on to the rubbish heap, he picked them up and looked at them.

'They are not worth your trouble, Mr Ogilvie,' cried Mistress Millam. 'They are but those I used to wear when I did the washing. And they are so broke up that my husband has bought me a new pair.'

'Nevertheless, Mistress Millam, they may be good for another washing day or two,' said Thomas. 'Have I your leave to take them?'

She nodded and smiled, wiping her hands on her sides. And Thomas took them back to his own house. Kate Campbell was in the kitchen, crooning to herself in Gaelic, and rubbing his shirts. She jumped as he addressed her by name, and dropped an awkward curtsey. He looked at the reddened eyes and swelling stomach, and pitied her. He would have liked to bid her be of good cheer, to invoke the hospitality of his roof, to offer her protection; but his womenfolk were too strong for him. So he held out the cast-

104

off shoes, which were better than bare feet, and smiled at her.

'Here, Kate,' he said. 'Here is a pair of shoes for you.'

And he patted her shoulder and walked out again.

'There are three handkerchiefs missing from my drawer!' Kitty cried, and burst into a tempest of tears.

'What ails the girl?' demanded Lady Eastmiln tetchily, for she had not yet sipped her morning tea.

'Mrs Ogilvie has missed three handkerchiefs, ma'am,' said Anne.

'Well Kate Campbell cannot have taken them?' said Lady Eastmiln, with dry humour, 'for she always wipes her nose on her sleeve!'

'We shall find them presently, Mrs Ogilvie,' said Anne. 'Do not distress yourself, I beg.'

'But my *mother* worked them for me, Miss Clarke. She worked a full dozen in fine lawn, and they had my initial on one corner and a sprig of heather – sewn very small – just below it. And now there are but eight, and the one I have in my sleeve.'

Anne walked unobtrusively into the kitchen.

'Kate,' she said quietly, 'Mrs Ogilvie is much upset. She has missed three handkerchiefs. Now I stand your friend, Kate, and I will not see you harmed. But you must tell me – and then we can set all right – have you taken them?'

The servant shook her head in idiotic emphasis, and Anne pressed her red hand reassuringly.

'Then all is well,' she said.

'Come, come, cease your noise, child!' Lady Eastmiln was saying sharply. 'Where could the girl hide them? Bring Kate Campbell here, Miss Clarke!'

Poor Kate turned out her pocket, disclosing all the treasures that poverty allowed her: a sprig of heather, two or three coloured pebbles that had caught her fancy, and a piece of cold fried sour cake she had been saving against a hungry hour.

'There is her bed,' cried Kitty, adamant now for justice.

Terror had taken what speech Kate Campbell possessed, and she stood red-faced and open-mouthed as Kitty flounced past her and shook the straw mattress and sleazy blankets. Three fine white lawn handkerchiefs were hidden in a hole in the ticking.

'Did not,' said Kate, beseeching, hands outstretched. 'Did not.'

Patrick had joined the chaos and hung about, shaking his head in amused astonishment.

'Get your things and go!' Kitty cried, strangely peremptory.

The servant was trying to collect her wits, but knowing herself to be no match against Kitty or the evidence, she attempted another argument.

'I could be – 'venged, mistress,' she said, with a limp gesture of defiance.

'Revenged? For stealing my handkerchiefs?'

'The Capting is too free,' said Kate.

'Why, you vixen!' cried Kitty, enraged. 'How can *you* talk of anyone being too free?' And she indicated Kate Campbell's rising belly.

Kate whimpered, and huddled on the side of the box bed, wholly defeated.

'Come, Kitty,' said Thomas, pushing his way through the assembly, 'let the wench stay for today, at least. You would not turn a dog out in this rain without so much as its breakfast. Then tomorrow we shall see.'

Kitty was silent, fingering the treasured handkerchiefs, already sorry that she had been led to say more than she meant, for her carelessness was not unkindness. But though Thomas urged Kate Campbell's suit in the matrimonial bed that night she resolved to have no further trouble and when he had gone about his work the following morning she swept into the kitchen.

'You may be well enough with the laird,' she said, 'but you do not deceive *me*, Kate. Pack up your things and go!'

Kate looked about her for her champion, but he could not be found. So she put together a very small bundle. A thought struck her.

'Wages, mistress,' she said, having received not a penny since she arrived.

'You'll get no wages,' Kitty said. 'You are fortunate to be allowed to go. Another mistress would have called the locksman, and had you whipped through the streets!'

'Wages.'

'No wages! Get you gone, Kate Campbell.'

Dimly, Kate looked about, seeing no help in any face. But Anne Clarke put a parcel of buttered bannocks in her hand.

'Here, Kate,' said Anne softly. 'Here is your breakfast.'

Silently, the servant picked up her bundle and her bannocks, the tears coursing down her cheeks, and made her way through the garden gate. On the drove road she stood helpless, not knowing where to go, then set her face towards Alyth, thinking vaguely that Martha might take her in.

A clatter of hooves reminded her what Kitty had said about the locksman, and she ran to the shelter of a wall and crouched clumsily in the heather. But hearing Thomas's voice, she ventured out again, tear-stained and dishevelled.

'Here, Kate,' he said. 'You had best go back to Mrs Spalding at Glenkilry. I have wrote a letter for you, and she will take you in. Put it safely in your pocket, lassie, and I will point you the way. And here, Kate, here is a shilling for you. Get yourself a pillion ride on the way, if you can. And – God bless you, Kate, you washed my shirts finely.'

'Did not steal,' said Kate, weeping and curtseying. 'Did not.'

'No, Kate, I do not think you stole. But who did is a mystery yet to be discovered. So go your ways, lassie, and God protect you and your bairn.'

'Home,' said Kate. 'I'm gang home. But there is two seas. Two seas to cross. North.'

Thomas soothed his horse and wrinkled his brows in an effort to understand her.

'Why, lassie, Ireland is not two seas away, but one. Have you no friends nearer than that?'

'The miller – at Braemar – his wife is kin.'

'They will take you in when the child is born?'

Kate nodded.

'Will they keep the child?'

She nodded again, though woeful at the thought.

'Well go to Mrs Spalding first, for Braemar is a bonnie distance, Kate. And they will see you are provided for. God bless you, lassie.'

She could not reach his hand, so kissed his stirrup instead. A thousand imprisoned thanks and blessings burned in her breast, but she could not have spoken, even if she were able, for crying. So she wiped her arm across her eyes and set steadily out along the road to Glenkilry; chewing at a bannock and sobbing from time to time, as recollections tormented her.

And Thomas watched her go, seeing that all was very wrong, and not knowing how to right it. So rode slowly home again.

XI

April passed, and Patrick was taken several times by fits of shivering, in which neither blankets nor fire could warm him; and then by such heat that he lay on top of his bed clad only in a nightshirt. And Kitty complained that she was not well, and sent to Edinburgh for salts and laudanum, and also stayed abed. Sometimes, showing neither good sense nor discretion, she and Patrick lay together in his room or hers, when Thomas had gone about his morning work. Lady Eastmiln noticed nothing, and Anne kept her counsel. But Lizzie and Annie whispered and giggled together over every creak heard through the unplastered ceiling, and raised their chapped hands in horror. Their gossip was substantiated by reports from outside the house, through farm servants and tenants, of kisses and embraces on afternoon walks. These morsels were rendered less exciting by news of endearments even in the presence of Thomas and Anne Clarke. Mistress Kitty, apparently, hung round Patrick's neck and curled his hair on her fingers, and played a dozen naughty tricks whether they were alone or in company. They agreed that her behaviour was highly unbecoming, and they wondered that the laird allowed himself to be shamed. But the upstairs door was always open, and every conversation could be heard if one stood on the landing, so the scandal, though very palatable, was also a puzzle to the scandalmongers.

'One morning,' said Annie Sampson, ladling water from the iron pot, 'I believed the Captain to be in Mrs Ogilvie's room. So I took her a dish of tea, to see if this was so. And there stood the Captain in his night shirt, and when he saw me he walked from the bed to the window and pretended to be looking out!'

'Even when I have been at the spinning wheel,' said Lizzie, anxious to cap the story, 'I have heard them shuffling their feet at the bedside, and I have heard them go from one room to another many a time!'

'And I – and Kate Campbell, too – have seen him put his hand down her bodice!' cried Annie.

A silence fell between them as they searched up more tittle-tattle to shock one another. Then Lizzie smiled, seeing the empty ale cask.

'We have run out of ale,' she said, very bright and practical. 'Shall I ask Mrs Ogilvie what kind I should fetch from the Kirkton?'

'You are better to ask Miss Clarke,' said Annie, 'for Mrs Ogilvie knows nothing of the ale.'

Lizzie looked at her with contempt for her stupidity, and then drew closer, smiling.

'But Mrs Ogilvie is the laird's wife,' she whispered behind her hand, 'and it is she who should give the orders!'

Comprehension came to Annie's freckled face, and she pushed Lizzie away coquettishly.

'But I think Mrs Ogilvie has gone early to bed,' she said, and jerked her head pointedly at the ceiling.

'Then I must go *up* and ask her!'

'Well do not put on your shoes, as you did that time we heard the bed rocking like an old ferry boat – else they'll hear you, and stop, and you will know nothing.'

They clung together, tittering. Then Lizzie crept softly up the stairs, tiptoed across the landing and peered curiously round the door. Patrick lay on top of the covers, clad only in his shirt and breeches, and across his breast curved a round creamy arm, the wedding ring plainly visible on one pretty finger. Quickly and noiselessly, hands to mouth, Lizzie ran down again and called from the bottom of the

110

stairs.

'Mrs Ogilvie! Mrs Ogilvie! What ale shall we fetch from the Kirkton?'

She heard a movement of the alcove bed as though Kitty sat up.

'Oh, fetch a barrel of tuppeny ale. That will do very well,' Kitty called down, surprised to be consulted.

Another creak and roll suggested that the Captain was stirring.

'Fetch something stronger than that, Lizzie!' he shouted. 'Tell Fergie Fergusson that the Captain wants a bonnie ale to wet a soldier's throat – he'll know the one I mean!'

'I'll tell him, Captain,' Lizzie managed to say, without giggling, and hurried to the kitchen with yet another tale.

They did not know how long Anne Clarke had been standing in the doorway, nor how much of their conversation she had heard.

'Why are you not about your work?' Anne asked quietly.

Lizzie made a great show of being off to the Kirkton, and Annie ladled hot water into a bowl with more haste than accuracy.

'Mrs Ogilvie and the Captain are not in good health,' Anne continued. 'If they lie abed at odd hours of the day it is to recoup their strength. And they must not be disturbed. Do you understand me?'

'Yes, mistress,' said Lizzie, subdued.

'Your employers know their business best,' Anne Clarke concluded. 'So take care that you mind your own.'

Annie Sampson's mouth opened, and shut again at the expression on that small pale face. Something was brewing here beyond her comprehension. Once, she had consulted a wise woman on a love matter, and experienced the same clutch of superstitious fear. And though the love potion had not worked at all, and her good sixpence lay in the woman's pocket, she had neither complained to her nor spoken of it to a living person, out of that same fear.

'We was saying that the Captain and Mrs Ogilvie seemed too free,' Lizzie dared remark, 'and Kate Campbell told the Captain so, the first week she was here. And something she heard one night in the laird's room had frightened her.'

'And you saw what happened to Kate Campbell,' said Anne, smiling, 'so take care it does not happen to you.'

They hurried to be out of her way. And yet, as Lizzie whispered to Annie that night in the box bed, it was strange that Miss Clarke seemed pleased with their gossip even as she scolded them for it.

Thomas alone took an objective view of Anne, uninfluenced by her efforts to please him. An introspective man, he saw that his mother had become Anne Clarke's mouthpiece, that Kitty and Patrick were too light-headed to go anywhere but where the wind blew, and that the servants were afraid of her. Vaguely, though intrigue was foreign to his nature, he suspected her of engineering Kate Campbell's dismissal, but could neither prove it nor suggest a motive. And though his home was cleaner and more comfortable than it had ever been, he did not forget that she had come to it with another purpose. He had seen her talking to William Craig the chapman, who carried all manner of goods and messages between Alyth and Edinburgh. And he reasoned that a man who could bring salts and laudanum for Kitty's persistent ill-health, could take letters to Alexander. He worried about Alexander's silence, too, since apart from his bill at *The Creel* no more debts had been incurred and no money demanded.

'Something's afoot,' said Thomas to his horse, sorely puzzled, 'but I cannot think what.'

'Did you find a use for the shoes, Mr Ogilvie?' cried Mistress Millam, as he dismounted.

'Aye – a poor wench that left our service had them. I'll have a word with your good man, Mistress, if he's about.'

James Millam, the tacksman, hailed him in great good humour. They were both reserved in speech, saying nothing that did not relate to the matter in hand; and they could also confide in one another and know that the confidence would be respected, even in the marital bed. So Thomas, walking away from Millam's cottage, leading his horse, availed himself of this trusty pair of ears.

'I am short of ready money for a while, Jamie,' he said, 'and I wondered if you would lend me ten shillings? You shall have it when the sheep are sheared and I have sold the fleece.'

'Aye, aye,' said Millam comfortably. 'Take your time, Mr Ogilvie. Take your time.'

He did not ask why Thomas needed it so quickly.

'I have a cousin, a Miss Clarke, staying at East Mill with us.'

'A tidy little body, Mr Ogilvie, and very pleasant-tongued.'

'That may well be, Jamie, but I shall have no peaceable possession of my house until she is gone. So if you will lend me her fare to Edinburgh I'll set her on her way.'

'I'm sorry to hear that, Mr Ogilvie. And is Mrs Ogilvie well?'

He had heard the gossip, and discounted it.

'Not well enough for my liking. But she'll mend, Jamie, she'll mend.'

'You'll pay my respects to Lady Eastmiln?'

'I will indeed, Jamie.'

'And is your brother the Captain no better?'

Thomas shook his head, and as he seemed disinclined to talk further they concluded their business.

'The laird carries enough troubles on his shoulders, I'm thinking,' said Mistress Millam, anxious to hear what had passed. 'They say in the Kirkton that his wife goes walking with the Captain every day, and John Lamar has seen them with their arms about each other in broad daylight!'

'Hold your tongue, woman,' said James Millam, 'until you have seen them for yourself – which I have not, for one. I'll have no scandal spoken about the laird in *my* house.'

XII

Not all the flowers in Scotland could lighten East Mill House for Kitty, though daffodils blew in the morning breeze, stocks scented the night wind, lupins promised abundance, and the lavender border would provide fresh sachets for her linen. The Grampians, which she had seen as guardians of the stronghold when she first came, now seemed to imprison her. The forests, gleaming gold and green in the May sunshine, were remote from her. And the solitary cry of eagle and falcon reminded her of a lost freedom. So she drooped at the window, and was only aroused by Patrick's smile and Patrick's fiddle and Patrick's stories of foreign lands.

'What ails the goose-cap?' Lady Eastmiln demanded daily, querulous at the sight of pale cheeks and unsmiling eyes and lips. 'She was as merry as a cricket when she arrived. Miss Clarke, see that we have some crabs or a lobster from the creelman when he calls. And a salmon pie would not be unwelcome, after all the broiled and salted meats we have been eating all winter.'

'Come, Mrs Ogilvie,' Anne coaxed, 'let us see what the packman carries the next time he is round. You could buy a length of sprigged muslin, and I will help you to sew a new gown.' And in her ear she whispered, 'Are you sure you are not pregnant? For, if so, I know a dozen remedies to abate sickness and discomfort. I stand your friend, Mrs Ogilvie.'

'I am not pregnant so far as I know,' said Kitty, tearful, 'but I am not well, and what is to become of me?'

Anne Clarke turned to Lady Eastmiln.

'I think that as the Captain is indisposed, ma'am, and the family is going to the kirk, I shall take Mrs Ogilvie for a walk – if you can spare my company.'

'Aye, take the child, and get a little colour in her face. I cannot bear to see so many sad creatures about me. God's love, I have been hearty all my days, and the only son who ails nothing I could do without!' She leaned towards Anne confidentially. 'Why is she not with child by now?' she asked. 'They have been married above three months. I knew my duty better, miss, when *I* was a bride!'

She watched them walk down the garden path and through the gate, and rested her head against the back of her chair while Lizzie fetched her best black cloak from the chest.

'I am too old,' she told herself, closing her eyes, 'for all this trouble.'

'Now what ails you, Mrs Ogilvie?' asked Anne briskly. 'You have a good husband, enough to eat, enough to wear, and good friends all about you. Ask me to do anything, and if it is in my power I will – from listening to a confidence to cutting out a new shift.' Her real question was delivered lightly. 'Is the laird not attending to your bed at nights?' she asked, and laughed.

'Oh, he is well enough,' said Kitty, forlorn, 'but how can I talk to *you* of such matters, Miss Clarke? You were never married.'

Anne reflected, ironically, that she knew rather more about coupling than the entire Ogilvie clan put together, but assumed a modest aspect.

'That is true, Katherine,' she said, and added timidly, 'I may call you Katherine, may I not? Now that is good in you, for we can talk as friends! I have eyes and ears, Katherine, and have served many women in many houses, and I know a great deal by hearsay.'

Kitty struggled with herself, uncertain what was proper to reveal.

116

'He likes my company more than I like his,' she said at length.

'Well, that will improve with time,' said Anne easily, dropping her usual formal tone. 'A man is born, apparently, knowing all about such matters, but a woman must come to them gradually. And a good wife does not refuse her husband.'

'So my mother and my sister told me. But whereas my mother said that I must bear with his fancies, my sister laughed and said it was good sport. And I have seen her clasp her husband's hand when she thought no one was looking. And though she has a child nearly every twelve month, and is ill in her breasts with every one, she makes a boast of it and says she is not surprised they have so many. And from the way she has spoken I thought it might be the same for me. But it is not.'

Well, pleasure is one thing, thought Anne, and performance quite another, and many a woman has borne a child by the man she did not care for.

'The first night he was sick in the stomach,' said Kitty in a low voice, gathering courage as Anne neither mocked nor chided her, 'so he turned over and fell asleep.'

'But no doubt your beauty changed his mind and stomach the next night?'

'Oh yes, but it was not as I thought. And it *has not been* as I thought. And now I do not want him.'

'Did he rouse no feeling in you when you first met?'

'I thought him very kind.'

Keep me, Anne reflected. What a weary business!

'Did you never have a suitor that made your heart beat quick?'

Kitty shook her head, and then hesitated.

'There was a Dutchman,' she confided, 'but I was only sixteen and my family would not have him. He was a little like the Captain,' she added shyly, 'in that he made me feel blithe.'

Aye, thought Anne, you can hardly keep your fingers off the buttons of his breeches!

'The Captain is not for you, Katherine,' she said, firm and cool.

Kitty's face fell.

'Then what is to become of me?' she cried again, as she had done half an hour before.

'I do not know what you mean,' said Anne. 'You are the laird's wife and will live in his house and bear his children, until death alone parts you.'

The prospect reduced Kitty to such a torrent of tears that Anne switched her policy, while administering comfort. She saw no hope of persuading the goose, by subtle means, that her only way out was to poison her husband. But she knew more about Kitty than Kitty did, and perceived that the romping and giggling had turned her mind to love-making of a more serious order.

'Don't grieve, my bonnie,' she implored, putting her arms round the weeping girl. 'You know nothing of the joys ahead of you, or you would be blithe to meet them. You are not awake to a man yet, Katherine, but you will be. It happens so with most women. At first they endure the man as something strange, even unlovely. And then, one day, a touch of the fingers or a glance brings happiness with it, and your sorrow will be of a different order. You will lie awake at night when you are apart, and watch the road by day for his coming, and live every moment over again. And rain on the roof or firelight on the ceiling, a tone of voice, a turn of head, the scent of flowers in a close room, will bring him to mind again.'

'You speak as though you knew,' said Kitty, wondering.

'Oh, that's another tale,' said Anne. 'A woman can love and her love be unreturned. I am long past youth, Katherine, and must content myself by pleasing others, and trying

118

to keep a family contented.'

'Poor Anne!' cried Kitty, touched. 'What should we do without you? Do you know what I wish – though it sounds both wrong and foolish? I wish that you and I and the Captain lived by ourselves, and were merry together!'

'That's a saucy thought!' said Anne gaily.

Kitty peeped at her timidly.

'I did not mean anything improper,' she said. And then, absorbed by their conversation, 'And shall I feel all those things for the laird?'

'Aye, for sure you will. And I envy you, Mrs Ogilvie, for there is no joy on earth comparable to that between man and wife – or so I am told, and I believe it. It can make a hovel into a palace, and bare boards into the finest bed imaginable. And when you lie together the world is forgotten, and neither money nor hunger can trouble you.'

'Oh you are good to me, and good to all of us!' Kitty cried. 'I love you as well as I love my sister Bethia!'

Her thoughts wandered again.

'I was thinking, Miss Clarke, how *is* the Captain?'

'How should I know?' said Anne, smiling. 'He lies abed still. Let us go back and you can take him a dish of tea, and tell him it is near noon.'

Kitty sat on the side of the alcove bed and could say nothing, so held out the dish of tea. The Captain stopped in mid-joke.

'What ails you, my bonnie lass?' he asked.

'Nothing. Only – do not be so light with me, Patrick!'

The air of inconsequence left him, and he stroked her curls.

'Are you home-sick still, Kitty?'

She shook her head and her tears fell on his arm.

'What then?'

'Oh, I am sick for *you*, Patrick – and what will become

of me?'

They had spoken quietly, fearful of being overheard, but then she sobbed outright and he put one hand across her mouth to hush her.

'Oh, it is just as Miss Clarke said,' cried Kitty, in despair. 'I lie awake at night, remembering you. And I smell the flowers you have given me, even when they are faded. I think of the firelight on the ceiling that night you came into my room with the ague. And I want to go away with you to some foreign land, and for us to be together always. And we could live at Malabar and be happy all our days . . .'

What little control he possessed – for like most of the Ogilvies he acted first and thought later – had been loosed. While she flirted and giggled he could keep their friendship on a light level, but her tears and trouble put an end to the loyalty he had for his brother.

'Where are they all, now?' he asked.

'They have gone to the kirk, for once, and will be above an hour. But Miss Clarke is in the parlour.'

'She will hear nothing, and does not seek to hear anything. It is the servants who cock their ears.'

'They have gone to the kirk, too. But if Miss Clarke came up the stairs?'

'Why should she? I tell you what I like best about Miss Clarke – she keeps a still tongue and minds her business, and besides she is our friend.'

'But not in this,' said Kitty sobered, aware of what she was doing. 'Never in this. No one could be.'

Anne Clarke stood in the shadow of the staircase, listening. She had not spent all those years in a bawdy house without knowing what to listen for, but her purpose was in no way lecherous nor her absorbed face the face of a voyeur. She was simply collecting evidence for a future date.

120

XIII

When she judged the love-making to be over, Anne moved quietly up to the landing, lifting her skirts so that they did not sweep on the stairs. And gliding into the Captain's room she walked over to the fireplace and lifted the kettle, as though she had forgotten something. Still without looking round she paused at the window a moment or two, and then turned to see the effect of her presence.

Patrick had sprung out of bed, his shirt hanging over his breeches – which he hastily buttoned. But Kitty lay motionless and careless, one round arm above her head, the other outflung. None of them said anything, and the Captain whistled softly and kept his eyes averted as Anne, still silent, walked past him and so out of the room.

All morning she watched them, under her usual cover of attending to their wants and comforts. Patrick joked and chattered, and entertained them with his fiddle as usual; but Kitty spoke very little, and sat on the parlour press bed dreaming until Anne moved to her side and spoke softly so that no one else could hear.

'Mrs Ogilvie, I know what passed between you and the Captain this morning, and I shall say nothing. But what you do is very wrong, and must cease!'

She looked into the pretty bewildered face and added judiciously, 'Now, ma'am, I know you will contract a hatred at me.'

Kitty, seeming not to understand her, only smiled. All her life she had been accustomed to having her own way. That this way meant betraying her husband with his own brother no longer entered into her considerations. She only knew that what had been desert was all light and blossom, and that Anne had been kind to her and meant her well. So she put her hand on Anne's arm and smiled.

'No, Miss Clarke,' she answered. 'I never will.'

The following day, as the servants chattered and clattered in the kitchen, as Thomas went his rounds of the farm and Lady Eastmiln dozed lightly, Kitty and Patrick went hand in hand to his room. And Anne again listened at the foot of the stairs. And on the Tuesday and the Wednesday the same thing happened. Their lack of caution aroused Anne's contempt, and their indifference to either her presence or her opinion enraged her. But she bent her head over her sewing and kept her counsel, until the old lady awoke with a start, crying that there were horsemen galloping on the road with news of the Prince.

'No, ma'am, you were dreaming,' said Anne quietly. 'Those horsemen came and went above twenty years ago. But in your house at this moment,' she said easily, 'your daughter-in-law has gone to bed with the Captain – and that is ill news enough!'

Lady Eastmiln felt for her stick, frowning.

'Come, miss,' she said. 'High spirits are not the same as lewdness!'

'I told you on Sunday night what I had seen and heard,' Anne went on, in the same even conversational tone. 'I told you again on Monday and Tuesday, but you would have none of it. And today, just as soon as you nodded, ma'am, they were off upstairs again.'

The old woman flushed up, became tart and imperious.

'You have been an old maid over-long, Miss Clarke,' she observed sharply. 'You see and hear a man and woman in every bed!'

Oh, God in heaven, thought Anne, I'll make you smart for that! Must I sit here and sew like a dried thing while those puppies tumble upstairs, and an old woman amuses herself at my expense?

'I am sorry you should think my wits are wandering, ma'am,' she said aloud. 'Do you not hear footsteps overhead?'

Lady Eastmiln paused, and cocked her better ear. But the faint creaks and muffled voices were silence to her.

'No, miss. I hear nothing.'

'Then you must take my word for it, ma'am, or call me a wanton liar.'

'Have you a spite against my son, Miss Clarke?'

'No, ma'am, I have a spite against *none* of your sons. But it is not right that a man should cuckold his own brother. You know the laird has no great liking for me, so I shall not be believed if I speak. Therefore, I beg of you, ma'am, speak to him yourself before Mrs Ogilvie and the Captain become an open scandal.'

The old woman pursed her mouth and pondered, then shook her head as though a wasp plagued her.

'I cannot believe it. I do not believe it. I *will* not!'

'Then let all go on as it has begun,' said Anne calmly, 'until one day the laird comes home early and finds them together. And when he confronts you, ma'am, and asks you why you said nothing you must plead what cause you can. But, whether he sends me about my business or not, I shall tell him the truth. And I shall say I warned you, and you did not heed me, ma'am.'

For a long time Lady Eastmiln sat staring in front of her at this latest spectre.

'Well, I will mention it to the laird in my own way and in my own time,' she said finally. 'And now, Miss Clarke, if you can tear yourself away from listening at the ceiling I should like a dish of tea – and a dram!'

Later she said, 'I spoke harshly to you, Miss Clarke, and it was not right. For since you came you have said no unkind thing of anybody, and even in this matter you have been discreet and judicious.'

Anne accepted the apology with an inclination of her head, and shook out the shirt she was mending.

'You see, ma'am,' she said, 'there is enough trouble already, and we do not wish the laird *further* harm. So let us stop *this* affair, and thereby prevent *another*.'

Her slight emphasis on the words brought Lady Eastmiln to attention.

'*Another*? Has Mrs Ogilvie set her cap at someone else as well?'

'Why no, ma'am. But she has been indiscreet in her remarks, and let fall that she wished her husband ill. And should she and the Captain get very thick she might slip a dose into the laird's tea.'

Lady Eastmiln sat, mouth fallen.

'She is not a clever girl,' said Anne, in excuse, 'and I am sure meant no real harm in what she said. But nevertheless, ma'am, we had best be certain to give her no cause.'

'I *will* speak to the laird,' said Lady Eastmiln, resolute.

But her resolution faltered at the enormity of the warning. So in the end, craving Thomas's private ear, she merely said that she thought Kitty was being troublesome to the Captain.

'The house is full of trouble,' said Thomas drily. 'I thought I had laid it by bringing a pretty head and a gay heart here. Well, I will speak to her, mother – and you were right to tell me so.'

He hesitated, nevertheless, because he could do nothing with Kitty these days. She flinched when he touched her, wept at the least thing, and seemed normal only when Patrick teased her. And there lay another resentment, for fond of Patrick though he was the accumulation of gossip and warnings disturbed him, and it seemed hard that his wife should prefer his brother's company.

He watched the three of them walking on the hillock:

124

Patrick talking to Anne Clarke quite earnestly, and Kitty running here and there after a flower and then returning to pluck at a sleeve and demand attention; and his heart was sore.

'Miss Clarke,' said Patrick, holding Kitty off, 'since you have established yourself as peacemaker in the house, might I ask your counsel on a delicate matter? Kitty! You are a goose-cap – run away and pick yourself a posy!' And as she danced off, unperturbed, he said lightly, 'I find there are two kinds of women, the foolish and the wise – and I cannot confide this matter to our giddy moth.'

'Well, Captain, I am honoured,' said Anne smiling. 'I had thought you a little giddy myself, and am delighted to find it is not so! And, as you know, no secrets pass my lips.' And she looked at him meaningfully.

He offered her his arm and smiled back, though his colour came high for a moment.

'I know full well, Miss Clarke. And, meaning no slight to your charms, I respect you as I would a brother-officer – whose clear head and steady eye might save a life in an emergency. Now what I want to say to you is this. I am not penniless, Miss Clarke. My father left each of us a bond of provision, out of which my commission was bought. When I came home some months ago, I asked the laird for the balance, and he put me off by saying it was bound up in the estate, and should take time to recover.

'I know my brother is paid oftener in kind than in cash, and has not ready money, so I have lived on his bounty and waited. The laird is generous with his hospitality, Miss Clarke, but I should like him to be less generous in that and more generous with what is mine. Now how would you advise me?'

Anne thought of the murderous suspicions already voiced

to Lady Eastmiln, and the gossip relayed to Thomas. She reckoned up Kitty's impulsiveness and the extent of her commitment to Patrick. She gauged the Captain's tale of his desire to be independent against its probable outcome – a long wild spree until the money ran out, and then back to his brother's roof. She weighed Thomas's patience under his yoke, and judged it to be at breaking point.

'Why, Captain Ogilvie,' she said, sweet and clear, 'I knew nothing of this, I promise you. But it seems something of a hardship that a man should be made to eat the bread of charity when he can buy his own and enjoy his freedom. The laird, I do not doubt, has hardly thought of the matter in this light. I think I should speak of it without hesitation. He is a just man, and an honest one. Make him a just and honest demand.'

Patrick's face shone with relief and pleasure.

'When should I speak of it, Miss Clarke?'

'This very day, Captain. Why leave the question to fester and bring bad blood between you?'

He picked up her hand and kissed it gaily. And then, serious matters over, ran after Kitty who was looking woebegone at his neglect.

XIV

Even Thomas had colour in his cheeks, and Patrick's were red with anger.

'I am only asking you for what is mine by right,' the Captain cried. 'I have eaten the bread of charity long enough. If you give me what is due I can pay for my own!'

'And when it is spent, what then?' Thomas shouted.

Anne Clarke, seeing that the servants hung open-mouthed at the doorway, sent them scurrying back to the kitchen. Kitty stood puzzled and frightened, and Lady Eastmiln looked from one son to the other, trying to find the right words and a gap in which to say them.

'Come, brother,' said Patrick, attempting humour. 'I have fiddled for my supper long enough. I want only my portion and my freedom.'

'Fiddled for your supper!' cried Thomas, enraged. 'Aye, and more besides! I counselled you to see that my wife was merry, you villain, and you have made a scandal of her in the Kirkton. My labourers stop speaking when I appear, and every old wife's head pokes from her window when I pass. Do you take me for a fool that you should win away my wife's affection while I work for the pair of you? Aye, and for all of you!' he cried, beside himself. 'I work, and have worked, these twenty years, and the house is not my own for women's tongues and women's grievances! I used to think it over-quiet with only my mother and myself to nod before the fire of an evening. But now, by God, I would give your portion and more besides to have that time back again. At least we were at peace with one another, and now all is trouble from morning to night – and my wife playing

127

the whore with my brother!'

He did not honestly believe this, and Patrick thought it best to defend the honour of a soldier and a gentleman with a fine blustering front.

'Why, Thomas, think shame to yourself. I have kept Mrs Ogilvie merry and comfortable as you asked me – and that is all there is to it, upon my word!'

'But not so much amused that she has no time for my company,' said Thomas bitterly, 'and not so merry that my labourers laugh at me behind my back.'

'If you will listen to your workmen, Mr Ogilvie...' Kitty began, conscience-stricken.

'Silence, woman! This is between my brother and myself!'

He still hoped; and in his heart thought that with Anne Clarke packed off to Edinburgh, Kitty sobered into motherhood, and his hearth quiet, he and Patrick might make up their differences over a dram. But for the moment the gossip must be scotched.

'Now pack your trunk and be off!' cried Thomas, and walked out immediately, lest he weaken.

Patrick stood quite amazed, reddening from neck to forehead. Then turned quickly on his heel and ran upstairs. The three women heard him pulling drawers open and flinging his belongings together. Leaning out of the bedroom window he shouted, 'Saddle my horse, Willie, and fetch it round to the front as soon as may be!' They were still silent when he clattered down again to take his leave of them.

'Where will you go, my son?' asked Lady Eastmiln, bereft of her favourite.

'To William Shaw at Little Forthar for a day or so, to collect my wits, madam. I shall be but four miles away from you. After that – God only knows, but you shall hear from me.'

He kissed Kitty's hand and his mother's cheek, and

bowed to Anne. They looked so wretched that he slipped into the role of humorist out of habit.

'Why, it is three o'clock already!' he cried, swinging into the saddle. 'I shall be in time for the four hours at Mistress Shaw's. Give me my fiddle, Willie, and take care not to put your fist through it – it must be in good shape for supper-time!'

Then he spurred his horse and set off at a gallop.

Kitty picked up her skirts and ran from the garden, but he was out of earshot, riding as though speed could wipe out anger. With a shriek that brought the servants into the parlour, she clapped both hands to her head, cried out that they would all drive her mad, and fled to the comparative privacy of her own room. They could hear her throughout the house, sobbing and crying and beating the bedpost with her fists.

'Mercy on us!' said Lady Eastmiln. 'The girl is quite distraught, Miss Clarke. Shall you go and comfort her?'

'I think her husband had best do that, ma'am.'

'Well, send Lizzie for him if you think it wise. For as God is my judge, Miss Clarke, you have been right in all other matters, and are no doubt right in this.'

The laird's timid intervention roused Kitty sufficiently to make her words coherent.

'Out of this room!' she shrieked, so that everyone could hear her. 'Out!'

Above her sobs and cries and thrusting hands Thomas's voice came clearly to the listeners below-stairs.

'Your conduct has been highly improper, Mrs Ogilvie. And for you to meddle with my decision would be the ruin of all of us. I have no more to say to you. Now attend to your husband and your duty, madam.'

He came downstairs so suddenly, and with such a dark face, that the women scattered. Pausing before he went back to his work, and looking them in the eye, he spoke firmly.

'I shall have no more of this, either. Hands should be busy enough to keep tongues idle! There has been too much talk in my house.'

He looked no harder at Anne Clarke than at anyone else, but she knew he had resolved to be rid of her.

'Should you like me to calm Mrs Ogilvie?' she asked.

'I should like you, Miss Clarke, to convince Mrs Ogilvie that my brother is best gone.'

'Then I will do that.'

And she went quietly to Kitty, while Thomas was still in the house, taking care he should hear every word of advice, and each word delivered as he wished.

'You will leave me Miss Clarke, at least,' said Lady Eastmiln stiffly to the laird. 'For without her I shall have no one to care for me.'

But he would not answer her.

Upstairs, Kitty sobbed into Anne's immaculate fichu and cried, 'You are the only friend I have now in the world!'

And Anne, relishing the irony of the situation, replied, 'Why, Katherine, look up and be cheerful. I shall be as good a friend to the laird as I am to the Captain and yourself. And in the end you shall all be together, with Anne Clarke to thank for everything!'

Though he was sorry for Kitty's trouble, and sorrier perhaps for the breach with his brother, Patrick felt free. He had been a long time at home, telling stories to the same audience, playing the same tunes on his fiddle, seeing the same bare hillock outside the same front door. And he remembered his conversation with George Spalding, two months earlier, when he had talked to Patrick of a soldier wanting a horse between his legs and a foreign horizon before his eyes. So he walked up and down the waterside at Little Forthar with William Shaw, and another splendid evening lay ahead of him, and a great many complications behind him, and he was content that the episode should pass. Tomorrow, he thought, would be another day, and he would find something else to do and somewhere else to go.

He was therefore taken aback by the sight of Lizzie Sturrock, with importance beaming in her face and a letter bulging in her pocket.

'Well, Lizzie, my lass,' said Patrick, pinching her cheek, 'what brings your bright eyes to Little Forthar?'

'A letter from Mrs Ogilvie, Captain,' said Lizzie, admiring him greatly, and inclined to blame Kitty for everything. And she dropped a curtsey to both gentlemen.

Patrick smiled at her as he broke the seals, and then walked a few paces away to read his letter in privacy. Kitty's careless scrawl was wild, her spelling had gone to the devil, and the paper was blotched with tears.

'Oh, Lord, Lord, Lord!' said Patrick under his breath. 'What a crackbrained jackanapes I've been!'

He was not a man to brood over a woman, and in Kitty's absence he inclined to worry more over the wrong he had done his brother than the hurt he had caused her. In any event, he reasoned, he was well away from East Mill House if the girl was hankering after him, for how could such an affair go on?

'If she hadn't come dropping her tears on my nightshirt,' he said to himself, 'I should have lived on a squeeze and a cuddle, and made up the rest with some whore from the Kirkton!'

'Lizzie, Lizzie, bright-eyed Liz,' he said aloud, gaily. 'Give my best compliments to Mrs Ogilvie, thank her for her concern, tell her I am very well, and bid her keep up a good heart. But tell her, if you please, not to expect me back because I am visiting Baron Reid, and from there shall go on to Glenkilry. Can you remember that?'

'Aye, Captain,' said Lizzie, deprived of the secret mess-

131

age she had hoped to whisper in Kitty's ear.

'Then here's tuppence for you, sweetheart,' said Patrick, 'and off you go home!'

And he slapped her behind for good measure.

The marital bed at East Mill that night was a stormy one, and Lizzie and Annie Sampson lay awake listening as the laird and lady quarrelled.

'What sort of a husband would drive his brother from the house and insult his wife because of servants' gossip?' cried Kitty, distracted.

'The sort of husband who sees his brother and his wife as frequent together as kirk bells on Sunday!' Thomas replied, sticking to his point.

Bereft, Kitty sobbed, 'But I was very dull in a strange house, and never the mistress of it, and the Captain made me laugh. And I have not been well since I came here. And now he is gone I feel worse. And he had medicines in his chest that he would let me have. And all my salts and laudanum that came from Edinburgh are used up. And what shall I do?'

Knowing that even in her misery she would not turn to him for comfort, only question and accuse him further, Thomas shouted, 'Do as you will, you spoiled queen! I'll have no more of your nonsense!'

The servants heard her crying and talking for over an hour, and just before dawn Lizzie Sturrock woke to the sound of light footsteps pacing the room overhead. To and fro, to and fro, accompanied by tears and pleading.

On the following afternoon Thomas sent James Millam over to Little Forthar with a letter. He was, he wrote, going to Edinburgh for perhaps as long as a month or six weeks. He regretted that more had been said than was actually meant. He wished to take back his remarks on Patrick's conduct and was sorry he had dismissed him from the

132

house. He would be pleased to find his brother re-instated at East Mill, and merry with the fiddle, on his return.

'Do you know the purport of this letter, Jamie?' the Captain asked, as they enjoyed a dram.

'Aye, sir, the laird read it over to me before he sealed it.'

'For no doubt you have heard the rumours that ran about Glenisla?'

'I have, sir.'

'Did you believe them, Jamie?'

'No sir, I did not. The laird himself asked me, and I said the same to him.'

'Jamie,' said Patrick, folding the letter, 'I think it best that I stay where I am if my brother is to be away in Edinburgh.'

'Well, sir,' said Millam, accepting the offer of another dram with more enthusiasm than he had shown so far, 'I think you are in the right of it!'

'Then since the laird is on his way to Edinburgh I shall address my reply to Mrs Ogilvie. I shall tell her that all is well, and that I thank them both most heartily, but I have promised my friends a visit each and shall be away some weeks myself. That way, Jamie, no one can take offence and no further harm be done.'

A second letter from Kitty followed him to the Spaldings.

Dear Captin

I was sorrie I missed you this day. I sat at the water side a long time this fornoon; I thought you would have comed up here; if you had as much mind of me as I have of you, you would have comed up, tho' you had but stayed out-by as there was no use for that, there is more rooms in the house then one. God knows the heart that I have this day and instead of being better its worse, and

133

not in my power to help it. You were not minding the thing that I said to you, or you went out here and what I wrote for. Meat I have not tasted since yesterday dinner, nor wont or you com here, tho' I should never eat any it lyes at your door. Your brother would give anything you would come, for God's sake come.

Ketty.

Patrick was not a man who found it easy to write, nor did he know what to say. So he let the blotched and ill-spelled scrawl lie in his pocket unanswered, and hoped time would settle the matter without his help.

XV

'Why, ma'am, I did not get a wink of sleep last night for the dogs howling!' cried Anne, as she laced the old lady into her stays.

'Dogs? Dogs? Do you mean Rabbie, miss?'

'No, ma'am, for I can tell his bark anywhere. It was a pack of wild dogs, ma'am, of that I am certain. And if they are not put down they will spoil the game.'

Lady Eastmiln had run the farm alone during the Rebellion, and played the part of listener and adviser to Thomas for twenty years. In his absence she assumed responsibility.

'Then they must be put down, miss,' she said briskly, 'or else we shall go hungry. Well, Mrs Ogilvie,' she cried, as Kitty drooped downstairs for her morning tea, her red and white calico bedgown crumpled and her hair out of curl, 'what ails you? Are you with child, then, and feeling sickly?'

'No, ma'am,' said Kitty wearily. 'I have slept badly, and there is no more laudanum and salts. And the carrier does not come from Edinburgh for above a week.'

'Then ask the Captain, girl!'

She paused as Kitty flushed, and then threw up her arms, impatient with the lot of them.

'All that nonsense is over,' she cried. 'The laird wrote to his brother and received a civil reply. We *are* speaking to each other, I hope? Come, child, no harm will arise if you write to the Captain, and ask him for a little medicine until the carrier brings your own. It is better than seeing a wheyface every morning, miss!'

'And when you write to the Captain,' said Anne smoothly, raising her eyebrows as Lizzie slopped porridge on the table and wiped it off with her petticoat, 'you might ask him to obtain some arsenic for the wild dogs that kept me awake last night.'

'Wild dogs, Miss Clarke?' cried Lizzie, all eyes and ears.

'Yes, Lizzie, but I doubt if you heard them yourself, being at the back of the house. And luckily Lady Eastmiln was not disturbed, being a little deaf.'

'There are advantages, I perceive, in deafness,' said Lady Eastmiln drily. 'Don't stand there gaping, Lizzie. Fetch the shortcake. The laird is not the only one who likes a finger with his breakfast!'

'Oh, but, Miss Clarke and ma'am, have you no' heard that the dogs are ghosties?'

Anne and Kitty burst out laughing, and even Lady Eastmiln smiled.

'No, ma'am, it's the truth. Did you hear them round about the sheep-cote, Miss Clarke? For that's where they say the ghosties howl loudest. It's to do with the minister's curse, for that's where Laird James hanged himself!'

'Why, Lizzie,' said Lady Eastmiln, very grim, 'I see that a quick servant can pick up twenty years' gossip in a few months! Never let me hear such nonsense again. Away with you girl, and fetch that shortcake here.'

'Well, ma'am,' said Anne, still laughing as she set the table to rights. 'I think it best to tie Rabbie up at night, and set poison for the other dogs just the same. If they are ghosties it won't hurt them – and if they are not it will silence them! And now, ma'am, your tea.'

So Kitty, happy to be given an opportunity of writing to her love, scrawled yet another letter, begging a small quantity of laudanum and salts from his chest, and asking him to procure some arsenic for the wild dogs that threatened to spoil the game.

136

On the last day of May 1765, Patrick Ogilvie and his friend Lieutenant George Campbell of the 89th Foot set off for a reunion at Brechin. It was good to be trotting a fair road in fine weather with a brother officer, and Patrick's handsome face was merry with the present and confident of the future. A sliver of the past, lying in the breast pocket of his coat, troubled him only for an instant.

'My brother's wife writes that they are troubled with marauding dogs, George,' he said easily, though the thought of Kitty gave him a pang of conscience. 'The laird being away, and the house full of women, she asks me to procure some arsenic to put the dogs down. Now where the devil am I to get that?'

'Why, shall we not be dining with your father's old army surgeon, Dr Carnegie, tonight?' said George. 'He will sell you a few penn'orth of arsenic and no trouble, surely?'

'So he will – and some laudanum too, perhaps, for I have the gripes. George, my guts ache abominably.'

The Lieutenant grunted. Few soldiers returned from the East without some token of their service there.

'I know a cure for all ills,' said George, grinning, 'and you have been mewed up at East Mill House these many months without it. We'll find ourselves a couple of lassies in Brechin!'

Patrick's smile grew broader.

'Then why are we creeping along like two old women?' he cried, spurring his horse.

They galloped along the road together, raising a cloud of dust and scattering a flock of sheep, whooping like boys let out of school.

John Gillock, walking home through the dusk past East Mill, saw a man and a woman conversing. He could not hear what they were saying, nor discern their features clearly; but observing the graceful figure of the girl and the height of the man who bent over her, he assumed them to be the Captain and Mrs Ogilvie.

Intrigued, he went on his way, shaking his head and surmising the worst. For had he not heard all the rumours, and seen them easy and light with each other that morning he fitted locks on to the chest of drawers?

On 3 June, Patrick was back from his brief and pleasurable carousel at Brechin, and dismounting in the Stewart's yard at Alyth. Martha, plump and happy as he had never seen her before, overwhelmed him with greetings. Together they sauntered into the house, arm-in-arm, attempting to tell all their news at once.

'We had heard such fearful things from East Mill,' said Martha, setting a tankard of ale at his elbow. 'Is all well now?'

'Aye, very well indeed,' said Patrick comfortably. 'I took myself out of the way and have been visiting friends here and there for almost two weeks. But Thomas has written to me most amiably, and the Kirkton will no doubt turn its tongues to other matters in time.'

'And what will *you* do, Patrick?'

'Lord knows yet, but I mean to find something. Scotland is a little pond, Martha, for such a restless fish as myself. I'll get abroad again somehow. And meanwhile – can I set my feet on your hearth tonight? For I'm off to Glenkilry soon.'

'For as long as you please,' said Martha. 'We are very quiet here, and shall welcome the sound of your fiddle in the evenings.'

'How should I live without a song to add relish to other people's suppers?' cried Patrick gaily. 'Is that a brace of ducklings I see on the spit? Why, Martha, I am ready to do your cooking justice – and birds sing all the better for a bit of seed!'

138

'Wherever you are, Patrick, there is a party,' said Martha shyly.

He pinched her cheek and said it was a pretty compliment paid by a pretty lass, and asked after her husband.

'We are very well together,' said Martha, smiling.

'Then you must make haste and seal his happiness with a clutch of bairns.'

'Oh, Patrick,' said Martha, remembering something else, 'poor Kate Campbell called on me for a night's lodging, and she was very weary and low in spirits.'

'Aye, aye,' said Patrick carelessly. 'Someone had stolen her virtue, and she stole Kitty's handkerchiefs.'

'But she is so simple and she works so hard. The Fleemings at Blackhouse in the West Forest of Alyth have taken her in, needing a washerwoman. And there Kate is, poor soul, near her time and working from morning to night. Mistress Fleeming is a kind woman, but she cannot get Kate to give any account of herself. Only the poor wretch saves every penny they give her to pay for the journey home. And she cannot say where she is going, only that she has two seas to cross. And I have such a pity for her.'

'Well, well,' said Patrick. 'Kate is built like an ox and will survive her trouble – and the child is not mine, Martha!'

'I did not say it was,' said Martha, blushing. 'But she has suffered, and will suffer, and no one cares.'

'I must send some cambric to East Mill House,' said Patrick, seeing no point in discussing a matter he could not mend. 'I am all of a tatter, and need new ruffles.'

'I would sew them for you, Patrick.'

'You have a husband of your own, and there are three women to care for Thomas. A shirt or two won't hurt them – and they can gossip as they stitch! Martha, those ducklings are making my mouth run water – when do we sup?'

'I did not know that Mrs Ogilvie was such a frequent correspondent!' said the Captain, as Lizzie Sturrock ate and drank her fill in Martha's kitchen, the following day.

'What news does she send?' asked Martha, staring at the length of the letter.

'She writes a great scrawl that says nothing, Martha, like most women. But mainly she asks for some drugs I promised her, and I will scribble a note to go with the shirts. Lizzie! Lizzie!'

Lizzie came in, curtseying and wiping her mouth.

'Lizzie, light of my understanding, I have a secret assignment for you!'

'Aye, Captain?' said Lizzie, agog.

He looked at her mischievously.

'Can you keep a secret, Lizzie?'

'Oh yes, Captain.'

'I'll lay you cannot, but I trust you, Lizzie. When you take this reply to Mrs Ogilvie, will you also collect a parcel of linens from Little Forthar? I had it sent there, not knowing where I might be. And give both letter and parcel to Mrs Ogilvie alone. Do you understand?'

'Oh yes, Captain.'

'Why, Patrick, what a tease you are!' said Martha, disturbed. 'Surely, there has been enough trouble without your making a great deal of a little matter?'

He winked, and put his finger to his lips.

'Not a word of this to anyone but Mrs Ogilvie, Lizzie!'

'Cross my heart, Captain,' said Lizzie, unable to get home fast enough in order to tell Annie Sampson.

Patrick watched her clatter out of Alyth on a pillion, and laughed until the tears came into his eyes.

'Can you not see how she will urge her rider on?' he cried. 'And all over a request for new shirts?'

'Patrick, you are not wise in this,' said Martha gravely.

He put his arm about her waist and gave it a brotherly

140

squeeze.

'My dear lassie,' he said, 'there are too many gloomy faces in the world. I'll raise a laugh whenever I can, and think it my bounden duty. And I am not so foolish as you think. I did not trust the drugs to Lizzie. I thought Andrew could take them when he visits East Mill tomorrow.'

'Yes, so he can,' said Martha, comforted. 'You did well in that, at least.'

'Mr Craig,' said Anne, smiling, 'will you help me in a little wager?'

'Aye, if there is no harm in it, Miss Clarke.'

'No harm in the world, and I will give you a shilling if all goes well.'

And she drew out a piece of the money Thomas had given her the evening before, to get herself back to Edinburgh – from whence he had returned unexpectedly.

'Mrs Ogilvie has received a parcel of cambric from the Captain, Mr Craig. All you have to do is to ask the laird to pay for it.'

'But the cambric was not got from me, Miss Clarke,' said the carrier, bewildered.

'Of course it was not – and so it shall be revealed. This is a joke to be played on Mrs Ogilvie by the Captain. The laird will refuse to pay for his brother's linen, so there is no harm done and no one loses by it – and you have the shilling for your trouble.'

'Well, Miss Clarke, I do not see . . .'

'Mr Craig, this is but a family joke – and you know how merry the Captain can be?'

'Oh, aye!' said William Craig, smiling.

'Then do this for him. Here is your money – and say nothing of it, or the wager is over and the fun spoiled.'

'As you will, Miss Clarke, and when shall I ask the laird?'

'Why, now. For he will be out with his workmen in half an hour. And I will take these things we have paid for to Lady Eastmiln. Now make it a stern request, Mr Craig, and sound most injured!'

'Aye, I will,' said the carrier, slipping the shilling into his pocket. 'Can I speak with the laird?' he called out, at the top of his voice.

In a moment Thomas appeared, frowning at the tone.

'Why, what's this, then, Mr Ogilvie?' the carrier blustered. 'Am I to go hungry and my wife and bairns have no porridge on their platters? I'm a poor man, Mr Ogilvie, and cannot go unpaid for a parcel of cambric.'

'Miss Clarke has just settled with you,' said Thomas, annoyed.

'Aye, for what my lady ordered – but not for what Mrs Ogilvie has taken. Here's the money in my hand for the ribbons and fine stuff. But who is to pay for the cambric?'

'Mrs Ogilvie!' Thomas called. 'What is this about cambric?'

Kitty was paler and more listless than William Craig remembered, and for a moment he felt uneasy. But the shilling in his pocket, and his acquaintance with Patrick's humour, restored him.

'I have no cambric but what the Captain sent us to make him some shirts,' said Kitty.

'I will not pay for my brother's shirts!' Thomas cried.

'Then who's to give me the money?' the carrier demanded.

'Ask the Captain for it!' said Thomas angrily. 'And tell him from me that he pays for his own linen!'

'But that parcel came yesterday,' said Kitty, trembling. 'Lizzie brought it, herself!'

Lizzie stood grinning at the fun, and holding twopence that Anne Clarke had given her. But her evidence was not called for.

142

'You can tell the Captain, William Craig,' Thomas shouted, 'that I've settled enough debts for my brothers in the past. In the future they must settle their own!' and he slammed the door.

Shaking his head and clicking his tongue, the carrier flicked the reins upon his horse's neck, and jolted off on the long road to Edinburgh. In his pocket, along with the shilling, was a letter to Alexander.

All was in an uproar at East Mill. And Kitty, clenching her fists against her skirts, cried over and over again, 'I hate you, Thomas! I hate you! I wish that you were dead!'

'Come, Mrs Ogilvie,' said Anne quietly. 'You had best lie down.'

Very pale, Thomas stalked off to his work. The servants whispered in the kitchen of the Captain's joke that had gone amiss. And Lady Eastmiln, shaking her head at the knob of her stick as though it were the head of a listener, said, 'Wherever that girl is these days there is trouble, always trouble!'

XVI

Andrew Stewart, arriving at East Mill that afternoon, detected rather more ill-feeling in the atmosphere than Patrick had led him to expect. But Miss Clarke was polite and solicitous, and Lady Eastmiln gracious enough. Only Kitty skimmed over the civilities, begged a word in private, and hurried him up to the Strangers Room where they might be undisturbed. He saw that she was nervous and distracted; and the flush of excitement, which had coloured her cheeks as she greeted him, now faded into an unusual pallor.

'Mr Stewart, I believe you have some message and medicines from the Captain?' she began abruptly. 'May I have them, if you please?'

He was an honest and a conscientious man with little imagination. She watched him impatiently as he drew out the letter and packet, and embarked on a fussy commentary.

'Here is the message that the Captain gave me . . . is that the one? Oh, yes, for I recollect he sealed it with both a wafer and wax. And round it he wrapped a paper of directions for use of the laudanum – which is in this parcel in a phial, Mrs Ogilvie. For laudanum can be fatal if the dose be exceeded, or so I am told, though no doubt you know best, Mrs Ogilvie, and with the Captain's instructions . . . And here *is* the packet that contains your medicines, which I believe the Captain wrapped up and marked separately, for I saw him busy among the salts in his chest. And in the packet is certainly a phial of laudanum – or is it salts? – but no doubt the Captain will have written upon it, and something stronger, too. I cannot, for the moment, recollect

144

what he said, but surely he will have . . .'

'I thank you most heartily, Mr Stewart,' said Kitty, anxious to read her letter in private. 'I will not keep you from the ladies.'

He saw her thrust the parcel carelessly into a drawer, and after a second's hesitation she put the letter with it, lest he think her too eager.

'I shall be down in a moment, Mr Stewart,' she said, as he stood there awkwardly, his mission accomplished.

'Indeed, indeed, Mrs Ogilvie,' said Andrew, bowing his way out.

He was not halfway down the stairs when she pulled out the letter, tore it open and began to read. Her exaltation faded as she scanned the easy scrawl. When she came to the signature she paused for a minute, and then began to read again, lest she had missed some secret indication that he loved and missed her. There was none. She folded the letter, trembling, and slipped it into the bodice of her dress. But the intimacy of its resting-place, and the absence of intimacy in its tone, troubled her. She stuffed it into her pocket, instead. For a long time she wrung her hands and paced the room, then finding that one sob came upon another, each faster and heavier than the last, she threw herself on the bed and shrieked for loss of him.

'Well, Mr Stewart,' said Anne Clarke, smiling and sewing, 'did you bring anything for Mrs Ogilvie from Alyth? For she was impatient at your late arrival, and looked for you so often that I thought she was expecting something.'

'Sit down, sir,' Lady Eastmiln commanded. 'Don't stand there gawking!'

'Thank you, ma'am, thank you,' said Andrew, and cleared his throat and looked about him for rescue; because the Captain had asked him to be discreet over the letter and packet, since there had been trouble enough already.

'Did you bring anything at all, Mr Stewart?' Anne asked

145

relentlessly.

'Why no, Miss Clarke,' he said, reddening, and felt so guilty beneath two pairs of sharp eyes that he amended the answer. 'Nothing of consequence,' he added.

'And what do you call nothing of consequence, Mr Stewart?' said Anne, smiling. 'I think you must be a great tease, sir, to say "nothing of consequence" when we ask a simple question!'

Lady Eastmiln gave a short sharp grunt of amusement.

'Why, Miss Clarke, it was but a note and a small packet. Nothing of consequence.'

'Now what can be in the packet, ma'am?' asked Anne, addressing herself in pretty mockery to Lady Eastmiln, 'for the Captain sent his cambric yesterday.'

'What is in the packet, Mr Stewart?' Lady Eastmiln demanded. 'Speak up, man, speak up!'

'Why, ma'am and Miss Clarke, nothing but some drugs that the Captain got out of his chest.'

'Then why did you not say so at first?' said Lady Eastmiln.

'The Captain,' said Andrew, very red, 'told me I was not to mention it.'

'It is some new nonsense of his,' said Lady Eastmiln, uneasy for her favourite. 'We all know that Katherine has need of salts and laudanum.'

But Anne, her needle poised, said very quietly, 'At the risk of displeasing you, ma'am, I must remind you that when Mrs Ogilvie wrote to the Captain she asked for poison to put down the wild dogs. Could this be the reason for her secrecy on the matter? I believe these are black drugs, and that through the help of the Captain she means to poison her husband.'

'You will say no such wicked thing, miss!' cried Lady Eastmiln, bringing her stick down with considerable emphasis.

146

Very pale and resolute, Anne replied, 'I must say what I believe to be true, ma'am, even at the risk of your displeasure. For a good man's life is in danger. I could not rest in my bed, knowing that I might have prevented it.'

In his chair, Andrew Stewart floundered like a captured fish and could only say, 'Oh, Miss Clarke! Oh, ma'am! Oh, Miss Clarke! Oh, ma'am!' until Lady Eastmiln told him peremptorily to hold his tongue.

'Why else should Mrs Ogilvie request a private interview?' Anne asked. 'Why did she look for Mr Stewart so often on the road, today? Why take him up to the Strangers Room if it was but a friendly note and a packet of medicines? Why could she not have said, "Here is a letter from the Captain, and he has sent my drugs and some arsenic to put down the dogs!"'

Then she was suddenly silent, and picked up her sewing, for Kitty stood hesitating at the foot of the staircase. Seeing the embarrassment her presence had caused, Kitty assumed that they had been gossiping about Patrick. Her eyes were still red, but she had curled her hair round her fingers and put on a fresh sprigged gown.

'The laird said that when Mr Stewart had come we were to go to the Kirkton,' she explained. A glimmer of her old childish excitement at the prospect of a jaunt showed through her misery. 'We are to go to Fergus Fergusson's, and the gentlemen are to have their drams and the ladies their wine, and we shall all be very merry!'

'I will follow you to the Kirkton, Mrs Ogilvie,' said Anne smoothly. 'I have some work to finish for Lady Eastmiln first.'

'Then, Mr Stewart, I am to have both gentlemen to myself!' cried Kitty, 'and that is what I love above all things!'

She remembered the scandal over Patrick, and the coquetry left her face. Sedately, the joy wiped out, she took

147

Andrew Stewart's arm and walked down the path to the garden gate to meet the laird.

'Now, ma'am,' said Anne quickly, 'what are we to do? Should I tell Mr Ogilvie?'

'Oh, that would be improper, surely. Katherine will say the drugs are to make her healthy, and we know of no others. And then she will turn against you, and how will that help us?'

'Then what do you advise, ma'am?'

Lady Eastmiln had survived many experiences, but prospective murder was not among them. She pondered, stroking an invisible pattern on the bricked floor with her stick. At last, upright and correct, she said, 'I think, Miss Clarke, that the proper method is for you and me to warn my son privately not to accept food or drink from his wife's hands.'

'Should I not, on my way to the Kirkton, call in on the minister and ask him what he advises?'

'If you think fit, Miss Clarke. We rarely see the minister, but no doubt he would like to be consulted – and may even be of help.'

But the minister was out, and with habitual absent-mindedness had locked his door and left the key in the lock. So Anne walked on to Fergus Fergussons and joined the other three. Thomas seemed even more withdrawn than usual, but Kitty was chattering to Andrew Stewart; and when they left the Kirkton she walked on with him rapidly, to avoid her husband.

'Mr Ogilvie,' said Anne quietly, taking Kitty's place at the laird's side, 'I know that you have never returned the liking and respect I feel for you, but that is no matter. A woman in my position is used to difficulties.'

Thomas gestured uncomfortably that she should not speak of it, but she took his arm and proceeded in the same quiet voice to warn him obliquely.

'Your mother and I think it very necessary for you to go

148

away from East Mill for a while, lest some harm befall you.'

'Well, I cannot, Miss Clarke. And that is why I returned so soon from Edinburgh. There is work to be done – and there's an end to such notions.'

'Mr Ogilvie, I do not like to speak very plain, for fear of hurting you, but delay could be dangerous.'

He looked from her intent face to Kitty's sauntering figure, and frowned.

'I know very well what you mean, Miss Clarke. I have ears to hear and eyes to see, as well as another man. I form my own conclusions. And now let us join my wife and Andrew Stewart.'

'Then if you will not listen to me, listen to your mother, I beg.'

He did not answer her, and she had to wait until they were home in a bustle of supper preparations, and Kitty was removing her bonnet upstairs. Again she repeated the warning, and turned to Lady Eastmiln for support.

'What do you say to this, mother?' Thomas asked, very grey.

The old woman sighed, shook her head and set her chin, perplexed and sorry.

'I would say we have no evidence that your wife can do you harm, Thomas. But I, too, think it best that you take neither food nor drink from her hands except at the table.'

'Why, ma'am,' cried Andrew Stewart, astounded. 'Why, Miss Clarke. This is not well in either of you! All I brought from the Captain was a packet of drugs.'

'Laudanum,' said Anne, 'taken in excessive quantity, can do for a man. I was talking of it once to a Dr Dougall in Edinburgh, who used it for his gout. He said there had been instances of fatal cases, when it was used incautiously.'

'Sit down, my son,' said Lady Eastmiln, tired, 'and hear Miss Clarke out. For she has warned me of this and other things, and all that she has feared has come to pass. If your wife is innocent then no harm is done – except that harm we do ourselves in thinking such things. But if she is guilty then you must be protected. There is no need for a scandal!' she said, looking sternly about her. 'None but the family is present, and what we say does not go beyond these walls. But it would seem that Katherine was over-fond of the Captain, and grieved at his departure. At the moment she might be tempted to do something foolish. Later, when she has recovered her commonsense, she will be glad we prevented her.'

Andrew Stewart stood open-mouthed, contrasting his placid little daily round with the Ogilvie's capacity for violence.

'There is no peace in my house,' Thomas said, at length. 'But I will do as you advise.'

The table was laid Ogilvie-style, inelegant but plentiful, and Andrew made a good supper. But Thomas picked and pushed and fretted at the food on his plate, and refused ale.

'Come, my son,' said Lady Eastmiln, concerned for him. 'You work hard enough. You must eat to sustain yourself.'

'I can drink no ale,' said Thomas, and as his mother looked to see if he was worrying over Kitty, he added in explanation, 'I fainted on the hill today. The old trouble, I have no doubt.'

He glanced at Kitty as he spoke, but she made no sign of having heard or cared. He compressed his mouth and put one hand to his eyes.

'Why, man, you need a dram!' cried Andrew Stewart, attempting to lighten the atmosphere.

'You are in the right of it, Mr Stewart,' said Lady Eastmiln, grateful to him for this at least. 'My son needs a dram.'

Unobtrusively, Anne slipped out of her chair and

150

brought the brandy bottle and the glass.

'Drink up, man, and have another!' Andrew cried.

A little colour came into Thomas's face and he smiled. With the exception of Kitty, who might have been blind and deaf, they urged and cheered him on until he turned to his supper with a better appetite.

'When are you going back to Alyth, Mr Stewart?' Lady Eastmiln inquired genially.

'I should like to leave at seven tomorrow, ma'am,' he said, 'but I do not wish to inconvenience you.'

'No inconvenience at all,' said Lady Eastmiln stoutly, accepting the undoubted inconvenience of being awake and dressed, with her bed made by six o'clock in the morning. 'Shall we sit by the fire a while?'

But Andrew Stewart, struggling with a sense of injustice at Kitty's plight, contrived to speak to her as she knelt on the press bed and stared into the twilight.

'Mrs Ogilvie,' he said with difficulty, for he wanted to do what was right, but did not want to offend anyone either, 'if you should ever need good friends, my wife and I are at Alyth and would welcome you.'

She was pretty in her sprigged lilac gown, her black curls caught up by a lilac ribbon; but her face was very pale and she seemed on the point of tears.

'Oh, Mr Stewart,' she said, quietly and bitterly, 'I have no friend on earth since the Captain went. Even Miss Clarke has chided me on my behaviour. Lady Eastmiln thinks of none but her sons, and my own husband calls me a liar in front of the chapman. How can you help me?'

'These things soon pass...' Andrew Stewart began, but she silenced him with a lift of the fingers.

'Nothing will pass, Mr Stewart,' she said, so unlike her former self that he was dismayed. 'I shall live here until I am old, and every day will be the same. No friend on earth can save me from it.' She turned away to hide the tears that

were running down her cheeks. 'I am just twenty, Mr
Stewart, and have been married for four months, but I tell
you that I wish my husband were dead – or that I were
dead – rather than live like this.'

She made an excuse to retire early, and hurried away.
And Andrew Stewart sat by the fire pondering six of her
words, over and over again. 'I wish my husband were dead.
I wish my husband were dead. I wish my husband were
dead.'

The laird went to bed soon after his wife, saying he felt
unwell again. And Andrew Stewart was drawn once more
into the little circle of apprehension.

'I see you are not convinced, Mr Stewart,' said Anne
relentlessly, 'and therefore, hurtful though it is to say such
things before Lady Eastmiln, I must tell you that Mrs
Ogilvie walked up and down the road all morning, waiting
for you to come. And when I asked her why she was so
eager she replied that the Captain had written to her the
day before, and told her he had got poison the length of
Alyth, but would not trust Lizzie with it – only send it by
his brother-in-law.'

Lady Eastmiln rocked herself gently in her chair, and
shaded her eyes from the blaze on the hearth.

'I told Mrs Ogilvie that matters would not come to such
a pitch, and exhorted her most earnestly not to say or think
such wickedness. I said that she would only bring disgrace
upon the family she was come of, and upon the family into
which she was married. But Mrs Ogilvie told me to leave
her alone for the conversation was disagreeable to her, as I
must know, and she was determined to do it whatever the
event.'

Andrew Stewart poured himself another dram,
uninvited, and wished himself safe at home and in his bed
with Martha.

'I begged her to live in friendship with her husband,'

152

Anne went on, 'but she said she did not love him and never could. She said he had used the Captain ill on her account. And then, either to make me a part of her concern or to persuade me to hold my tongue, she said how happy she and the Captain and I could live at East Mill if no one else was there – are you not well, ma'am?'

'I am as well,' said Lady Eastmiln resolutely, 'as a woman could be, hearing such things.'

'I would not torment you, ma'am, but Mr Stewart must see that I do not speak idly. Then, Mr Stewart, I said that even though all were dead or gone she still could not marry the Captain since he was her husband's brother. But she said that they could go abroad and live in some of the countries where he had been. She said that in Persia they tolerated such things, and that the Captain knew Persia bravely and had been in it.'

Andrew Stewart sat for a long time in silence. The old woman watched the fire and shaded her eyes. Anne picked up the ruffles she was making for Patrick, and sewed her stitches very small and fine.

'Well, Miss Clarke,' said Andrew slowly, 'I see I was mistaken, and must help as best I can. Mrs Ogilvie put the packet into a drawer in the Stranger's room, where I shall sleep tonight. But she locked it. Now is there any way we can get her keys and remove the drugs? Or, failing that, can we get a carpenter to break it open tomorrow?'

'I do not think that a wise procedure, Mr Stewart,' said Anne. 'We do not want a scandal in the family.'

'No sir, no scandal,' said Lady Estmiln. 'As for getting her keys we can do that tomorrow, by some ruse or other. Miss Clarke is clever at thinking out such things. And until then we must see that the laird takes nothing from her hands. Mr Stewart, may I now ask you to retire, for I am very weary?'

He jumped up at once and made his bow, but took the

stairs as slowly as a man going to his execution.

'Oh, Miss Clarke,' said Lady Eastmiln, as Anne helped her to undress by the fire, 'I have sat tearless through bloodshed and violence and sudden death, but tonight I could weep fit to break.'

'Well weep away, ma'am, if it comforts you,' said Anne gently, 'and I will fetch you a posset.'

'I have left softness too long, I think,' said Lady Eastmiln. 'I do not know how to take trouble, except in silence with a straight back.'

XVII

Anne lay awake until the first light came through the window, and the first cock crowed, then crept softly from Lady Eastmiln's side and dressed. Her face was pleasant, her appearance composed, but inwardly she burned with a gambler's fervour. Whether or not Kitty's packet contained poison, Anne knew that she must act while everyone thought that poison was in the house, and poisoning in Kitty's mind. Against this moment, whenever it should come, Alexander Ogilvie had sent a paper of arsenic and a letter of directions. And now Anne memorised the letter as she moved about the room, with the arsenic safely in the pocket of her dress.

Best of all, [Alexander had written], mingle it with porridge or a viscous substance. Secondly, stir it into a hot liquid and skim off any film of powder. Thirdly, mix it with a cold drink if nothing else is to hand. But the rate of solubility is slow and might easily be detected. And if the poison is concealed in honey or treacle and added to a milky drink it will take time to settle, and leave a greasy residue behind. The rest I leave to your good sense.

A theatrical groan from the kitchen brought her soft-footed to Lizzie Sturrock's box bed.

'Oh, Miss Clarke,' said Lizzie, choosing her words as delicately as possible, 'I have an ache in my belly such as is common with me at times.'

'Stay where you are, then,' said Anne, 'and someone will

fetch you a dish of tea when it is brewed. Annie, get up and take hot water to Mr Stewart to wash his hands. I must look to Lady Eastmiln.'

'Lack-a-day! Lack-a-day!' the old woman was muttering as she crawled out of the press bed. 'Oh, Miss Clarke, how can we eat breakfast knowing what we do?'

'Why ma'am, you complain before we are hurt!' said Anne cheerfully. 'We shall all eat a good breakfast and keep our eyes open, and unless there is some unlucky chance naught can happen.'

And she slipped her fingers into the pocket of her dress, and felt the paper cornet of powder.

Andrew Stewart came down looking like a man who has slept badly, but automatically rubbed his hands at the smell of porridge and sausages. He was followed in a moment by Kitty, still in her scarlet and white bedgown.

'The laird has been awake much of the night,' she whispered to Anne, 'and he does not seem well this morning. Where is Lizzie?'

'She is sick abed herself, Mrs Ogilvie.'

'Then I will make tea. No, sit down, Miss Clarke!' she added, with quick displeasure. 'I can make tea for my husband in his own house, I dare say.'

Anne saw the sugar bowl being moved from her reach, but did not dare to insist, and mentally crossed out a dose of arsenic in the laird's dish.

With her usual slapdash movements, Kitty pulled a bowl towards her, filled it with tea, reached for the milk, yawned and looked about her vaguely. And in that instant Anne divined that she meant to take Thomas a piece of the short-cake that usually stood on the side-table, and the basket was not there.

'Why, Lizzie!' said Anne, pleasantly chiding, 'you have forgot half the breakfast things!'

And gliding into the kitchen she felt in the cupboard for

a single piece of shortcake, slipped the cone of arsenic from her pocket, and powdered the biscuit well. The sugar bowl still stood at Kitty's elbow, as she got back, and Anne added a final sprinkle of sugar on top of the arsenic, and put the shortcake in the basket. Her heart seemed to beat in her throat as Kitty picked up her husband's tea and, yawning, made for the stairs. If Anne had guessed wrongly then she must make sure that no one else ate the biscuit. But Kitty paused briefly at the side-table, scooped up the sugared slice, and went on her way.

So Anne turned round and sat looking out of the window, seeing to Lady Eastmiln's comforts, and making a pleasant third in the conversation while she waited.

Downstairs came Kitty, filled another bowl with tea and took it out to Lizzie Sturrock, and sat down with some satisfaction.

'Well, the laird and Lizzie are well off this morning,' she announced, 'for they have got their tea first!'

Neither Lady Eastmiln nor Andrew Stewart was accustomed to noting every movement, but Anne did not intend that they should miss this particular opportunity.

'What?' she cried, turning round, 'has the laird got tea?'

There was a little hush at the table as they took in the import of this remark.

'Why yes, of course he has, Miss Clarke!' said Kitty sharply, annoyed.

Anne said nothing, but glanced at Lady Eastmiln, who frowned a silent question.

'*You* may pour the rest, Miss Clarke!' said Kitty, 'I shall take mine upstairs.'

She swept off, injured; and in a moment was down again, disturbed, asking Lizzie for a bowl and water, and returned to her husband.

'Can Mrs Ogilvie not sit with the rest of us like a Christian?' asked Lady Eastmiln, peevish at these interruptions

157

to her breakfast.

Her deaf ears prevented her from knowing what was going on above. But hearing sounds of distress from the laird's room, Andrew asked nervously if aught was amiss.

'Annie! Annie! Come up here at once!' Kitty cried suddenly.

The urgency in her tone brought them all to their feet; and Annie went at a run up the stairs, to return for a clean towel almost immediately.

'What's amiss, girl?' cried Lady Eastmiln, as the servant ran past.

'Oh, ma'am, the laird is taken ill, with purging and vomiting, and I have but two hands,' said Annie, distracted. 'Lizzie! Will you not help me?'

A groan of dissent from Lizzie, who intended to be ill in comfort.

'Miss Clarke,' said Lady Eastmiln, 'you are younger and quicker than me. Go up, if you will be so good, and see what is the matter. And you had best finish your breakfast, Mr Stewart.'

'I cannot, ma'am,' said Andrew, and pushed his plate aside.

In the bedroom, Kitty opened the window and pulled the soiled covers from the bed. Her momentary anger with Anne Clarke had faded.

'Oh, help me, Miss Clarke,' she cried, as Thomas fell back on the pillows, 'for the laird is very sick, and Annie like a hen with its head off.'

Anne brought clean sheets from the chest, and between them they stripped the bed, moving Thomas as little as possible, and made him comfortable.

'We need more water, and these things out of the way,' said Anne, efficient and calm in the crisis.

She noticed the plate by the bed, empty of everything but crumbs, sugar and powder, and swept it up with the linen as she passed, saying, 'I will take these downstairs, and be back immediately.'

She heard Thomas retching and vomiting again as she ran down, and Kitty's despairing voice as she tried to comfort a man she no longer cared for, in a state that would revolt the hardiest stomach. But the only thing Anne could think of, as she clutched the bundle of linen and the plate was, 'Did I give him enough?'

'Well, Miss Clarke?'

'Oh, ma'am, the laird is very ill. He has got a bad breakfast!'

Then she burst into tears, finding them easy in the excitement and hysteria of the moment.

'Hot water!' Kitty cried. 'Annie! Miss Clarke! I cannot manage alone!'

And she appeared among them in a tempest of fear and anger.

'For God's sake, woman, are you daft?' she demanded, seeing Anne Clarke weeping.

'Aye,' cried Anne bitterly. 'I am daft, Mrs Ogilvie, to weep when the laird is dying!'

Kitty turned pale and then red, but made a derisive noise in her throat, and pushing the servant before her up the stairs told her to hurry.

'I think I will see for myself, ma'am,' said Andrew, following them.

He stood by the door, horrified at the stench and disorder in the room, and the wracked body trying to rid itself of irritant. As the vomiting abated Thomas fell back in dull amazement, and looked about him.

'I am here, Thomas,' said Andrew, and gripped his hand.

'Thank God for that, then, Andy. Too many women around me. Too many women. Fickle cattle, Andy. I am all wrong within. I have got my turn.'

And he cried for something to drink.

'Milk is very soothing, Mr Ogilvie,' said Annie Sampson.

'Water. Only water. My guts burn.'

'Mrs Ogilvie,' said Andrew, drawing Kitty aside, 'may I have a private word with you? Should I not ride at once to Alyth for a surgeon?'

'But he will be better presently,' said Kitty, harrassed. 'He has had such bouts before, Mr Stewart, though not so violent.'

'Mrs Ogilvie, this seems to be no ordinary nausea. I would strongly recommend that you call in professional assistance.'

Kitty's eyes filled with tears.

'But Mr Stewart,' she said, 'Miss Clarke has just said such bad things of me that I am afraid to call a doctor, lest he think it is my fault.'

'Mrs Ogilvie, I have some little experience of these things. The laird was ill yesterday, of his old trouble. That bowl of hot tea you brought him may have caused further inflammation. And Dr Meik of Alyth is not a man to listen to gossip, and will consult with you without prejudice.'

Her face cleared.

'Then go as quick as you can, Mr Stewart – and God bless and thank you.'

'Thomas is right,' said Andrew to himself, as he mounted his horse. 'There are too many women in the house, and they all clack too much.'

But before he was properly on the road to Alyth he heard his name called, and reined in. The girl who ran to his stirrup was one of those who helped at harvest times.

'Annie Robertson, is it?' he inquired.

'Aye, sir, and the old mistress says you are to ride for the surgeon as fast as may be. For the laird is so badly, Mr Stewart, that she fears for his life.'

'Tell her I will spare neither my horse nor myself, Annie.

160

Here is a penny for running so hard after me. Go back now, like a good girl.'

'Bring me my clothes,' said Thomas, pulling himself up. 'I must feed the horses.'

The women were round him like a flock of birds, crying that he must rest.

'Away with you!' Thomas commanded, as sternly as his weakness would let him, and he began painfully to pull on his breeches.

He swayed downstairs, holding on to the wall at every step. And they scurried before him, begging Lady Eastmiln to persuade him back to bed. But she grunted her way out of her chair and came to meet him, as resolute and pale as himself. Patrick had always been her favourite, but now she saw something of her own indomitable spirit in Thomas's face, and honoured him for it.

'Will you not speak with the laird, ma'am?' Kitty cried. 'He will do himself a hurt.'

'The laird is a *man*,' said Lady Eastmiln proudly, looking round on them. 'The laird is not a sick child. He does as he thinks best.'

And she went back to her chair and would not speak to any of them, and they were very quiet.

Slowly, Thomas crept from horse to horse, leaning on a glossy flank here, patting a soft inquiring muzzle there, speaking their names and attending to their needs. And when they were fed and watered he braced himself to ride to Shilling Hill to visit his tenants. He was back again before ten, slipping helplessly from the saddle, vomiting.

'Lizzie!' cried Kitty, running to the kitchen, as two labourers brought Thomas in from the yard. 'Get up! You are well enough, and have drunk your tea!'

The servant made a sulky face and stuck one dirty leg out of the bed.

161

'Hurry yourself!' said Kitty impatiently. 'And you, Alex, carry the laird as gently as you are able! Annie, fill the pot and set it on the fire again!'

At the foot of the stairs Anne Clarke stood composedly, a little smile on her mouth.

'I have made the bed ready, Mrs Ogilvie,' she said.

'I can manage without you, Miss Clarke, I thank you,' said Kitty coldly. 'You have done and said enough already!'

For a moment the grey eyes were surprised. Then Anne turned away to sit with Lady Eastmiln, who was crying, 'What is amiss? Why will no one tell me anything, in my son's house?'

'I fear, ma'am, that the laird has had a dose with his morning tea,' said Anne.

'Then go upstairs to him, Miss Clarke, and keep him from those two women!'

XVIII

The servants being occupied, Anne Clarke made the laird a bowl of hot tea, skimmed a film of powder off the surface, and sugared it well. Then she powdered and sugared another slice of shortcake and went softly up the stairs. Thomas was quiet now, against the pillows, his eyes closed and sunk in his head.

'I said I did not want you, Miss Clarke!' Kitty cried impatiently.

'I am here by Lady Eastmiln's orders, Mrs Ogilvie.'

'Then if you stay, I go!' Kitty said, and looked to Thomas for support.

But he was too weak to argue with them, and as Kitty ran out in a flurry of tears Anne sat at his bedside composedly, and began to spoon the tea into his mouth and persuade him to take a bit of biscuit for nourishment. Minutes afterwards he was crying, 'I cannot keep it down, Miss Clarke!' And she held his head while he was sick.

Downstairs, Kitty sat at one end of the parlour and Lady Eastmiln at the other, and neither spoke. For the first time in her twenty years, Kitty was attempting to assess a situation instead of dancing through it. She clung to Andrew Stewart's theory that Thomas was suffering from grievous inflammation, and hoped that the surgeon might cure him quickly. But she knew that Anne Clarke, who had said she was her friend, had given them all to believe that Kitty poisoned him. She recollected a dozen foolish phrases, spoken in temper and thoughtlessness, which could be made to seem incriminating. She was afraid that her affair with Patrick would come out, and provide a motive for murder. She admitted to herself that she did not love Thomas, and remembered she had said so to at least two witnesses, but she did not wish him dead. Indeed, with Patrick lost and her reputation at stake, she prayed that he might live. She pondered his dislike of Anne Clarke, when all others had praised her. She thought of his attempts to get rid of her. And looking at Lady Eastmiln's grey head and sad mouth, she saw Thomas as he had been when they were first married: shy and gentle and kind. She recollected the expression on Lady Eastmiln's face, and her reproof as her son went out to feed the horses. 'The laird is a *man*!' Lady Eastmiln had said proudly.

Tears ran down her cheeks and on to her white fichu. She had dressed, but her hair hung out of curl, and she had not had the time nor the heart to bite her lips and make them red.

I shall be kinder to him, she promised, and think what I can do to make him happy. And we shall send Miss Clarke packing, between the two of us. And with the Captain gone I shall be with Thomas as I was six months ago. And if the Captain comes again I shall be friendly but nothing more.

'I am going upstairs, ma'am,' she said timidly, 'to see how my husband does now.'

But Lady Eastmiln did not answer.

'God knows how we shall get all this bedding washed and dried!' said Lizzie, grumbling down the stairs with a fresh bundle. 'I wish we had Kate Campbell here to set about it, for our hands are full looking after the laird!'

His face was clay-coloured and his forehead wet, and Kitty wiped it with her handkerchief. Anne Clarke stayed obstinately in the chair by his bed, and would not make room for her, so Kitty sat by his knees and took his hand.

'Thomas,' she said softly, 'it is Kitty. Thomas, I am sorry for this – and for all other things.'

He opened his eyes a little and looked at her, but she

could judge nothing from his expression.

'Thomas, we shall be merry together, again, when you are well. And all will be forgotten. Do you remember how we rode to East Mill after the wedding, and I raced you down the hill?'

A very faint smile touched the corners of his mouth.

'Do not disturb the laird, Mrs Ogilvie,' said Anne sharply. 'He must have rest.'

All Kitty's temper went into her voice as she cried, 'Thomas, make her go! There was no trouble between us until she came. And I will nurse and care for you, all day and all night if need be. But make her go!'

Anne Clarke held her breath, but her management had been too thorough to let her down.

'Miss ... Clarke ... stays,' said Thomas.

'But if she stays then I will go, Thomas. I *will* go! I will not be treated so in my husband's house!'

His face contracted with pain and he called for water.

'Thomas!' cried Kitty, clutching at his wandering hands. 'Tell her to go!'

But he repeated weakly, 'Miss ... Clarke ... stays!' and drank as though he would never stop.

Kitty released his hands gently and stood up.

'Well, Miss Clarke,' she said, 'you are to have all your own way, it seems. I have been a sightless fool, but I am wiser now, and I shall not forget this.'

Anne's smile followed her out of the room, and haunted her for hours afterwards.

No one had any heart or stomach for food, and about one o'clock Lady Eastmiln got Lizzie to help her up the stairs. She found Thomas restless and thirsty, calling continually for cold water. He complained that his heart hammered in his breast and there was no air in the room.

'Open the windows wider, Miss Clarke,' said Lady Eastmiln, and watched with pity as he rolled his head from side to side, and his hands gripped and twisted the sheets, and he tossed and groaned in an effort to find relief.

'Oh, my son,' she said, 'you promised me to take nothing from your wife's hands.'

'Well . . . mother . . . it is too late . . . now.'

'Can I not do anything for my son, Miss Clarke?' Lady Eastmiln asked.

'I think it best if you leave him to those stronger and nimbler than yourself, ma'am,' said Anne gently. 'We are up and down the stairs all the time, and the room is very small.'

'Help me to my feet again then, Lizzie, and I will sit below.'

She put one hand on Thomas's cheek for a moment, seemed about to say something, shook her head and made her way out. She was glad that Kitty was walking in the garden. She could not have borne to speak to her. So, for want of anything to do, she ordered Annie Sampson very sharply to go and clip the sheep.

'Shall I not be needed here, ma'am?' said Annie, wiping her nose on her sleeve.

'No, girl. Miss Clarke and Lizzie will see to everything. I cannot bear to have you clattering in the kitchen. Get you gone.'

In the little garden, Kitty walked to and fro, hands clasped, oblivious of the riot of scent and colour. Once she paused over a bed of herbs, and wondered whether any of them might alleviate her husband's sickness. But the virtues of pennyroyal, hyssop, camomile and rue, faded before the magnitude of his ailment. So she walked and thought and wrung her hands helplessly, and sometimes put them to her ears to shut out the sounds coming from the bedroom above.

Anne Clarke was tireless in her attendance, trying to persuade Thomas to take milk with his water, substituting small ale for nourishment. But he brought back everything

166

the moment it had been swallowed. And he threshed his limbs to escape the pain and cried that the brawns of his legs must burst, and asked Anne Clarke to bind them. At first she brought a pair of Kitty's silk stockings, but he would not have them near him. So very carefully she bound his legs with strips torn from an old shirt, and he thanked her. But his lungs laboured for breath, and though they had removed the timber leaves from both windows he could not get enough air. And they observed that he drew breath like a child with the croup, in a rasping fashion.

James Millam was the first to inquire about Thomas's health, calling at mid-day and then an hour later, and so through the afternoon. He bore himself with dignity and was courteous to all the ladies, though once or twice he glanced at Anne Clarke and wondered about her dismissal, since she appeared so anxious to do her utmost for the laird. The rumours of poison, whispered throughout Glenisla, he ignored entirely, taking care to inform Kitty and Lady Eastmiln that this illness did not surprise him.

'The laird was at my house four days ago,' said James Millam, upright and decent, 'and he complained to me of gravel and colic. And he told me that if he did not get the better of it he could not live – though we must pray that the surgeon thinks otherwise. And but two days ago he walked into my house talking of the cold, though Tuesday was as fine and warm as anyone could wish. He asked for some shilling seeds to be set to warm. And my wife offered him a bowl of broth, but he would not eat, saying he wanted no supper but the fire. And as he held his hands to the peats he said he was fading as fast as dew goes off the grass.'

'You are most kind, Mr Millam,' said Lady Eastmiln, as upright as himself, 'but I think my son suffers a worse hurt than the colic.'

'Well, I will inquire of him later, ma'am and Mrs Ogilvie, and hope there is better news.'

He bowed to both of them, pulled on his woollen bonnet, and strode out of the house.

Thomas grew worse, and Kitty caught Lizzie by the arm as she hurried downstairs for yet more water.

'Go and fetch the precentor as fast as you can,' Kitty whispered. 'I do not wish to worry Lady Eastmiln but I think a clergyman should be sent for – and, oh, *where* is Dr Meik?'

The spurious excitement of a sudden illness was vanishing under the labour involved. Lizzie dumped the calf's bucket full of hot water by the laird's bed, snatched a bannock from the kitchen cupboard, and ate as she ran – glad to be out of the sights and smells of the sickroom.

In ones and twos the neighbours, drawn by the news, called to pay their respects and ask how the laird progressed. Lady Eastmiln was garrulous, grateful to talk at length to so many listening ears. But Kitty was brief with them.

'My husband is very ill and must not be disturbed,' she said, blocking the way up the stairs. 'He will see you when he is better.'

Remembering what they had heard of her, they turned back discontented, and gossiped among themselves as they went back to their homes.

But when the precentor came, Kitty took him to the bedroom herself, and knelt with him in prayer, and tried to coax Thomas to speak to her. His eyes were inflamed and looked on her without kindness. His swollen tongue did not allow him to speak plainly; but from his aspect and his mumbled words, and the gestures of his wandering hands, she understood that he had finished with her. Very white and silent she saw the precentor out, while the voice of Anne Clarke tormented her.

'Would you be so good, Mrs Ogilvie,' said Anne coolly,

'as to fetch a glass of wine for the laird? He can keep nothing else down and it may do him good.'

This much I will do, thought Kitty, as she wiped the glass on her handkerchief and poured the claret, but no more. I will not stay where I am not wanted. And when he is well again I shall go back to my mother.

The wine stayed down for an hour and Thomas lay back with his eyes closed, though from time to time his limbs jerked involuntarily, and he burned from throat to guts. Then the agony began again, and he moaned and retched, and Anne Clarke did all she could to ease him.

At the four hours, Lady Eastmiln and Kitty were sitting at opposite ends of the parlour, taking their customary glass of wine, when Andrew Stewart clattered into the yard with Martha.

'Where is your doctor?' Lady Eastmiln demanded, without preamble.

'I have left a message for him, and he will come as soon as he is back,' said Andrew. 'I have not been idle, ma'am. I have sent a message to the Spaldings at Glenkilry, and indeed I have hardly got off my horse since I left this morning.'

And he drank off two tankards of small ale in two draughts, and dropped into a chair unasked.

'Well, well,' said Lady Eastmiln, gesturing to Martha not to fuss, 'you have done all you could. The house is in disorder and none of us has eaten. If you are hungry you must look to yourselves!' A ghost of Highland hospitality stood reproachfully at her elbow. 'Forgive this poor welcome,' she added, weary with waiting, 'but we cannot help it.'

'How is Thomas?' Martha asked, making tea and trying to find clean bowls.

'He is dying, I think,' said Lady Eastmiln, cold and clear and steadfast.

'I will help you, Martha,' said Kitty, glad of something to do.

But the rap of Lady Eastmiln's stick on the brick floor arrested her.

'Sit where you are, Mrs Ogilvie!' said Lady Eastmiln. 'My daughter will prepare the tea. One of us has suffered from your ministrations already!'

Kitty looked to Martha and Andrew for support, but they avoided her eyes.

'I will walk in the garden, then,' said Kitty, stupefied.

In a few moments Lizzie was at her side, dirty, tired and scandalously delighted.

'Oh, Mrs Ogilvie,' she cried, 'Miss Clarke said you was to be sent for, and the laird said he did not choose that you should come, but Miss Clarke says you must come whether he will or not, and she says to tell you that he is dying.'

Kitty had never felt so solitary in all her life. A dozen protests trembled on her tongue. A gale of tears threatened her eyes and hurt her throat.

'I do not choose to come where I am not wanted!' she cried, and turned away. 'I do not wish to watch my husband dying!'

Lizzie's eyes grew rounder. She put both chapped hands over her mouth in horror, and then ran indoors to tell everyone what Mrs Ogilvie had said.

The summer day waned and Thomas waned with it. Afraid to stay indoors, to eat or to drink, Kitty walked the braes and hung about the house. The evening brought a breath of reason with George Spalding, who came outside and put his arm round her shoulders.

'How is poor Thomas?' Kitty asked, afraid to hear.

'He is a little eased,' George Spalding answered, choosing his words with care. 'They were giving him ale and I advised against it. Will you not come in now, Kitty?'

She shook her head: a child afraid of punishment.

170

'Come,' he said kindly, 'I am here and will stand by you. I have heard what they are saying, but that is all a nonsense. Thomas has been in poor health for years. I wrote to tell your mother so, shortly after your marriage, and that was why I urged the signing of the infeftment so eagerly. His own tacksman, honest Jamie Millam, says he has been ailing since Sunday. It is not *your* fault, Kitty, but poor Thomas's insides!'

She allowed herself to be led to the parlour, and sat quietly in a corner avoiding everyone but her brother-in-law.

At nine o'clock Annie Sampson trailed in exhausted, to eat a hasty supper in the kitchen. Cold meat, bannocks, cheese and ale was set on the table for those who felt they could manage a little food, but it stayed untouched. Anne Clarke, refusing all offers of help in her long vigil, stayed upstairs, and they sent her glasses of claret to keep up her strength.

'Miss Clarke has been exceedingly good,' said Andrew Stewart, into the uncomfortable silence.

'Most assiduous,' Martha agreed.

'I do not know what we should have done without her watchfulness and quiet devotion,' said Lady Eastmiln, very loud.

Kitty's head drooped.

'Miss Clarke has done excellently with the nursing,' said George Spalding, shrewd and easy, 'but I must be honest and say that I never cared for her. I do not trust a woman who sees so much and says so little, however great her devotion.'

And he crossed his legs and drank his wine, and smiled encouragement to Kitty. No one had the strength to argue with him, and conversation ceased.

'All is uncommonly quiet upstairs,' said George, setting down his wine. 'Can poor Thomas be easier, do you think?'

171

'Well, Lizzie? How is the laird?' Lady Eastmiln demanded, as the wretched servant stumbled downstairs for the hundredth time.

'The laird is quieter, ma'am, but I think no better. Miss Clarke does all for him and he looks kindly at her and speaks soft.'

'Why does that fool Meik not come?' cried Lady Eastmiln, imperious and afraid at once.

No one could answer her.

Anne Clarke sat wearily by Thomas's bed, hands clasped in her lap. She was ready to hold or change him or fetch the basin whenever he should need it, but now he rested and so did she. Her purpose had been accomplished and she lavished all her care upon her victim. No one could have done more for him, nor done it better. She bore him no malice and took no pleasure in his suffering. He had simply been in Alexander's way, and could she have dispatched him in an easier manner she would have done so. She had taken his life, and in its place she gave him assistance. Her love of order and cleanliness, so rare in that day, prepared him to meet death washed and combed, in a fresh shirt between the folds of a decent sheet. He blessed the gentleness of her hands as she turned him, and was grateful that she preserved the remnant of dignity left him. And as they neared the end of their curious relationship she went with him, perceptive and imaginative, as adaptable as water, following every twist and turn of the failing mind so that he should not be entirely alone.

Thomas, who had wandered through the labour of the Rebellion again in his delirium, now drifted into happier and less responsible times, and let loose the cows in the minister's pastures with a phantom chuckle. He no longer knew who Anne was; aware only of a comprehending smile, of deft hands and attentive ears; and addressed her by a

172

dozen names. She answered to every one of them, though most were strange to her. And Lizzie dozed on the chest near the window, and did not care what happened so long as she was not troubled.

'Janet,' Thomas whispered, quite clearly. 'Janet.'

'I am here, Mr Ogilvie,' said Anne, and saw by the light of the candle a change come over his face.

'Lizzie!' she said sharply. 'Fetch Lady Eastmiln and the others!'

'Yes, Miss Clarke,' said Lizzie, feeling that the day would never end. 'Is the laird gone then, Miss Clarke?'

'Be quiet,' said Anne, soft and imperative, 'and do as I tell you.'

'Janet,' Thomas whispered, smiling at her. 'Janet.'

His hand wandered towards hers and she clasped it.

'Your hair's right bonnie, Janet,' he whispered. 'Right bonnie, Janet. Put your arm round my shoulders, Janet.'

Very delicately she moved so that she sat behind him and pillowed his head on her breast. His momentary clarity of speech had left him, and he mumbled and gasped, but seemed happy enough in her arms. And she sat there, as lonely as she had ever been, and pitied him, and wondered how many years ago he had stroked that girl's hair and found it bonnie.

He stiffened, paused a moment, eyes wide, and then vomited as though he would bring up his heart. She could do nothing but receive him in her arms again as his head came to rest. So strange and pure and solitary she felt, in this moment, that she forgot herself altogether, and was with him as one human being is with another when all earthly considerations are swept away.

'Thomas!' she cried, wiping his face for the last time and looking into his eyes.

The years were moving from him, leaving his counten-ance curiously young and vulnerable. And she saw how he

173

must once have been, before time and circumstance had changed him.

They were coming up the stairs, too late to bid him farewell. But Anne did not heed them, weeping and rocking over his dead face, calling on God to bless him – who had been a good man and done nobody any harm.

XIX

Peter Meik, a fresh-faced sandy man of twenty-seven, rode into the yard at two o'clock in the morning; but could do nothing for Thomas, except to pronounce him dead and advise a dram as the best restorative for the company.

'Did you not have a copy of *The Poor Man's Physician* in the house, ma'am?' he asked Lady Eastmiln. 'There is none better than John Moncrieff's book of homely medicines when a physician cannot be got quickly. Well, well, I am very sorry for it. I could have let his blood or applied a few leeches had I been in time, and that would have eased him considerably. Thank you, sir, I could do with a dram and a bite myself. I have been riding all day, here and there, and this is my second death since morning – may Christ have mercy on them both. The other was a child with pestilential fever. I did all I could, had a cataplasm of snails beat up and set to the soles of her feet, but she expired at sun-down. Well, well, that is the way of it, and who are we to question the will of Almighty God?'

'Amen,' they murmured. 'Amen.'

The house was filling with friends and neighbours from all around, and the nightmare was complete. The weary women began to wash tankards and dishes that had lain all day, to fetch sack and ale and claret, to set the table with all the food they could muster, and prepare for a night's heavy drinking.

Alone with her dead, Anne Clarke washed and laid out the body of the laird. She drew the customary woollen stockings over his thin legs, wrapped him in a woollen winding sheet, covered the furniture with white linen, and

175

lit tallow candles at his head and feet. Every window and door in the house had been opened to let the soul go free, and now she placed a dish of salt upon the laird's breast, and left him ready to be viewed.

'Mr Millam,' said Kitty timidly, 'would you not ride and find the Captain?'

'Indeed I will, Mrs Ogilvie.'

'No need of that, Mr Millam,' said George Spalding, pulling on his coat. 'I am off to Glenkilry this very hour, and I shall find him myself. He should be here by sun-rise, or a little after.' Over the confusion of drinking and talking and weeping he said, 'A lyke-wake was never my notion of pleasure, so I must bid you farewell for the present, Kitty. It would be kinder of them to let you all go to your beds, but it seems that no one intends to sleep tonight.'

'I wish you were not going,' said Kitty, holding his sleeve. 'I shall have no friend here to stand by me.'

'I think that Mr Millam is your friend,' said George kindly, 'and Patrick will be here in the morning. And after the funeral you must come to stay at Glenkilry for as long as you please.'

She said nothing, but her mouth and chin quivered, and two tears rolled down her cheeks.

'Come, Kitty,' said George, 'you are young and pretty and have much to look forward to. Your family has seen to it that Thomas's death does not leave you in poverty. We shall all help you to recover. Lady Nairne will be glad to have her silly puss back again, and poor Frisk will wag his tail off!'

She nodded and sobbed and tried to smile.

'Mr Millam,' said George to the tacksman, who stood a little to one side, affecting not to hear, 'Mrs Ogilvie has suffered a grievous shock. And there is some wicked talk to worry her, on top of it. Will you see that she takes some nourishment and is not pestered by gossip?'

176

'Aye, sir. No one shall talk to her while I am by, I promise you.'

'The laird would have thanked you for those words,' said George. 'Though there have been trouble-makers between them, these last weeks, she was always dearest to him.' And he shook James Millam's hand.

Lizzie was collecting eggs from beneath the hens on the midden when Patrick Ogilvie galloped into the yard on a lathered horse. It was six o'clock in the morning, and the last of the mourners had reeled off to work as best they could. He looked older and sadder than she had ever seen him. Nor did he pinch her cheek or her behind in his usual fashion, but nodded at her curtly and asked a boy to care for his horse.

'Mrs Ogilvie! Mrs Ogilvie!' cried Lizzie, running in. 'The Captain is come!'

'Do not shout it all over the house,' said Kitty, coming out of the corner where she had been sitting, 'but ask the Captain if he will kindly speak with me privately in the stable.'

'He is walking with Dr Meik and talking very stern!' said Lizzie, all eyes and ears.

'I will wait in the stable until he is done.'

She stood by Patrick's sweating horse and stroked its muzzle, glad to touch something that had been near him. But her thoughts and feelings were so confused that she did not know what to say, so dropped him a formal curtsey when he came up to her.

'I am very sorry,' said Patrick, pale and stiff in his bearing. 'When did my brother die?'

'At midnight.'

'Dr Meik says it was a recurrence of his old trouble.'

'Yes, so I believe.'

The silence was more than she could bear, and she cried that she had suffered very much and feared she had no friends. His manner did not alter but his eyes softened. And he said to her, as he would speak to a child or a pet, 'Come into the house, Kitty. You are distracted.'

She caught at the cuffs of his jacket and shook them.

'But Miss Clarke says that I poisoned my husband! And I am very much afraid!'

Still he said, 'Come, Kitty. You are distracted!' and led her into the house.

Lady Eastmiln sat erect and dry-eyed after the night's wake, weary for her morning tea. But she trembled as Patrick embraced her, and said, 'My son, my son,' and stroked his curly head. Then she recollected herself, and was very sharp with Annie Sampson, and told her to take the Captain upstairs to view the corpse.

'Your brother looks well out of this troubled world, sir,' Peter Meik observed.

Patrick stared at the peaceful face, now looking no older than his own, the waxen hands folded in prayer. He remembered a hundred little kindnesses from the brother who had been more like a father to him, and the quarrel between them that had driven him away. Then he fell on his knees and wept without restraint, and the physician bowed his head in prayer and was very sorry for him. But a duty remained to be done.

'Lieutenant Ogilvie,' said Peter Meik, as Patrick wiped his face and got to his feet, 'do you not find your brother's wife distraught?'

'It is very natural, sir.'

'Yes, yes. Certainly. But I feel I must tell you, sir, as the head of the family, that she has made the strangest of suggestions to me. She asked me what, in my opinion, her husband died of; and hearing the history of his poor health, and judging from his symptoms, I said it was an acute inflammation of the intestines. Whereupon she begged me that should I discover it was anything else I would conceal

178

the matter from the world! Now what, sir, do you suppose Mrs Ogilvie thought I *should* discover?'

'I do not know,' said Patrick, disquieted.

'I believe,' said Peter Meik judiciously, 'that the lady is suffering from shock, but I thought I had better mention the matter.'

'You were in the right,' said Patrick, concerned, 'but I think it best that you should not repeat this to anyone else.'

'Why no, sir, I spoke to you as your brother's heir, and the head of the family.'

It was the first time that Patrick had realised his new status, and the enormity of it rendered him silent over breakfast. After he had eaten a bowl of porridge he escaped to the burn-side, east of the house, to think it over. No more roving, no more haggling for money. Much more responsibility, and his life laid down, hour by hour, and burden by burden, until the day he died. As he strove between the advantages and disadvantages of this new situation he observed the neat figure of Anne Clarke approaching, and took off his bonnet.

'Well, Captain,' said Anne, smiling, 'shall we walk a little way?'

He gave her his arm and they sauntered on.

'Now you see, Captain,' said Anne coolly, 'what this woman has brought you to!'

The hair rose on his neck, though why he could not have said, for they had always been good friends. Only there was something so baleful about that bland smile and equable tone that he stood still, and asked her what she meant.

'Why, Mrs Ogilvie desired *me* to get poison for her, months ago, but I thank God I never had a mind to do it!' And as he stared and stared, she added, 'The late laird died of poison, Captain, did you not know? Everyone in the house knows it, and in Glenisla too. Did you not consider what was in her mind when you sent Mr Stewart over to her with his secret packet?'

'The arsenic?' said Patrick. 'But that was to put down the wild dogs that were spoiling the game.'

'Oh, Captain, what a story to believe!' Anne chided. 'We have had no dogs. I thought I heard some, one night, but no one has seen any.'

He stood quite aghast.

'But Good God!' he cried. 'I never dreamed that she would give it to Thomas. How could I?'

'She was not happy with him,' said Anne smoothly, 'and *I* know how happy she was with you. Have you never heard her say, "Divil burst him! I should like to give him a dose!"?'

'But that was in play, Miss Clarke. Kitty's tongue always runs ahead of her thoughts. She meant no harm by it.'

'Well, he is dead,' said Anne calmly, 'wherever her tongue and her thoughts ran. And her ill-doing will implicate you, Captain, since you were her lover and provided her with the means to dispatch him.'

She let go his arm, still smiling, and said she would return to the house.

Alone on the brae Patrick stared after her, mouth fallen. From time to time he said to himself, 'Good God! Good God!' in terrible disbelief. Then he began to run across the hillock to find Kitty, and discover how much truth was in the tale. He had thought himself beset by problems, on becoming the laird of East Mill, and now he saw those little problems as most precious and desirable things beside the threat of murder.

He found Kitty in a pitiable state, whispering and crying to Lizzie Sturrock, whose face betrayed an interest that was quite unseemly.

'I beg of you, Lizzie,' Kitty was saying in a low voice, 'if any should ask, that you tell them you drank the tea that the laird could not finish, out of his own bowl, and that I gave it to you with my own hands.'

'But who *should* ask me, Mrs Ogilvie?'

'How should *I* know? Anyone. Anyone who asks. Tell them you drank the tea before and after the laird had it, and that you saw me make it. And while I have a ha'penny in the world, Lizzie, you shall share it with me!'

'Aye, Lizzie, be a good lass,' said Patrick, putting his hand in his pocket, 'and do as your mistress says.'

Lizzie took his twopence and put one finger to the side of her nose to indicate secrecy. Then ran off to tell Annie Sampson.

'Kitty,' said Patrick, taking her arm, 'for God's sake tell me the truth. Did you poison Thomas?'

'No, no, no,' she cried, and became so distressed that he took her to the back of the barn, lest she be observed. 'Oh, I am going mad!' she cried, putting her hands to the sides of her head, and wept hysterically.

Words and sobs strangled each other as she tried to explain.

'They say I gave him poison in his dish of tea, and I did not. I did nothing wrong. I would not. But I am so afraid that I am trying to make it sound right, lest they fetch the Sheriff. And if Lizzie says she drank from the same bowl...'

'Kitty,' said Patrick, 'we cannot rely on Lizzie. Where is the packet of arsenic I sent you?'

'I have burned it.'

'But why? Why burn it? Had you opened it, or had anyone else opened it?'

She shook her head and fairly screamed dissent.

'Then you could have shown them it was still sealed and whole, Kitty. And I should have said where I got it from, and for what purpose. But now they will not believe you. *Why* did you burn it?'

'Because it was poison,' she cried, unable to think. 'Because it was poison and they must not find it.'

He made a sound of exasperation and pity, and said, looking at her face spoiled with weeping, 'No man will ever love you for your wits, Kitty, so you had best dry your tears!'

'But what shall we do?'

'We shall do nothing,' he said at last. 'No one has accused you openly. This is all gossip and rumour. My mother would do much to avoid a scandal. The servants can be turned off if they threaten to speak. So there is only Miss Clarke – and we must send her packing. Then Thomas will be buried, and however much tongues clack they can't *unbury* him.'

Kitty wiped her eyes and re-tied her ribbon, slightly heartened.

'I will send her off myself,' she said.

'Annie,' said Lizzie, 'did you notice aught amiss with the tea Mrs Ogilvie made for the laird yesterday morning? For she wants me to swear that I drank from the same bowl.'

Annie thought.

'Why, I swear that is the same bowl I rinsed out and took fresh water in when he was ill,' she said, and then saw the disappointment on Lizzie's face. 'But now I remember,' she said, 'that the laird did not like it. I think he said something about getting his death from it.' Her fancy ran ahead of her. 'Yes, he said, "Damn that bowl, for I have got my death in it already!" and he told me to take it downstairs and fetch his water in the tea-kettle.'

Lizzie's expression was all that she could have desired.

'And I looked into it,' said Annie, 'and there was grease in the bottom of it, for all the rinsing!'

'Where is it? Did you wash it after?'

'It is in the press. Why should I wash it when it had held nothing but water? I emptied the water out and put it in the

182

press.'

They found the bowl and examined the grease at the bottom as though they were unused to slovenly cleaning.

'It smells like mutton fat,' said Lizzie, uncertainly. 'Here, put some broth in it from the pot and give it to Rabbie.'

The sheepdog trotted in, wagging his tail, and emptied the dish with relish. They watched him lolling his tongue and winking with pleasure, none the worse for it. And an hour later he was still on his legs.

'I think we should give it to Mrs Stewart,' said Lizzie hopefully, 'and tell her what you know, and ask her to take charge of it.'

'Now I remember something else,' said Annie Sampson, honest in this at least. 'I saw Mrs Ogilvie take up the tea when Lady Eastmiln and Miss Clarke was there, and I wanted some beef from the closet so I followed her up. And she was stirring the tea round and round, and frowning, standing just inside the closet door. And when she saw me she told me to get downstairs because she was not ready to give me the beef yet. And she was in a passion at me, and said I was always wanting something.'

'Did anyone else see her stirring the poison in the tea?'

'Aye, Alex Lindsay, the new servant. He was going up to the garret, and I saw him from the stairhead, near the closet. And he must have seen both of us.'

'Fetch him!' said Lizzie.

Alex Lindsay was a raw-boned lad of twenty-one, very red about the hands and face, and glad of a tankard of ale to refresh his memory.

'Aye,' he said, 'I was going up to the garret to take down a wheel when I saw Mrs Ogilvie standing in the closet doorway on the landing. But I did not see what she was doing, nor what she had in her hands.'

'But she had a bowl of tea, and had set down the plate of

shortcake, and was stirring and frowning!' Annie cried, robbed of her tale.

'Well, that's as may be,' said Alex Lindsay, 'but I cannot remember. Only she did tell me not to walk over the closet ceiling when I was in the garret, for fear of shaking something down.'

'But you saw *me*, did you not, you daft creature?' Annie persisted.

'Aye, I saw you right enough. You were at the stairhead near the closet, and Mrs Ogilvie took a scunner against you about the beef!'

'They have shown Martha the bowl that held Thomas's tea,' said Patrick, very white. 'They have told her that they saw you stirring poison into it. Two of the servants saw you.'

For a moment Kitty could not get her breath.

'I stirred nothing into it. Nothing.'

'For God's sake, did you stir the tea at all?'

She was as white as himself.

'Why, yes, I did,' she said slowly, 'for that slut Annie had given me a greasy bowl that stank of mutton fat, and I was trying to get the grease out with a spoon. But still it floated back on the surface. And I was angry with her for bothering me about the beef.'

'When did Thomas first vomit?' Patrick asked, trying to make sense of chaos.

'When he had drunk a little of the tea and eaten his shortcake, and he was drinking again and suddenly he cried out and vomited.'

'Did no one but yourself touch the tea?'

Kitty thought back, and shook her head.

'It is the very devil,' said Patrick, 'that they should think he was poisoned, for Dr Meik swears it was an inflammation. But all is hanging together as though it was planned.'

184

'I know that *you* had nothing to do with it,' said Kitty, trembling, 'but you do believe, do you not, that *I* am innocent too?'

He said quickly, 'I know that.'

But now and again he glanced at her because the sequence of events seemed so strange, and he remembered the distraught letters she had sent him, and cursed the day he had so much as smiled at her. And the burning of the arsenic seemed so futile if she had not indeed used some of it to procure her husband's death.

'Good morning, Mr Millam,' said Anne, 'are you come again so soon? That is most kind.'

'The laird was my good friend, Miss Clarke,' said the tacksman soberly, 'and if I can do anything for his family I will.'

The borrowed ten shillings lay between them like ten stones, and each wondered how much the other knew or guessed of Thomas's intention to send Anne back to Edinburgh.

'If you are the Captain's friend, or Mrs Ogilvie's friend,' said Anne lightly, 'you will tell them that I have not so much as a mourning apron to wear in the laird's honour, nor the money to buy one.'

'That would come better from you than from me, Miss Clarke.'

'I should prefer them to know that others observe my lack,' said Anne, 'and if they are not so good as to provide me with an apron I shall make it as dear to them as if it was a gown!'

'With respect, Miss Clarke, you must carry your own messages!' said James Millam sturdily, and left her frowning.

The servants toiled all day with the washing, for there was not an item of clean bedding in the house when

Thomas died. Their labours were rewarded by a brisk wind and a fine morning, and by nightfall everyone was ready for their first sleep in forty-eight hours. Martha and Andrew Stewart had been lodged at the Millam's house. The laird's body occupied the West room, so his widow had to sleep in the Strangers Room with Patrick. But the properties were observed by his sharing one bed with Thomas's tenant, Donald Shaw of Downie, while Kitty slept in the other. Fifteen drops of laudanum and two days' misery gave her that sleep, and the Captain drank himself drowsy.

XX

The funeral was going to be a fine one, not only for the honour of the dead Ogilvie laird but to still the rumours whispered in Glenisla. Whatever the nature of Thomas's passing no one should be able to say that his burial lacked respect. East Mill house did not run to such luxuries as mirrors and clocks, but Kitty swathed her small looking-glass superstitiously, and Alex Lindsay had spattered the front door with white paint to show that the family tears flowed. Each night a watch was mounted over the corpse, and a solemn dance led by Kitty to the woeful sounds of a piper's lament. And Patrick ordered the best and blackest mourning, including a dress for Anne Clarke, and made his neighbours welcome to bread and cheese and ale.

The cortège on the coming Tuesday promised to be long. Pibrochs would wail, attenders would weep. From miles around every beggar would claim his bellyful, and every mourner drink himself stupid on sack and wine and whisky and rum. Under the cost of this lugubrious celebration Patrick turned to his mother, knowing they would spend in a few days what it would take to keep the household for a year. But Lady Eastmiln said it was proper and fitting, and they must find the money somehow.

Apart from the night following Thomas's death, when nothing could have roused them, the family slept fitfully and uncomfortably: cramped by visitors, disturbed by the continual coming and going. On the Saturday night Mr Shaw of Downie took his leave, and Anne Clarke offered her services as chaperone in the Strangers Room, lest Kitty and Patrick be tempted to renew their love-making. The

187

Captain said nothing, but Kitty glared at Miss Clarke as she slipped into the bed beside her. Then she snatched up Anne's pillow, dumped it on top of her own, and lay on it with her back to her companion. But Anne, making herself as easy as Kitty would let her, remained awake doing arithmetic in her head.

She had given the carrier a letter for Alexander on the Wednesday, advising him to come home. With luck he might receive it on Friday, or early Saturday, and should be at East Mill on the Monday. Until then she must bear with her reluctant hosts and wait.

But James Millam was not the only man to distrust her. Andrew Stewart, after much cogitation, told Martha that he disliked the way Miss Clarke had accused Kitty without proof.

'I could have taken the poison from the drawer and so prevented matters,' he said, reproaching himself, 'but Miss Clarke was against it. Now Dr Meik says Thomas died of inflammation, and he is a fine surgeon. So how do we know it was poison? And even now, though Miss Clarke is forever whispering with this and that person, she makes no attempt to have the chest unlocked, and still shows no evidence. I think she is a trouble-maker, Mrs Stewart. I do not like Miss Clarke!'

Martha, a good wife, found that she agreed with him entirely. Nor did Lady Eastmiln greatly regret the loss of her bedfellow. For now, it seemed, Patrick would stay with her until she died, and run the estate; and Kitty would certainly dance off with her settlement to find another husband; and when the mourning had ceased Patrick could play his fiddle in the evenings and make them both merry. So to her confidante's hints and whispers Lady Eastmiln turned her deafer ear, and said that Patrick had no hand in this, and that she thought Kitty and Thomas had got on better in the last weeks and seemed comfortable with each

188

other. Annie Sampson, speaking too freely in the kitchen one morning, found herself packed off in the afternoon with her wages. And Lizzie, shown the consequences of idle talk, said no more. The Ogilvies, mindful of family loyalty, were not prepared to make an issue over Kitty, and Anne Clarke's power was at an end.

Anne watched them close ranks in profound dismay, but could do nothing. And when Martha approached her on the Monday morning, with that silly embarrassed smile on her face and money in her hand, Anne knew that her long visit was over.

'Mrs Ogilvie wishes to thank you, Miss Clarke, for your unfailing devotion and kindness,' said Martha, translating Kitty's brief command into a more digestible one. 'And she begs you to accept this silver as a token of all our gratitude. Alex Lindsay can take you on his pillion as far as Alyth after breakfast.'

Anne took the money with a smile.

'Tell Mrs Ogilvie I thank her for her generosity,' she said drily, 'and tell her I shall never forget what she has done for me, and that I shall repay her by all the means in my power. Will you remember that message, Mrs Stewart?'

'Oh yes,' said Martha, smiling, 'it is such a handsome one.'

Merrymaking was forbidden in a house of mourning, but that Monday evening as Kitty sat with Lady Eastmiln, and Lizzie moped companionless in the kitchen, and the corpse lay in the outhouse, Patrick played two or three laments on his fiddle.

There was an air of relief, almost of contentment, at the breakfast table. They wore their black clothes soberly and spoke little. Kitty endeavoured to take Anne Clarke's place by seeing that the bowls and dishes were well-washed, and the cloth turned so that the stains did not show. Even Lady

Eastmiln, looking to a brighter future, was genial.

'I daresay you will visit the Spaldings after the funeral, miss, and then stay with your mother?' she inquired.

Kitty looked at Patrick, but his head was averted, and even their proximity in the Strangers Room had not softened him.

'Yes, ma'am, if it pleases you,' said Kitty, with a short sigh.

'You are young and bonnie,' said Lady Eastmiln, 'and your family will want to find you another husband. That is only right and proper. You need not consider my son and me. We do not expect you to mope here.'

'Thank you, ma'am,' said Kitty politely, given her leaving orders.

She glanced again at Patrick, and Lady Eastmiln looked to him also, willing him to answer.

'Yes, Kitty,' he said heartily, 'you must think of yourself now. Poor Thomas has gone, and we do not expect you to hide yourself away at East Mill. The Spaldings will look to a husband for you.'

'Some city merchant, perhaps,' said Lady Eastmiln, spreading honey thickly on her bannock. 'I have always felt you would do very well in a livelier circle.'

A tear fled down Kitty's cheek and she whisked at it with her handkerchief, trying to appear unconcerned.

'Well, well, it is not kind – nor perhaps very proper – to talk of such matters at such a time,' said Lady Eastmiln, missing nothing. 'But I was always one of those who speak frankly, and it is best to know how we stand with each other.'

The door was flung open, even as she spoke, and a dark man clad from head to foot in deepest mourning, strode into the room. He was grinning and triumphant, and though he strove to be dignified he could not hide his delight.

'My compliments to my lady mother,' said Alexander

190

Ogilvie, bowing deeply, 'and to the new laird and the lovely widow. I have come home to pay my respects to the dead. Lizzie! A plate of porridge, for I have fasted in my attempt to reach here early. A dish of tea would be acceptable, Mrs Ogilvie. Mourning and widowhood become you immensely. Ah! What a sight is this! Thank you, Lizzie – the porridge is not burned, I hope? And where is Miss Clarke?'

'I gave her money to return to Edinburgh,' said Kitty, challenging him, for she was no longer part of the family and sick at heart with the lot of them. 'She made trouble between my husband and myself. I will not trouble you with the details, Dr Ogilvie, since they are no concern of yours. But I assure you that Miss Clarke tried to do me – to do *all* of us – great harm.'

'I am sure she did,' said Alexander smoothly. 'I know the doxie well. So she has slipped back into the arms of Auld Reekie, has she? Ah, there is a city for you. Lizzie! Tell that lad to look after my horse well or I'll give him a thrashing! Cow hairs in the butter again, Lady Eastmiln? Why, this is a very countrified habit. You should go to Edinburgh and see a little high life. And so should the laird and Mrs Ogilvie. They may do yet, of course.'

But Lady Eastmiln was not to be bullied at her own table, though her foreboding was reflected on the faces of the other two.

'Enough of this!' she said. 'Eat your breakfast and get back to your porter's daughter, sir! And hold your tongue. You are no longer a member of this family. You were not invited to the funeral.'

'I have not come to *attend* it,' said Alexander, smiling, 'but to *prevent* it.'

'Brother,' said Patrick, aware of the danger in provoking him, 'there is no need for a quarrel. You will walk with me and with Mrs Ogilvie and our mother as chief mourner.

191

That is only proper.'

'I shall walk with nobody, brother. I have come post-haste from Edinburgh to see that justice is done. Dr Meik of Alyth, Dr Ramsay of Coupar, and Dr Ogilvie of Forfar are following to inspect the corpse. The funeral is postponed.'

They sat quite silent, and he observed them with pleasurable malice.

'Why, my Lady Eastmiln,' he said, 'what a fond hypocrite you are to cover up your son's death! Had *I* cuckolded him and given him poison you would have brought the Sheriff very quick. But the Captain must be allowed his pleasures, must he not? And you, brother, what a sneaking coward you have turned out to be, to fumble your brother's wife behind his back and give her the means to dispatch him. And as for the widow herself, what crimes fester in that pretty, silly head! The Nairnes and the Spaldings had best shut their ears and close their doors when incest and murder are mentioned.'

'Be silent!' cried Lady Eastmiln, enraged by the noise of Lizzie dropping plates in her excitement as she gaped in the doorway.

'But the servants should hear,' said Alexander. 'They have evidence to give. Lizzie! Fetch me a tankard of ale, girl. And I see only one servant. What has become of the other?'

'Annie Sampson was dismissed,' said Lady Eastmiln, 'and that is enough.'

'Lizzie!' Alexander roared, and gripped her arm cruelly as she quaked beside him with the ale. 'Lizzie! If you do not speak the truth I will have you whipped naked through the Kirkton and let them cut your ears off! Why was Annie Sampson dismissed?'

'Oh, Dr Ogilvie,' Lizzie whimpered, for he was hurting her and she was terrified of all of them, 'do not make me

192

say or *I* shall be turned off, too!'

'Oh, terrible, mother, quite terrible! The witnesses disposed of because they speak the truth. Tell me, Lizzie, or shall I break your arm.'

'Oh sir, sir, Annie saw Mrs Ogilvie stirring poison into the laird's bowl of tea, and Alex Lindsay was in the garret and swears he saw it, too. And Mrs Ogilvie and the Captain has given me many a tuppence to say that I drank from the same bowl and it was not dosed. But I did not, sir, and that is the truth!'

Patrick and Kitty sat quite motionless, staring at their plates. And two red patches came unbecomingly into Lady Eastmiln's withered cheeks.

'What else, Lizzie, what else? I'll protect you, Lizzie. No one else can, now. But if you do not tell me the truth they will hang you from a tree, and let your feet swing, and then Dr Munroe will cut up your corpse for the students!'

And he twisted her arm until she fell to her knees.

'Oh, sir, do not let them harm me. But the Captain and Mrs Ogilvie was too free with each other. And Kate Campbell heard the bed rocking and creaking, and we have all seen him with his hand down her bodice.'

'Kate Campbell? Was that the stupid one? Where is *she*, then?'

'Mrs Ogilvie said she had stole some handkerchiefs, and she was turned off. But Kate swore she did not, sir, and that she was dismissed for knowing what went on. And Annie Sampson and me believed her, sir.'

He let go her arm and she retreated, whimpering, and rubbing at the marks his nails had made.

'Oh, what a pretty story, Lady Eastmiln! You did badly, mother. You should have sent them all packing while you were about it. This one knows enough to start a fire.'

'*And* Alex Lindsay,' said Lizzie from the doorway, throwing in her lot with the stronger party, '*and* Mr Gillock, *and* Mr Lamar, and many others has seen them together. And so they will tell you, even under oath. It is not only me and Annie Sampson. Glenisla has been talking these many months. And the late laird turned the Captain out because of it.'

'We must fetch the Sheriff then, Lizzie,' said Alexander, addressing himself to her. 'We must see that the late laird does not go to his grave unavenged, must we not, Lizzie? Thank you, Lizzie, you can fill my tankard again and fry me two collops of mutton. I have an appetite, Lizzie, all of a sudden. And the rest of you,' he said, turning on them, 'may do as you please!'

One by one they pushed back their chairs and left the table, and he laughed and set about his breakfast with relish. And, as they sat pale and silent in separate corners of the parlour, he glanced at them from time to time to feed his humour, and laughed again.

'Why, Thomas, how you stink, man!' cried Alexander, as he and Patrick stooped to enter the shed. 'Come your ways in, Dr Meik and Dr Ramsay. I think there is enough light if you leave the door open.'

Patrick held a handkerchief to his mouth and nose, but the other three men, used to the disagreeable side of their profession, merely grimaced as they bent over the corpse.

'The discolouration of the breast and nails can be that of natural decomposition,' said Dr Meik, looking to his colleague for support.

'But the lips are more discoloured than they should be,' said Dr Ramsay, 'and the tongue is swelled so that it cleaves to the roof of the mouth, and that is a sign of poison.'

'But there are no ulcers on the tongue and lips,' Peter Meik observed, conscious that he was guilty of too hasty a diagnosis.

'No, no – but the tongue, man, look at the tongue!'

'We had best open him up,' said Peter Meik, 'and look at the organs.'

'I am agreeable to that,' said Gilbert Ramsay.

Patrick said nothing, sick and dumb at the side of the shed.

'But *I* am not agreeable to it,' said Alexander. 'Dr Ogilvie of Forfar will be here, either late today or early tomorrow, and I should like him to be present so that we have three open minds as to the cause of death.'

'I cannot wait on his arrival, sir,' said Peter Meik, thinking of his practice in Alyth.

'Nor I, sir. I must be back at Coupar this very day.'

Alexander smote the palm of one hand with the fist of the other.

'I had so hoped for Dr Ogilvie's opinion,' he said. 'Well, sirs, I can hardly keep you from your duties. Will you make a note as to what you are agreed upon?'

'Indeed, sir,' said Gilbert Ramsay soothingly. 'And in my professional opinion, sir, even were we to open up the body it would be in such a state of putrefaction that evidence of poisoning would be difficult to find.'

Patrick stumbled through the door, whipped off his handkerchief, and took great breaths of air. And though the yard was not as sweet as one might wish, it smelled like honey to him after the shed.

The news of the postponed funeral, and its reasons, had spread throughout the neighbourhood, and now everyone talked openly. Andrew Stewart, wishing to help and unable to think what to advise, suggested that Patrick might flee while there was still time. But this the Captain refused to do, knowing himself to be innocent, and believing that there was not enough evidence.

Kitty, on the other hand, feeling herself to be in a perilous situation and relying as always on her charms, begged a private interview with Alexander. Some vague notion of her family's power persuaded her that he might listen. When he refused even to see her, she threw herself upon her bed and screamed and drummed her heels, hysterical at the thought of what threatened her.

And Lady Eastmiln sat upright and unbowed, ready for the worst that could come upon her, and expecting no quarter from Alexander.

'No, sir,' said Dr John Ogilvie, physician of Forfar, 'I cannot undertake to open the body. Why, the flesh is livid and the nails are quite black. The jaw is locked, beside. Certainly, the tip of the tongue seems unusually white and rough, and looks as though the laird died in a convulsion from some violent cause. But otherwise, sir, I doubt that any could say what the man died of. I wish, sir, that I had been here yesterday, and then the three of us might have opened it up. But I do not care to risk it by myself, sir, and that is the truth.'

'I think we have enough evidence, nevertheless,' said Alexander, 'and now I have done all that I can I shall inform the Sheriff at Forfar. Perhaps you would be good enough, sir, to deliver a letter to him and ask him to come here with all possible haste?'

All the flowers in the garden seemed to be out when Kitty and Patrick were taken away, and she stooped to pick a sweet-scented stock and hold it to her nose as though it were the last breath of life.

Alexander watched them go, from the parlour window, and then turned to enjoy the spectacle of his mother's sorrow. Lady Eastmiln had attempted to withhold some of the household keys from Alexander, by offering them to Mr Rattray secretly. But he had refused, and she sat quite alone, bereft of every little power. One old hand grasped

196

the knob of her stick until the knuckles stood out white, but she was erect and looked back at Alexander proudly.

'Now this is a fine Friday, mother,' said Alexander, 'and if we were a kirk-crowding family I might even say it was a *Good* Friday! But you never could enjoy a joke. We should have an old friend and confidante of yours here today, Miss Anne Clarke. She has been staying at Alyth until I sent for her. And do you know what I am about to do now, mother? I shall spend a merry Saturday at Fergus Fergusson's and on Monday I shall sell the stock on East Mill farm.'

'You are not the laird, Alexander Ogilvie. I hold the farm in Patrick's stead for when he shall return,' she said stiffly.

'He will not return, mother, and I am master here. I shall not be greedy, mother. I shall drive no hard bargains that might keep me here for months. I shall take what is offered, in bills and ready money, and spend it as fast as I can. Someone will buy the house and land when the laird is hanged, and then you must go and live with Martha on your settlement. It will be very little, mother, but you are accustomed to live poor and genteel.'

'Why, you villain,' she said fearlessly, 'do you think that Almighty God will let you foul the earth so long?'

'He will not hear *your* prayers, mother. For you have not prayed often enough. And an old woman without protection, and but a few meagre Scots pounds a year to keep body and soul together, should be civil to those who call the tune!'

'You could drag me by the hair to my own grave,' said Lady Eastmiln steadfastly, 'and I would not open my mouth but to *spit* on you.'

'Aye,' he said quietly, 'I know that hardness in you as I know my own.'

'And the minister said, "If *any* of these men die in their beds, God hath not spoken through me!"' she continued implacably. '*You* are one of those men.'

He laughed and flung himself into the laird's chair, and put his boots up on the parlour table.

'I was not born when he said that!' he observed.

'Perhaps he had the gift of prophecy,' said Lady Eastmiln, pleasantly.

He was on his feet in a passion, but she did not flinch as he stood over her; and suddenly the tears were in his eyes in spite of himself.

'You never cared for me,' he cried. 'You never cared whether I lived or died. You did not *care*!'

She sat in solitary dignity for some time after he had blundered out, until Lizzie stuck her head round the door to see what had happened.

'Shall I brew you a dish of tea, ma'am?' Lizzie asked fearfully, in an effort to make all well again. 'You should keep up your strength, ma'am, for all our sakes.'

Lady Eastmiln looked as though she had discovered a louse in the bedclothes.

'Since that is all you are *good* for,' she said distinctly, 'you may brew the tea. One cannot, I suppose, expect to buy *loyalty* for twenty shillings a year and a new gown!'

The Outcome

XXI

In the city of Edinburgh, sedan-chairs swayed, women crushed hooped skirts in the narrow streets and kept the sun from their faces with green paper fans. Judges wore their wigs and carried their hats carefully under one arm. Advocates swept past in billowing gowns. Old ladies tapped by in pattens, and young ones in buckled or rosetted shoes. The merchants took snuff and talked business in little groups at the Cross near St Giles. Ragged caddies, whose night had been passed sleeping on a doorstep, threaded their way swiftly through the crowds with messages and parcels at a penny an errand. The ministers were grave in blue and grey, their bands white, their wigs severe, their tricorne hats sober. Porters carried coals. Musselburgh housewives bore creels. Sweeps and barber's boys and watermen went from place to place.

. In the high narrow houses of the Luckenbooths tradesmen hung their painted signs: here a quartern loaf, very brown and shiny; there a great cheese; elsewhere a pair of stays, buttons, jewellery and petticoats. And from basement to chimney towered and teemed the people's dwellings; reached by precipitous and filthy stairs, overcrowded and baldy lit. A stench of foul water and excrement from the running gutters outside – the Flowers of Edinburgh as it was called – was equalled in intensity by the stench of burning brown paper, supposed to render it inoffensive.

Worshipping apart, receiving the sacrament apart, the hangman sat in his appointed seat at the Tolbooth Kirk each Sunday. And afterwards he walked the streets of the city; while eyes glanced away from his grey bonnet, and skirts endeavoured not to touch his black velvet coat, resplendent in silver lace.

On 21 June a guard was sent to convey Kitty and Patrick to the capital. With some notion of looking well and behaving gracefully under difficulties, Kitty took special care over her toilet, and emerged from the open boat smiling nervously and seeming more fitted for an assembly than the Tolbooth prison. But news of the murder, coupled with her position in society, had flown ahead of her. The crowd, unwashed, unkempt, and righteously indignant, took her appearance as a personal affront – and picked up as many stones as they could find, to teach her better manners. Only the muskets and shoulders of the guards saved her, as she was hurried trembling between banks of ill-wishers. Anne Clarke in the same situation would have understood, and shrugged wryly. Kitty pondered the assault for a long time without ever comprehending it, and wept for her mother and the cold sweet nose of Frisk.

The justice begun at Forfar continued in Edinburgh, and a sorry jumble of false and true statements travelled with the prisoners. Kitty had already come off badly with doughty old George Campbell, Sheriff-substitute of Forfar. She declared that she had written only one letter to Patrick after he left East Mill house; feeling that to admit to more was a sign of complicity. She swore that Andrew Stewart had brought only salts and laudanum on the eve of her husband's death, and added that she had given the rest of the laudanum back to Patrick – lest they think Thomas had been poisoned with that. She denied stirring the tea in the closet, and said that Lizzie had drunk from the same bowl, and indeed of the same tea, shortly afterwards. And this she declared to be the truth; scrawling *Ketty Ogilvie* along the bottom of the sheet, and being witnessed by George Campbell and his clerk John Ure.

202

The following day she had made a further statement, in an effort to cover Patrick's other purchase, saying that the salts and laudanum came from the Captain's chest that he brought from the East Indies.

Patrick had also decided to repress the packet of arsenic carried by Andrew Stewart, and in two declarations he spoke only of the salts and laudanum, and denied the rumour that he had purchased arsenic from James Carnegie of Brechin. The result of this grievous error of judgment was to send his friend Patrick Dickson post-haste to Dr Carnegie, with the plea that the doctor should perjure himself. When they discovered that this suggestion was not to the doctor's liking, Patrick tried to amend his statement. But this, the Sheriff told him, was not possible. What had been written under oath must remain unaltered, to be used in evidence against him.

Neither Patrick nor Kitty was allowed to communicate, and so they were able to worry separately over their muddled statements as they entered Edinburgh and prepared for further examination. The city seemed a fortress in itself, walled and buttressed and battlemented, its gates guarded by keepers who closed them at nightfall. And within the fortress lay yet another, the Tolbooth prison built by the citizens of Edinburgh in 1561, and originally intended to house Parliament and the Courts of Justice as well as prisoners. But after 1640 only debtors and criminals lay within its sombre walls; and those who judged and ruled them used Parliament House, forty paces away across the broad stones of the High Street, past St Giles.

Between that cathedral and the jail snaked a narrow alley known as the Krames, whose profusion of little shops clung to the abutments and projections of St Giles like so many noisy supplicants. Here, among the hosiers and hatters, mercers, milliners and glovers, Kitty had shopped a hundred times and given no more than a superstitious glance at the Tolbooth looming opposite them. But now the Krames and the Luckenbooth held no comfort for her, and as she stepped from the carriage she saw nothing but the prison.

Its turrets reared against the sky, dominating that sliver of summer white and blue. Its aspect was ancient, its walls forbidding, its massive oak door studded with broad-headed nails, its portals bound with iron. At a word of command from the Captain of the Guard the door swung ponderously upon its hinges, to reveal the Outer Turnkey. He looked as frail as his charge was stout, but proud of his office, and he flourished an enormous iron key nearly two feet in length, to show where his particular power lay.

The place was full of odours and shadows, and as the catch sprang shut a dozen echoes haunted the corridor ahead of them. In the semi-darkness Kitty put out a hand to steady herself, and drew it back with a jump of repulsion as it touched slime and stone.

On 22 June James Balfour of Pilrig, Sheriff-substitute of the shire, began *his* interrogation of the prisoners. Hale old George Campbell had worried Patrick Ogilvie, but James Balfour terrified him. The Captain was a soldier, not a lawyer; a man of action, not of thought; and he would infinitely rather have taken his chance in a hail of bullets. The questions probed minutely. The implications were far-reaching and subtle. Mr Balfour did not ask for a brief outline of the case, nor simply the important points. He wanted to know everything.

Studying that legal face, which expressed no emotion; watching those thin lips compressing over each scrap of evidence; Patrick felt cold. His examiner betrayed only one weakness – he was extraordinarily proud of his hands, which were well-tended and beautifully shaped. He would stick out his fingers and observe them, wipe the palms with a handkerchief of surpassing whiteness, or just stare at them

204

idly and pleasurably as he waited for an answer. Lost in laudanum, salts, the health of himself and Kitty and Thomas, the conversations with his family, Kitty's letters and messages, where he had slept and when, and the exact date of his late brother's marriage, Patrick clenched his brown fists and would not speak. At the end of the interview, asked why he had refused the questions, he declined to find a reason – but gave James Balfour his signature.

Her friends, family and advisers having gained access to her, Kitty was told to say nothing until a counsel could be found. So she, too, refused to answer any questions. And at length she and James Balfour sat in silence together – he tending his nails and she twisting her fingers – until he smiled and shrugged and courteously ordered her to be returned to her cell.

Mindful of its honour and her life, the Nairne clan turned to Commissioner Sir William Nairne and begged him to do his utmost. A man of imposing presence, with an ironical manner, Sir William closeted himself with his niece for above an hour. As she tripped over each half-lie, contradicted herself, wept and wrung her hands, he watched her. His little eyes beneath the drooping lids missed nothing. His eyebrows remained in permanent peaks of astonishment. But he was affable, until she had finished lying and he had begun questioning, when Kitty was driven to the truth. Soberly, Sir William contemplated the dripping walls of the cell. Stiffly, he rose and made his bow.

Then he said, 'Well, miss. We must see if we cannot find you better lodgings – else you will feel the Tolbooth a greater burden than East Mill House!' Which made her smile for the first time since she stepped off the boat at Leith.

Walking over to Johnnie Dowie's tavern, he pursed his lips gravely, but once inside the crowded room became his usual quizzical self, and sat down as if by accident with one of the men he was looking for.

'Your servant, sir,' said Alexander Lockhart, Dean of the Scottish Bar.

'Come, sir,' said Sir William pleasantly. 'No man can call himself a servant that is one of the greatest lawyers in an age of great lawyers!'

'You are very complimentary, sir,' said Lockhart, shrewd and smiling. 'I believe you must be on business!'

'Let us say that I am excessively glad at this chance meeting,' Sir William replied, his eyes almost lost between lids and pouches as he sniffed the claret. 'Mr Lockhart, you have the reputation of enjoying a desperate cause – as indeed your pleading for a number of Jacobites would testify! I wonder whether you would undertake the defence of a case very near my heart? My niece, Katherine Ogilvie, lies in the Tolbooth under suspicion of poisoning her husband. And, though I am convinced of her innocence, she needs the best lawyer her family can obtain.'

'I have heard something of the case,' said Lockhart cautiously, 'but I should like to hear more, and to speak with the lady before I commit myself.'

Sir William ordered more claret. Then turning to the handsome man who lounged in his chair, he said, 'Sir, you are renowned for both a silver tongue and a hectoring manner. Believe me, sir, you will *need* both. For my niece is a silly pretty goose as ever was cooked – and the murder, my dear sir, if murder it was, is lapped about her like an apple sauce!'

His next port of call was John Clerihew's, the vintners, where people said more legal business was done over a bottle than was done dry in the Courts of Justice. And here he found another eminent lawyer, Henry Dundas, and drew him aside from an admiring circle, and put the case to him. But whereas Sir William had flattered Lockhart's tongue he now paid tribute to Dundas's brilliant perspicacity.

'You have rose very fast,' said Sir William smoothly, 'and it is on account of your wits, sir. Why, I have seen you drop like a hawk on some morsel of evidence that no one else had looked for. And believe me, sir, I hope you can do the same for my niece – for she is in a pretty way! I have already retained Mr Lockhart in her defence, and he is very fine. But with *two* such eminent men I shall sleep sounder tonight, I can tell you!'

'Who is helping the Lord Advocate and the Solicitor-General with the Prosecution, sir?'

'I have heard Sir David Dalrymple *mentioned*. And I believe there is talk of Mr Patrick Murray and Mr David Kennedy too.'

'They have fetched out some heavy cannon, sir! And for the gentleman – for Lieutenant Ogilvie?'

'I understand that Mr Rae and Mr Crosbie have been approached.'

Dundas made a face.

'Well, sir,' said Sir William judiciously. 'I grant you that Mr Crosbie is a mighty dull man, but he is ingenious and talkative enough in court. You must give him that. And Rae is prosy, very prosy, and a stickler for rules and etiquette – but he is most able, sir, and will no doubt sit on the Bench in time.'

'It is his voice that distresses me, sir,' said Dundas. 'For he grinds out each word like a grain of corn, and drones on until I feel myself nodding. And, besides that, he says some mighty foolish things. Why, only the other day, I heard him say that now he had proved some legal point to be *impossible* he would show how it was also *improbable*. I put it to you, sir, what a masterpiece of *improbability* that would be!'

'Aye, well, Mr Dundas, he is for the lieutenant – and I care not how Mr Ogilvie fares. It is my niece I am concerned for. Will you undertake her defence with Mr Lock-hart?'

'My hand upon it!' said Henry Dundas.

'More claret!' Sir William ordered, and every vein on his countenance stood out in relief.

Great legal names on both sides drew up lengthy documents, and chivvied their clerks. George Campbell, Sheriff-substitute of Forfar, searched the house at East Mill to find the supposed cause of death, and broke open the locked drawers of the chest in Patrick's room. But he only found two or three small parcels of saltpetre, purchased to cure hams, and not a grain of arsenic came to light. Andrew Murison, Macer of the Court, measured and drew up a plan of the rooms at East Mill, and a legion of witnesses was cited for the Prosecution. One name in particular came up again and again, as the statements were set down: that of Anne Clarke. But she was not to be found, and when Alexander was questioned he shrugged his shoulders and said she had disappeared, being afraid of the slanderous things said about her and fearing imprisonment.

Lizzie Sturrock was brought to Edinburgh. A description of Annie Sampson was issued, and the girl discovered. Poor Kate Campbell, speechless and bewildered, was tracked down. But of Anne Clarke, now publicly described as an artful woman of dubious profession, and a person capable of deadly malice and hatred, nothing was known. She had slipped into the labyrinths of Edinburgh, as safe in that maze of streets as Kitty was in the Tolbooth.

'A major witness!' said the Prosecution. 'Find her!'

But where? Beth's Wynd, Turk's Close, Libberton's Wynd, Horse Wynd, Forrester's Wynd? Where?

In the city jail, the Heart of Midlothian – dark, unventilated, undrained, insanitary – Kitty and Patrick made

208

their separate bests of a bitter confinement. He, perhaps, did better than she, being a professional soldier, for he knew that money could buy almost everything, even a lass to while away the hours. So the jailor became sightless when bonnie Peggy Dow slipped into Patrick's cell with a basket of food and wine. And he could not hear her giggles and protests on the straw mattress – for the chink of silver in his pocket.

But Kitty was frequently sick in the pestilential air, plagued by her old ills of sleeplessness and constipation, and mortally afraid. Sometimes the sun crept between the bars, and then she remembered a sprig of blossom or the sound of a throstle, and those long May mornings when Patrick was her world and the dull round of East Mill House was vanquished.

On the eve of the trial Anne Clarke sent a personal letter to the Lord Advocate, Sir Henry Miller, dated Sunday evening, eight of the clock. She said she had decided to put herself at the disposal of the authorities, and her tone was meek. But it was a bold, driving hand that stared the Public Prosecutor in the face.

Lord Advocat,

Upon my coming to town, I am informed that you have been searching for me. It would never bread in my breast to keept out of the way had it not been for the terror of imprisonment; but houping you will be more favourable to me I shall weat upon you tomorrow morning at eight of the clock.

Anne Clarke

She was to be aided by the extraordinary decision of the Crown to incarcerate her with the three maids from East Mill House, in one room at the Tolbooth. With their reluctant assistance, Anne immediately set the place to rights, and then proceeded to instruct them in the matter of their evidence.

Defence cried scandal, and presented a petition to the Court on 6 August, in which Anne's character and disposition was clearly set forth, and they begged for her removal to a separate room. This request was granted, for one night only, and then withdrawn on the pretext of the room lacking proper security. And back she went again, with her three pupils, to instruct and rehearse them in the line of their duty.

XXII

At a quarter to seven on the morning of 12 August 1765 Kitty and Patrick were escorted from the Tolbooth to Parliament House, through the people who already thronged the High Street. In view of Kitty's family connections, and the sensational nature of the case, the trial was to be held in private. The public, deprived of its opportunity to see two gentlefolk at bay and accused of shameful charges, showed some hostility. As soon as the prisoners appeared a ragged lad cried out that the murderers were come; and caddies and chairmen loitering at the Mercat Cross, citizens setting about their morning business, jostled for a sight of Kitty and Patrick, and impeded their progress. Elbowed and shouldered away by the guards, the crowd still flowed on like some great tide, even into the outer precincts of the Court-house. A regiment of feet stumbled over the handsome chequered wood floor, a sea of faces bobbed beneath the arched hammerbeams of the ceiling, until they were summarily halted by a line of muskets before the Inner House. So far and no further could they go, though they cried that they wanted to see justice done, and grumbled their discontent long after Kitty and Patrick had gone and the great doors slammed against them.

The Court-room was a square, low-ceilinged place, some forty feet in length and width, and it promised to become an oven as the summer day reached its zenith. Two of the windows had been opened already.

A vast stone fireplace gaped in one wall; and so that their Lordships should be warm in winter the Bench stood only a few feet in front of it, covered in green baize. Six high-backed chairs, covered in leather, gilt-studded, awaited the Judges; so did six inkhorns, six quill pens and six stacks of paper. A little below the Bench ranged a long, broad table covered in be-ribboned briefs; with the Counsel for the Crown whispering on one side, and the Counsel for the Defence conferring on the other. A little above the Bench, so short a distance than an advocate might strike his hand against it if he gestured too dramatically, ran the Spectators' Gallery – empty today, but able to seat an enthusiastic audience at other times. And on either side of the fireplace hung a black velvet sampler embroidered in gold thread: depicting the Lord's Prayer and the Ten Commandments.

A hush fell on the Court-room as Andrew Murison entered solemnly, bearing his mace; and everyone rose in respectful silence, as the judges in red and white robes followed him. Lord Kames, the Lord Justice-General, towered above the other five: a man of such startling height that in his youth he had contemplated a career in the King of Prussia's tall regiment. His robe of scarlet silk with tippet and hood, was all edged and lined with ermine. Instead of the bands worn in the English Courts he had a long white starched neckcloth. A full-bottomed wig flowed down his back, curled like a ram's fleece, and he sat down very slowly and deliberately – as though unwilling to lose one inch of that tremendous dignity. His first action was to cause the windows to be closed. Then he took a pinch of snuff while the jury were sworn in.

Three times, in batches of five, the jurors took their oath, that 'By Almighty God, and as you shall answer to God at the great day of Judgment that you will truth say and no truth conceal, so far as you are to pass upon this assize.' Then at a command the doors were opened and Kitty and Patrick brought to the Bar – which was indeed a bar, being no more than a brief length of wood sufficient to hold back two people. A City Guard stood by each prisoner, a number-

212

plate visible on his white cross-belt, his hat gallantly cocked at the side, his Lochaber axe to hand.

Kitty looked hopefully at the judges, who looked through and beyond her into some abstract realm of justice. She twisted slightly to survey the jury, headed by Sir George Suttie of Balgonie, and recognised a face. It was Mr Hamilton, her father's bookseller. But even as she smiled at him he ducked his head and avoided her eyes. She turned back again, discomfited, and then took a deep breath and a fresh grip on the Bar, because Sir Gilbert Minto, the Lord Justice-Clerk, was watching her as the interlocutor read out a double indictment of incest and murder. The charge was terrible, and sounded worse. She caught an avid glance from Lord Alemoor, known for his curiosity, and a leisurely stare from Lord Kames.

'He has a rough tongue, Kitty,' Sir William Nairne had told her, 'so do not let him unsettle you. He tried one Matthew Hay, twenty five years ago, for murder. The man had been his friend, and played chess with him regularly, and I should have thought Kames would act more delicate. But when a verdict of guilty was brought in he leaned forward, and giving a great grin of triumph he cried, "That's *checkmate* to you, Matthew!" So take no notice of what he says.'

They were reading out the sorry account of endearments and kisses and other liberties, of the lying in one bed on May mornings, and Kitty stole another glance at Kames's stout clean-shaven face, the nostrils arching like those of a horse, the full-lipped mouth and sarcastic brows. And he was looking back at her in a mixture of contempt and amusement.

The interlocutor paused to turn over a page, and into the silence Lord Kames spoke directly to Kitty.

'Eh, man, but ye're a queer bitch!' he said coarsely, and laughed and took more snuff.

213

Her cheeks the colour of his robes, Kitty stared at the samplers until she could have sworn every word he had uttered was worked on them in gold thread.

Counsel for the Prosecution opened, using the evidence of indecent familiarities as a sort of legal broth: a starter, a warmer-up for the main course that would follow. Anne Sampson and Lizzie did not look at Kitty as they spoke; but poor Kate Campbell did, attempting to convey the misery of rejection. Bitter experience had not robbed her of her simplicity; goaded and destitute, she still hoped, still looked for affection and security.

The wheels of justice moved slowly and sometimes halted altogether, since shorthand was not yet adopted as in the English Courts. Each witness was sworn in separately and at some length, assuring the Bench that he or she bore no ill-will towards the prisoners, had been offered no reward for testifying against them, and had not been told what to say. The clerks wrote down the substance of each person's evidence in longhand, which was afterwards read out, signed by the witness and by the Lord Examinator, and followed by interrogations from both counsels.

Officially, no one was allowed to leave the Court until the case was concluded, but there were opportunities for recess in rooms attached to the place of trial – and the judges never liked to leave their claret for too long. But though the prisoners were shepherded carefully to and fro, the rest of the assembly did as they pleased. The jurors got up and down, ate and drank, chattered with witnesses and counsels, and even dispersed to other parts of the building. No roll was called as they drifted back from their dinners, nor even the correct number of jurymen ascertained. The heat became stifling, but the windows stayed shut by order of Lord Kames. Whisky and ale, served to keep the jury attentive, fuddled some and rendered others belligerent – so that they argued with the lawyers. No chair was offered to Kitty, in

214

spite of her evident fatigue, and only bread and water served to herself and Patrick. At one stage all the judges but one had left the Bench, in search of relief and refreshment, and only Lord Kames dozed in solitary grandeur.

But everyone was ready for the Prosecution's chief witness, the meat of the occasion, Anne Clarke. She came forward, composed and neat in her grey dress and spotless fichu, very respectable and quiet-voiced, and gave her evidence with damning clarity. Since Lady Eastmiln was down on both lists Anne watched what she said about the old woman, taking account of her deafness on those occasions when she might have heard something of note, taking care to quote her accurately. But this care was only the culmination of her long preoccupation with facts and circumstances at East Mill House, and she did well for the Crown.

Evening drew on, and tallow candles were lit, smoking abominably in their tin candlesticks. And still the Prosecution called witness after witness, sixty-four in all, and Lockhart and Dundas chafed as the hours passed and the case was built up minutely against Kitty and Patrick. Hundreds of documents were sifted, thousands of words written and read. Heads were scratched, voices hoarsened, the air became foul and close. Noise and exhaustion and chaos reigned supreme. And when no one could stand or sit any longer, or listen or speak any further, the court was ordered to withdraw for the night; to make themselves comfortable as best they could, in a little incarceration of their own.

By three o'clock the following day all evidence for the Crown had been given, and at last Alexander Lockhart and Henry Dundas could bring forward the case for the Defence. Backed by a protesting jury, Lord Kames leaned across the Bench and asked how many witnesses they proposed to call.

215

'One hundred and eight, my lord,' said Lockhart, looking remarkably fresh now his chance was come.

'One hundred and eight, Mr Lockhart? Why, man, we have been here nigh on two days already! You had best re-order your list, sir. I want to see my bed again.'

'How long will your lordship allow me?' Lockhart asked in his most silvery tones, but he was apprehensive.

Kames stared at him through his reading glass, not displeased to have so much power over a lawyer of Lockhart's standing, and took snuff with great deliberation.

'Why, man, you have had your turn at the witnesses for the Crown. I have heard you milking them dry, sir. We see the drift of your argument well enough. You need only finish off with a few – say, a dozen witnesses. We *must* be done, sir. We must be *done*.'

The other judges nodded and whispered, in accordance with this decree.

'As your lordship pleases,' said Lockhart, with a bow.

He switched away his black gown with unwonted emphasis, set his wig aright, smoothed his ruffled jabot, and endeavoured to cram a gallon of evidence into a pint pot of time.

George Spalding established Thomas's long record of ill-health, and gallantly said that he *thought* an incriminating letter to Patrick was in Kitty's handwriting, but he could not be quite *positive*.

James Millam whisked away rumours of indecent familiarities between Kitty and Patrick, saying that for his part he never saw any. He also established the laird's last illness as beginning four days before his death, with gravel and a colic. He informed the court that the laird had borrowed ten shillings from him to be rid of Anne Clarke, that Mrs Ogilvie had given her money to be gone, and that Anne had threatened the prisoners in the matter of the mourning apron. His honest, straightforward manner made

216

a nonsense of the hysteria roused by the Prosecution. Skilfully questioned, he pointed out that Alexander Ogilvie – never examined by the Crown – was benefiting by his brother's death and the plight of Kitty and Patrick; and had taken possession of the estate and sold the stock.

Jean Wallace, servant to George Spalding, verified Thomas's ill-health. She remembered nursing him at Glenkilry for six weeks when he was bad of an ulcer, and she set her cross to the paper since she could not write.

Thomas Jack, Elizabeth Ferguson, John Paterson, Margaret Paterson and Margaret Reid of Glenisla all testified to seeing Thomas in a bad way, either on the morning or the day before his death. They had spoken to him, seen him take frequent rests and a sleep on the ground, and heard him say that his bones and bowels were sore and he had not felt so ill in six years.

Dr James Scott of Edinburgh told the Court that arsenic was never greasy, thus refuting Annie Sampson's implication that the greasy bowl had held arsenic. But he did point out that if arsenic was stirred into a mixture of tea, sugar and milk it would be suspended long enough to kill the person who drank it.

Dundas passed a note to Lockhart. It read, *We shall not have time to call Lady Eastmiln, and she is warm towards the prisoners!* The Prosecution had not called Lady Eastmiln either, possibly for the same reason. Upon another sheet of paper the infuriated Lockhart scribbled back, *I know! Damn all claret-drinking, snuff-taking old scoundrels!* And he saw Dundas smile ruefully as he crumpled the reply in his hand.

'You had best sum up your case, Mr Lockhart,' said Kames, consulting his watch and yawning.

Lockhart was not a man prone to despair, but he came pretty near to it. He saw the case so clearly, though one or two details remained obscure. True, it took a leap of the imagination to get over that business of Patrick buying the arsenic and lying about it; to convince the Court that Kitty asked for it in good faith, and destroyed it out of foolishness and fear. But think of that locked drawer in which the arsenic had rested overnight: the drawer Andrew Stewart had wanted to force open. Why had Anne Clarke not let him, and so removed any opportunity for poisoning? Her excuse of fearing to cause a scandal was too thin. No, Lockhart argued, Anne Clarke *wanted* the arsenic to stay there to provide a cover for her own activities. And what were those activities? Dosing the laird's tea with poison she herself had obtained – and probably obtained from Alexander? And how had she administered the dose, since Thomas Ogilvie vomited over his first bowl of tea – and his own wife had made it in full view of the company, and given it to him with her own hands?

Even Henry Dundas had not lighted on that heavily sugared finger of shortcake. Only two people knew of it: Kitty and Anne Clarke. And Kitty had picked it up without thinking, and would not have attached any significance to it had she remembered. And Anne Clarke, relying on good luck and good management, had never mentioned it.

Lockhart's shrewd, light, sherry-coloured eyes fastened on Anne Clarke, and she returned his gaze composedly.

By God, madam, Lockhart thought, you are the cleverest woman I ever have encountered. For you set the case up both ways. If Thomas Ogilvie had died of natural causes you could still have made it look like murder. And were I given time and opportunity I would set a noose about your neck as you would not shake off.

But in the brief space of three hours, at the end of a dragging trial when energy and patience were spent, Lockhart and Dundas had to leave the case as a suggestion that the laird had died of inflammation of the bowels, and Kitty and Patrick shown no more than ordinary family affection

218

for one another.

At two o'clock in the morning of 14 August the jury, having stood throughout the judge's address, retired to consider their verdict while the court recessed. They grumbled and yawned and wrangled among themselves, until sheer physical wretchedness brought them to a decision. Then fourteen hours later, at four o'clock in the afternoon, they returned with the slow tread that might have been due to weight of responsibility – but was most probably exhaustion.

A terrible silence descended on the Court-room. Lord Minto said, 'Have you agreed upon your chancellor, gentlemen?'

Sir George Suttie stepped forward, holding out a sealed paper. The jury remained standing. In his usual leisurely fashion Lord Minto broke the seals, read what was written, and handed the paper to the Clerk of the Court. No word was spoken, and Kitty and Patrick followed each gesture and expression endeavouring to guess the verdict. The Clerk entered it in his record book and passed it back to the Bench. Minto, still taking his time, folded it in yet another sheet of paper and sealed it with his signet. A candle was produced, and solemnly lit.

Then, so dramatically that the assembly drew in breath, a fantastic figure approached the Bench. Long and lean and haggard, clad in a garment of black and grey with trimmings of silver lace, stalked Isaac Gibbs the Dempster. And as he passed, all about him moved back as though the touch of his clothes might contaminate them.

At a motion from Lord Minto, the Clerk of the Court read out the sentence – guilty, on both counts. He ceased. The Court-room was hushed. But Isaac Gibbs, pointing full at the prisoners, cried, 'I pronounce for *doom*!' and turned to blow out the candle. It flared, wavered, and was suddenly nothing but reeking smoke.

XXIII

Alexander Lockhart, on behalf of both prisoners, put in a plea for arrest of judgment, and stayed up a great part of the night making a case against the informal and irregular proceedings in the course of the trial. He pointed out that thirty-three hours had been given to the hearing for the Prosecution, and only three for the Defence. That no time or attention had been bestowed on the examination of Alexander Ogilvie's conduct. That the records were defective, and certain favourable proofs for the prisoners had never been taken down. He spoke yet again of the conduct and obvious malice of Anne Clarke. He decried the injustice and stupidity of shutting up an exhausted jury for a further fourteen hours, after a trial of such length, when fatigue must surely impair their powers of judgment.

His Majesty's Advocate and the Solicitor-General described the plea as being groundless and frivolous; said the jury was of a highly respectable character; and the trial conducted with more attention and favour towards the defence than any trial occurring in the memory of any member of the court. And they repelled the objections.

Patrick had run his course, but Kitty's advocates had one last card to play for her. It was a piece of information at once vital and homely. She expected a child. At least, she *thought* she did, she was pretty sure. For the sake of decorum she could not go into medical detail with her counsel; but through the medium of Bethia, via George Spalding and Sir William Nairne, Mr Lockhart gathered that – though her cycle inclined to irregularity – she showed every sign of being three months pregnant.

When he first heard the news Alexander Lockhart had advised total secrecy. He saw that an earlier announcement could prejudice the jury against her – those May mornings in Patrick's bed, for instance. He also saw that if the verdict went the wrong way he could use her pregnancy as a reason for deferring the execution. So he stood, very grave and dignified and handsome, and begged to represent to the Court that the prisoner, Katherine Ogilvie, was with child.

On 16 August five honest midwives removed Kitty to a private room, and wagged their heads and tongues over her to no avail. They could not give a positive opinion, they said. They could not depone that the panel was with child, nor could they depone that she was not. Then, said the Lord Justice and Commissioners of Justiciary, they would order the said Katherine Ogilvie to be carried back to prison, to be visited and inspected by the five midwives, with the addition of Mrs Johnson, another midwife; and a further report would be made on Monday, 3 November, at twelve o'clock before noon.

But as to Patrick Ogilvie, Lieutenant of the 89th Regiment of Foot, and brother-german to the said deceased Thomas Ogilvie, he should be carried to the Tolbooth of Edinburgh, to be fed upon bread and water only, until Wednesday 25 September, when he should be taken to the place of execution in the Grassmarket of Edinburgh. There, between the hours of two and four of the clock after noon of the same day, he should be hanged by the neck, by the hands of the common hangman, upon a gibbet, until he be dead. And thereafter, his body be delivered to Dr Alexander Munroe, Professor of Anatomy in Edinburgh, to be by him publicly dissected and anatomised.

The Nairnes had procured everything that money and influence could buy. In a cleaner, lighter room, Kitty lay on her bed and watched the September sun slant through the bars. Her linen had been washed and her hair curled. She had just breakfasted on a dish of tea and a fine pear, finding that porridge sat uneasily on her queasy stomach. And though she could hardly be happy she was comfortable.

Alone, she pondered Anne Clarke's betrayal and Alexander's villainy. They seemed, against all the laws of justice and religion, to have triumphed; and she supposed they would enjoy the proceeds together. Her uncle, Sir William Nairne, the Commissioner, had been to see her. He was full of grave news on her dowry, now Ogilvie property; and the fate of the infeftment money due to Thomas's widow, also confiscated. He was concerned, too, with the many legalities threatening an income to Kitty's coming child, since Alexander would certainly contest its paternity. But money had never worried Kitty, and the fine points of the law were beyond her grasp. What did occur to her, though she said nothing, was the possible fate of the baby after the execution. The Nairnes would not see her child want, might even cherish it in memory of her, but suppose it became an impediment or a threat to Alexander's inheritance of the East Mill estate? Would not he and Anne Clarke devise some subtle way of ridding themselves of this new burden?

So she lay puzzling out means of smoothing the baby's path, of rendering it secure, and could find none. Even at times, child as she still was herself, she would put both hands over her belly and wonder at the miracle of life. And then she went back to those May mornings in Patrick's room, and dreamed of escaping with him to Persia, and living happily ever after.

'Here's your bread and water, you scurvy villain!' bellowed the jailor. 'And here is your cousin, Miss Ogilvie, come from London to visit you!'

And he winked as Peggy Dow slipped past him, with a

basket of meat and buttered bannocks and two bottles of ale.

Patrick had worked and walked with death too long to worry about the morrow, and play-acting had always delighted him.

'Will you starve me before you string me up?' he cried, dropping silver into the outstretched hand.

'Aye! Who cares what becomes of gibbet meat?' yelled the jailor.

'Mercy, mercy!' cried Patrick, grinning. 'Give me a dram to keep my courage up!'

'To hell wi' your courage,' roared the jailor, passing over a bottle of whisky and a bottle of rum. And in a whisper he added, 'Do you need aught else, sir?'

'Peg'll fetch it this evening,' Patrick whispered back, 'and every time she comes, my laddie, your pocket will be the heavier.' Then in a despairing cry, 'Don't lock me up like an animal, my good fellow, I beg of you!'

'You're no' fit for the name of animal!' shouted the jailor.

And he slammed the door of the cell and locked it, so that the lovers should not be disturbed.

Patrick fooled pleasurably with Peggy Dow, and his friends and lawyers struggled for a respite while certain fine legal points were determined. The Captain's service to King and Country was dredged up. The evidence was raked over and re-valued. Anne Clarke's disreputable character was again smirched. The jury's reliability came in for further rough-handling. And Kitty's own stay of execution was given as a reason for delaying the Captain's walk to the gallows.

The King's most Excellent Majesty granted four respites, seven weeks all told, while Patrick played his fiddle and entertained his new mistress.

Mr M'Carty, an English barrister, published a cogent

paper on the shortcomings of the Edinburgh Courts of Justice. He pointed to the lack of proof that Thomas Ogilvie was murdered at all, since inflammation of the bowels bears a strong resemblance to death by arsenical poisoning. His publishers were then accused of contempt of court. They apologised, and were dismissed with nothing harder than a mouthful of words. And at last the legal battle ended graciously in a shower of compliments, expressions of high esteem on both sides, and the general feeling that everything possible had been done.

On 13 November 1765, Patrick Ogilvie laid down his fiddle for the last time, and emerged from the Tolbooth prison blinking at the afternoon light. His final walk had quite a military air. City Guards wielded their Lochaber axes. Magistrates bore their white staves. And Patrick, clad in his grave-clothes, walked between two clergymen like some fearful spirit raised from the dead. Lest the occasion become too military, the authorities had confined Patrick's old regiment to their present quarters at Edinburgh Castle. For it was rumoured that they disagreed rather forcibly with the verdict, and might fly in the face of justice by attempting a rescue.

But Patrick strode jauntily enough, his shoulders well back and his head high. Up the Lawnmarket, down West Bow, and so to Grassmarket where the hangman waited for their appointment. And here his step faltered at the spectacle before him.

The Grassmarket had been chosen for public execution on account of its size, and every window of the mean tenements held its complement of wagging heads and gaping mouths. These towering houses had once seen better days, as homes of the Knights Templars and the Knights of St John; and the iron cross of those orders still clung proudly to fronts and gables. But the present tenants made a

224

mockery of chivalry, and cried to Patrick to look sharp –
for the 'hangie' wanted his pear trees to bear fruit! Nor
were these the only avid watchers. People crammed the
narrow winding street of the Bow, pressed against the
guards, jostled for a good place at the foot of the scaffold,
and shouted encouragement and abuse according to their
natures.

Patrick's momentary halt had gone unnoticed as the
spectators crowded to see him, and he recovered himself
and walked on – as well as they would let him. The battle-
ments and turrets of the castle seemed to rear higher and
higher as he approached, and against their sombre background grew the gallows-tree. He had heard that they kept
this monstrous instrument in one of the vaults beneath the
Courts of Justice; fetching it out at dawn before the popu-
lace were about and taking it back at night when they were
abed. And they built it high, so that all could see the two
ladders, by means of which the hangman and the prisoner
climbed up – and only the hangman climbed down. And
from the broad black beam an empty noose swung gently,
to and fro.

Alone on the scaffold in his black velvet coat, the execu-
tioner waited – affecting not to hear the rough jokes
directed at his office. The law appointed him, the public
crowded to watch him at his work, and yet they did not like
him. He was their scapegoat, and they kept him in a social
wilderness. They employed him, and decried that employment. At a safe distance, they taunted him and bade his
victim be of good heart – but would not have missed the
show for a world of charity.

Someone *had* tried to save the Captain. Someone had
frayed the rope skilfully, the noose slipped, and Patrick
swung out and dropped – dishevelled but very much alive –
clear to the ground. From the front of the crowd several
voices shouted, 'You canna hang a man *twice*!' and a little

forest of arms reached out to pull him to safety. But the authorities thought otherwise, and scuffled him back to the scaffold, where he stood trembling and breathing raggedly while the sweat dropped from his brow and chin.

'Now, sir,' said the hangman, annoyed by this reflection on his care and efficiency, 'we'll have no more ado, if you please.'

He looked into Patrick's white face and judged how best to coax him.

'You are a soldier, sir, are you not?'

'I am,' said Patrick with difficulty.

'You have said your prayers and written an account of your innocence, I take it, sir?'

'I have.'

'And freely forgiven every person concerned in this melancholy affair?'

'Indeed I have,' said Patrick, getting his breath – and a morsel of courage – back.

'Then sir, you have done your duty – and I pray you let me do mine. Sir, a soldier carries out many an order that goes against his humanity, for the sake of his King and Country. This is my work, sir – and much akin to your own – and I have a wife and bairns to find porridge for. So pay no heed to their shouting, Captain. They would shout louder had you got away!'

'You are an honest fellow,' said Patrick slowly, looking at the plain face. 'Let us make a decent end of it.'

'Why, sir,' said the hangman cheerfully, adjusting the noose, 'there's nothing to it. And you and I – in the line of our duty – have faced death too often to be afraid of him overmuch.'

226

XXIV

The five midwives pronounced Kitty pregnant, and she was given a stay of execution until 10 March, the following year. On 21 November her advisers petitioned the court to protect her unborn child; by securing and possessing Thomas Ogilvie's estate, and by appointing its own custodian to manage that estate, until the child was of an age to inherit; and to serve this petition on Alexander Ogilvie.

'Perhaps you do not entirely understand,' said Kitty humbly, 'what danger you place my baby in, sir.'

'My dear lassie,' replied her uncle. 'You are talking nonsense. Your child's care is my first concern.'

'But Alexander Ogilvie will not heed the petition.'

'He must,' said Commissioner Nairne, 'if the law says so.'

'The law did not save me, nor the Captain,' said Kitty, and lay on her bed and turned her face to the wall.

Alexander rose to the challenge, refreshed. His melancholy situation, he said, made it uncomfortable for him to live in his natural country, and he thought of going abroad. He said he would be grateful for a factor appointed by the court to manage his brother's estate, especially as he found that Thomas had died in debt. He mentioned the extent of the debt: one thousand pounds sterling. He remarked that his mother, Lady Eastmiln, was a helpless old woman existing on an annuity of four hundred merks Scots. He added piously, that though he was very doubtful whether Thomas was the father of the expected infant, he was entirely in the hands of the Court. He said that the doubt of paternity might be strengthened by consideration of other circumstances.

'I want to see Bethia,' said Kitty, very white, as her uncle reported Alexander's reply.

'Have you not been listening to me?' he asked patiently. 'Dr Ogilvie makes no objection in the meantime.'

'Sir, I wish to see Bethia.'

'Well, so you shall, so you shall. Have you everything you need, Kitty?'

'Yes, uncle. I thank you – but let me see Bethia.'

'You must not give up hope, Kitty,' said Commissioner Nairne kindly. 'Your family has not forgotten you.'

He wondered how much her poor featherhead might be relied upon to keep a secret, but decided against confidences and patted her hand instead.

Bethia arrived, well-wrapped against the December cold; bearing a pound of tea, two jars of preserves, and a bunch of dried camomile flowers.

'Why, Bethia,' said Kitty, laughing and crying and hugging her sister, 'do not tell me you are in the same way as myself!'

'May God forbid,' cried Bethia, 'with an army of little Spaldings at my skirts and one still at the breast! No, Kitty, I have not yet lost my flesh from the last infant, that is all. But George says he would not give up an ounce of me!'

Then she was stricken by her tactlessness and remarked that Kitty had more colour.

'Bethia, come and sit by me, for I am very much afraid someone might hear us. Bethia, I have a favour to ask of you – the greatest I have ever asked of anyone. Bethia, I want *you* to have my baby when I am gone.'

228

'But you had no need to ask me, my bonnie. George and I shall bring it up as our own. George himself says so – and he sends you his heartiest and most loving greetings.'

'Bethia, I am asking more than that. I want you to pretend the baby is your own. I want you to disclaim any inheritance from the Ogilvie estate and give my child the name of Spalding.'

'Disclaim inheritance?' said Bethia, troubled. 'Well, *I* do not care, my love, if the poor bairn has not a frock to its back – but what will the gentlemen say? Your uncle, your brother, even George, are so particular with regard to money and legal business . . .'

'I am not clever,' said poor Kitty. 'They do not call me a goose-cap for nothing. But a woman finds wit from somewhere when her child is involved. I have had a long time to think, Bethia, and I know I dare leave nothing to chance. I shall not like to die for I have loved living so much. But I could die gladly if I knew my child would live. Bethia, the doctor and Anne Clarke will try to prove that this baby was not fathered by Thomas. If they do, then it lives dishonoured and penniless. If they cannot prove paternity – and I do not see how they can – then they will find some way of dispatching the child.'

'Not under my roof!' cried Bethia roundly.

'You do not know them,' said Kitty. 'And I fear them – even here, even under the sentence of death. I shall be brought to bed about the end of February or the beginning of March. About that time, Bethia, you can go to my mother's house on a visit, having given out that you are far gone with child. My uncle is a wise man, and will arrange the details, I am sure. My own baby can be reported stillborn or sickly or overlaid – God knows its chances are poor enough in all my trouble. But if it lives then they can send it to you secretly. You report at Glenkilry that you were taken suddenly in labour, and in a month or so you return to your family with your new son or daughter.'

Bethia sat for a long time, smoothing her bonnet strings and thinking.

'I shall have to set the matter right with George,' she said, 'and we must persuade the Nairnes. There will be a number of outstretched hands, too, on the way from the Tolbooth to Dunsinnan – and a jailor and a midwife to be paid and trusted.'

'Yes, I know,' said Kitty confusedly. 'It makes my head spin to think of it. And I am not clever enough, even if I were free, to do all myself. But the gentlemen are clever, and I trust you, Bethia, to be clever *for* me.'

'That lost inheritance will stick in the men's craws!'

'And my child's future will sweeten or embitter my death,' said Kitty. 'It is all you will have of me, and the thought of death is not easy.'

'I will make us some camomile tea,' said Bethia suddenly, smiling. 'It will ease your labour when the time comes – and mine!'

'Now, niece,' said Commissioner Nairne, 'this enterprise will take all the wit and courage you possess, so listen to me and keep your lips sealed – or more necks than one will be stretched. I shall speak of a Mrs MacDonald, lest the walls have ears – though God knows these walls are buttered with good Scots merks!'

'My baby?' said Kitty, propped against her pillows, waiting.

'That is another enterprise, and all is arranged as you wished. But this venture of which I am about to speak concerns a Mrs MacDonald, who is at present unable to travel, being in a condition like to your own. *Poor* Mrs MacDonald,' he continued, looking full at her, 'is parted from her family and friends and has not the money to join them. She is a widow, like yourself, expecting her first child.'

230

Kitty's mouth moved, her eyes were intent, as she re-peated the sentence, puzzled.

'Do I know her?' she asked timidly.

'You do not remember Mrs MacDonald? Oh, but you should, for she was a Miss Nairne before she married. A close relative on your father's side. I have good news of her for you. Mrs Macdonald hopes shortly to be confined, and is then travelling to Holland. She is a friend of Pieter van Dukker who painted your portrait. Do you remember him?'

Kitty was paler than ever.

'I do not think it is kind of you to remind me of another folly,' she said with dignity.

'Why, my lassie, follies can become wisdom – given time and circumstance. Had we known that poor Thomas would bring you to such a pass, and indebted and sickly to boot, we should perhaps have found Pieter van Dukker a better offer than he first appeared. But it is too late to set your cap at him now,' he said, smiling and holding her eyes, 'for Mrs MacDonald is going to him, over the water. Aye, weep away, niece, weep away. Her case is different from your own, for she has a husband to look forward to – after a troublesome time – and will be easy in Holland.'

And as Kitty wept, puzzled and hurt, he leaned forward and whispered, 'She was a pretty lassie that had a dog named Frisk!'

Kitty stared into her handkerchief, wiped her eyes, and stared at him.

'So you need fear no longer for our mutual relative, Mrs Macdonald,' said Commissioner Nairne, picking up his tricorne hat. 'She is not alone in the world, as she thought. Her good friend Mary Shiells is sitting by her – though plagued by a tooth-ache. Mary Shiells should have that tooth drawn, niece, it could gnaw for weeks. I know she keeps a shawl to her face when she goes out of doors, and looks so poorly that she can hardly be recognised. I saw a play the other night,' he continued, in a different tone, 'that would have made you merry! I wish you had been there.'

'Tell me about the play, uncle,' said Kitty, sobered and suddenly older.

'Why, it was the usual nonsense about a young woman disguising herself, first as an elderly woman and then as a young officer, and running away to be married. But we laughed ourselves hoarse, for she carried it off with such style. She was a dark young lassie, and looked very well in the uniform.'

'Did all end happily?' asked Kitty, a touch of anxiety in her tone.

'Aye, very well indeed. Some friend or other had arranged for a coach to be waiting at each stage, and a companion to see her safely to her destination.'

'But would she not meet her family again – not be reconciled to them again? Ever again, uncle?'

'Why, Kitty, she could not have everything. She had a loving man to care for her, and her youth and her bonnie looks, and a new life ahead.'

'How did the play end, uncle?'

'It left much to the imagination,' he said sturdily, 'for she had been a thoughtless and a silly lassie in the past. And yet I felt she would make a fresh beginning, become a good wife, have children at her knee. And now, niece, I must take my leave of you, for dinner is waiting.'

Kitty raised herself with difficulty and held out her hands.

'I thank you – for your goodness – to me and to my child. I thank all of you. Will you take that message from me to all who have helped me?'

'I will. And when shall you be confined?'

'In another week at the most, they say.'

'Then Bethia will have two bairns to look after, since she is also expecting a child in March.'

232

'Am I – can I – see her again?'

'She is best not to travel at such a time of year, and in her condition. Though she talks of visiting your mother Lady Nairne, who has been unwell. We all think this is not wise, but Bethia has a mind of her own.'

Kitty wept and kissed his hands, and he withdrew them gently.

'Mrs Shiells!' he called at the door. 'Mrs Ogilvie is much distressed. I pray you come and sit by her for an hour or so.'

XXV

Scots Magazine, February 1766
BIRTHS
*Feb. 27. In Edinburgh prison, Mrs Ogilvie, of a
daughter.*

Scots Magazine, March 1766

On Monday, March 10, the day to which the diet in
the case of Mrs Ogilvie was adjourned, the High Court
of Justiciary having met, it appeared, by evidence of a
physician and two midwives, that she was still so weak
from her recent delivery, that she could not be brought
into court. The Lords therefore adjourned the diet till
the Monday thereafter, the Court to meet that day in the
Tolbooth of Edinburgh, when it was expected sentence
of death would have been pronounced.

'How is the lady, Mrs Shiells?' asked the jailor, as he
looked out his keys the following Saturday evening.

'Ask me rather how *I* am!' cried the midwife, 'for my
tooth plagues me until I could screech out! Ah! The poor
lady must be indulged a little, Mr Pringle. She is weak as
yet from her confinement – only a fortnight last Thursday –
and the child is but sickly. I pray you, since I am with her,
to leave the door open for a little air.'

'Well, I should not, Mrs Shiells, but as the poor lady is
abed...'

'And hardly able to raise her head, Mr Pringle. I keep
my ladies abed for six weeks after the birth, before I will so
much as let them set foot to the ground. But they will have

her half-fainting at the scaffold, more shame on them. Oh, sweet Lord, my tooth, my tooth! Thank you kindly, Mr Pringle. The lady will be grateful for a breath of air. And how do you find yourself, my lady? But poorly, yes. But poorly. Look, Mr Pringle, she can scarcely raise her head! And how is my bonnie bairnie, then? I will but set the door open an inch or so, Mr Pringle, for fear of a draught on the bed. I thank you, Mr Pringle. You will see me in half an hour or so, when I have set all to rights.'

'Now, my lady,' she whispered, as Kitty sat up, 'dress yourself in this uniform as speedily as may be. Though what will happen to your insides, rising so soon, I dare not think!'

'It is a good thing I do not put on flesh like my sister Bethia,' said Kitty, and she giggled as adventure beckoned. 'I could not get into these breeches, else!'

'I have never seen a lady in breeches,' whispered Mrs Shiells, rocking the fretful baby, and watching the door. 'You look fine, Mistress Ogilvie. You are narrow in the hips – which is why this bairn gave you such a tussle! Now set your hat well forward and cocked bravely – and walk with a long stride.'

Cheeks flushed, eyes bright, Kitty swaggered about the cell for practice; and gave the midwife a wink that made her laugh and clap one hand to her mouth. Then in another moment she was on her knees, weeping with grief and weakness, burying her face in the baby's small body.

'Now, my lassie,' said Mrs Shiells, 'you canna have the whole world! Thank God for honest friends and your life. The bairn will be in good hands, and I'll take care of her as though she were my own until a week tomorrow.'

'Is that when Bethia . . .?'

'Aye, Mrs Spalding should be confined soon after. But I must watch for this one. She is no' so strong and might be overlaid! Now compose yourself, my lady, for you must be off. Mr Pringle is looking the other way, and there is my mantle and shawl on the chair. My back will be turned so that I don't know when you leave. I'll sleep on your bed tonight, and mind the bairn. They'll no' find out you're gone until tomorrow forenoon when I am expected again.'

'Will you – you will not get into trouble, on my account, Mrs Shiells?'

'Why no, my lassie. You offered me a glass of wine and dosed it with laudanum and stole my mantle and shawl. I'll be found groaning on the floor with a headache on top of the toothache! And now, lassie, wrap yourself up well. It's close on seven of the clock. Aye, give me a kiss, that's thanks enough. And kiss the bairnie, too.'

Kitty took her daughter in her arms for the last time, smothering its small cramped fingers and soft wet cheeks. Then laid her gently in Mrs Shiell's lap again.

'I shall not see either of you again,' she said quietly, 'but I shall pray for you both as long as I live. May God bless and keep you both.'

She covered her uniform with the long mantle, pulled the shawl round her face, and groaned.

'Is that you, Mrs Shiells?' said Mr Pringle, as she closed the door behind her, still muttering and moaning. 'You need a dram to ease that tooth of yours!'

He looked at her as he locked the cell, making a great rattle with the keys. And she groaned reply.

'Good night to you, then, Mrs Shiells. I'll see you tomorrow forenoon.'

The turnpike stair echoed with her lament, and the keepers cried abuse and encouragement as the old howdie descended.

'Turn your hand!' came the order from the inner turnkey.

The outer door of the Tolbooth prison swung weightily upon its iron hinges.

'Begone with you – you howling old Jezebel!' cried the outer turnkey, and clapped her on the back as she whimpered past him.

She was free. She wanted to laugh, to dance, to cast Mary Shiells's cloak to the ground. But she had learned in bitter sorrow to keep her head. So she shuffled slowly towards Parliament Stairs where her uncle's house reared in sombre grandeur. Sir William Nairne himself opened the door when she knocked softly, and hurried her inside.

'Down here,' he whispered, and held the candlestick high that she might see her way down the cellar steps. 'Let's look at you, Kitty. Aye, you'll do, you'll do. You make as pretty an officer as ever I set eyes on! Now listen to me. My clerk, James Brenner, will be here in an hour with a post-chaise, to escort you to Dover. You will find food and drink on the table, here, and a candle to eat by. Sup as well as you can, for you will stop only to change horses. Give me the good Mrs Shiell's mantle and shawl to burn. No one must find *them*. And remember this, your life and all our reputations depend on your behaviour. If you are stopped you are Lieutenant O'Connor, a distant relative of James Brenner's wife, an Irishman on his way to join his regiment. Speak as little as may be, and gruffly. Mr Brenner will see you as far as Calais, to the *Lion d'Argent* inn. And there Meinheer van Duker will be waiting.'

Her courage failed her.

'Suppose,' said Kitty, 'that we do not care for each other, after all these years? So much has happened to me – Thomas, my baby, and the Captain.'

Sir William hardened, for her own sake and his.

'Katherine, Pieter van Dukker has been acquainted with the *facts* of the case – not the scandalmongering, the *facts*. He believes you, as we do, to have been wrongfully and maliciously accused. You go to him as a widow with no encumbrance and a dowry. He is offering you the security

237

of his home, and will wait until you feel yourself ready to accept him as a husband. There is no forcing you, Katherine, but you would do well to accept his name and his protection. For we have now done all we can, and perhaps more than we safely should. You will be on your own in a foreign country for the rest of your life. Come, lassie,' he said, as her childish face stared out from beneath the gallantly cocked hat, 'you were fond enough of the man to harry *us* with his intentions, barely four years ago!'

'I loved Patrick,' she said, all pretence gone. 'I loved him. If he was with me now, escaping even to Persia, I should be content.'

'He would not be with you now, even if he were alive and free,' said Sir William, 'since his easy fancy turned to a woman called Margaret Dow. They entertained each other for some months in the Tolbooth, and that villain Alexander has recently formed a bigamous marriage with the wench – which will do him no good in the eyes of the law. I had thought you would have heard.'

'I heard – but did not believe . . .'

'Then I must corroborate the news. And I will give you some excellent advice, seldom phrased so brutally, but for that you must forgive me, since time presses and I have your welfare dearly to heart. A woman's life can only be as good as her man makes it. With Thomas Ogilvie you led a sickly, cloistered existence. With his brother Patrick you were endangered, made light of and betrayed. But Meinheer van Dukker cares enough for you to wipe out your past, make safe your present, and offer you a happier future. No man could do more, Katherine, and few would do as much. The rest is for you to make or break.'

'I thank you,' said Kitty, in honesty.

He bowed and took up his candlestick.

'We shall have no time for farewells when James Brenner

comes, and I must be upstairs and ready with my story should they discover you are missing. Have you any message for your family?'

'My love and thanks to all of them, all of them. I should – if no one objects – like my daughter to be christened Katherine.' Sir William inclined his head. 'And will you tell Mamma that I am very sorry – and ask her to kiss Frisk on the nose for me?'

He bent and kissed her cheek gently, and then walked slowly up the cellar steps and bolted the door behind him.

She sat at the table for a long time, wiping her eyes. And she wrapped the food in a napkin, since she could not eat it.

Mr Brenner was not likely to forget the next four and a half days. A sober young man, well aware of the risks he was taking for his employer, he fulfilled his duty admirably but with some trepidation.

The wheels of the post-chaise gathered speed, drawing them faster and faster away from Edinburgh, going at a gallop through Haddington, pausing only to change horses at each stage. They rode day and night. Berwick, Newcastle, Durham, and down the London road, heading for Dover as fast as hooves could fly and a whip urge on the lathered steeds.

'Mrs Ogilvie, I beg of you,' cried Mr Brenner, as the chaise swung from side to side, and his teeth rattled in his head. 'I beg you to control your levity, madam. I am afraid we shall be noticed, and so discovered!'

Her head light with wine, her stomach empty, her heart sore, Kitty clasped her arms about her body and bent double with hysteria. And as she laughed and cried, and he scolded, her face was white and childish under the officer's hat.

At Dover, no ship was sailing, and they hired a hackney coach and went back on their tracks as far as Billingsgate. There at Gravesend they boarded a boat and were taken across to Calais for the sum of eight guineas. By this time, Mr Brenner reckoned, the authorities would be after them in full cry, and lest the boatman be suspicious enough to inform on them he hit upon a pretty deception. He paid the man a guinea a day, to remain four days in Calais harbour, with instructions to leave without them if they should not return in that time. Long before the boatman saw Gravesend again Kitty was established in the *Lion d'Argent*, and Mr Brenner well on his way home to Edinburgh.

'Sir William,' the messenger whispered, begging a word aside, 'Mrs Ogilvie is escaped from the Tolbooth last evening, about seven of the clock they reckon. But it was not discovered until the afternoon, and I am sent post-haste to tell you.'

'Good God!' cried Sir William. 'What are they about? I must see the city magistrates at once!'

He became cool and formidable, explaining briefly to his guests.

'They must issue the news imediately,' he said, 'and offer a reward. A hundred guineas, I think, would be a sufficient inducement to recapture Mrs Ogilvie.'

And looking round at the faces which struggled between shock and approval, he added, 'Mrs Ogilvie may be my niece, sirs, but I have a public duty to perform which must in no way be imperilled by private feelings.'

They agreed, behind his back, that the Commissioner's attitude might be admirable, but his heart was akin to the granite rock upon which the city had been founded.

In a private parlour at the *Lion d'Argent* Kitty sat waiting for the door to open. Her hair was newly curled and

240

caught up by a ribbon. Her velvet gown was brushed smooth. Her hands were folded meekly in her lap. Outwardly, she seemed ready for this latest meeting. Inwardly, she was afraid.

'Madam,' said Pieter van Dukker, bowing, 'I am honoured to renew our friendship.'

His painter's eye approved the dark glossy hair and crimson gown. 'I am amazed how – well – you look, madam.'

She had quite forgotten how charmingly his tongue stumbled over the foreign language, and the smoothness of his butter-coloured head and beard. She smiled and bowed, unable to speak, and he stood there awkwardly and turned his feathered hat round and round in his big hands.

'How was your journey, madam?' he asked, keeping to the formalities, since they seemed safest.

'The journey?' Kitty cried, in disbelief.

That awful journey, in hysteria and hunger and thirst, in discomfort and terror; and the final moment at Dover when their plans had to be reversed, and both she and the Edinburgh authorities were headed for London. And James Brenner doing his duty, and staring at her like a shot rabbit.

'The journey was tolerable, Meinheer van Dukker,' she began, but could not go on.

He watched her laugh, in utter astonishment, and as suddenly joined in. But she was near tears again, swinging from mood to mood with fear and excitement; and he patted her hands and proffered a fine large linen handkerchief, and ventured to put his arm round her as she wept.

'Now, now,' he said gently, slipping into his own tongue, 'everything will be well with us, Katherine. Cry as much as you please. Everything passes. Everything passes.'

She did not understand what he was saying, but translated the tone and his expression into comfort. So she wept

241

a little longer, for the pleasure of it, and then looked cheerfully enough at him, ready to begin again.

Scots Magazine, March 1766
DEATHS
Mar. 23. Mrs Ogilvie of Eastmiln's infant daughter.

XXVI

CRIMINAL LETTERS: HIS MAJESTY'S
ADVOCATE AGAINST ALEXANDER OGILVIE.
'... That the said Alexander Ogilvie, in so far as, He,
after being joined in holy marriage with Anne Rattray,
daughter to James Rattray porter in Edinburgh, by Mr
James Grant late minister of the Episcopal congregation
in Skinner's Close in Edinburgh, upon the thirteenth day
of January, one thousand seven hundred and sixty-five
years, and after having cohabited with the said Anne
Rattray as his lawful wife for some considerable time,
did during the life of the said Anne Rattray, who still
lives, and without being divorced from her, enter into a
second marriage with Margaret Dow daughter of the deceased James Dow of Bandeath, late a lieutenant in the
Royal Highlanders, the ceremony of which second marriage was performed by Mr John Warden one of the ministers of the Canongate, upon the twenty-fourth day of
February last, one thousand seven hundred and sixty-
six: And the said Alexander Ogilvie did, after the marriage, cohabit with the said Margaet Dow as his wife
... being found proven by the verdict of an Assize ... he
ought to be decerned, by decreet and sentence of Our
said High Court of Justiciary, to suffer the punishment
directed by the statute before recited, to the terror of
others from committing the like offence in time coming.'

Fourth day of August 1766
   'Alexander Ogilvie Compeared and gave in a petition,
craving Banishment, the pray of which was granted and

he was accordingly Banished from Scotland for Seven years, under the usual Certifications.'

Alexander looked up from his tankard and realised that nothing more could surprise him. There, as neat and purposeful as ever, stood Anne Clarke. He pushed the oyster wench from his knee, gave her sixpence, and told her to find another customer. And she, thick-limbed and coarse-featured, swore at him for a dull dog as she pulled down her skirts, and stared at Anne Clarke before moving away.

'Sit you down, Anne,' said Alexander, 'and tell me what brings you to an oyster tavern, to a twice-married man who has lost his fortune!'

'What brought me to you in the first place, I suppose,' she replied calmly, as she wiped the stool with her handkerchief, and settled her gown. 'I thought you might have need of me.'

'I have that slut Rattray, and bonnie Peg.'

'It is only a friend that can help you now, Alex, not a mistress.'

'But you were my mistress, too,' he mumbled, and smiled into his porter.

'And the only one who cared to wash your linen from the look of you. You fool!' she cried. 'I did *everything* for you. Lied and poisoned for you. Gave the estate into your hands. And you threw it all away for an impudent, yellow-haired baggage that had opened her legs for your brother first!'

The corbie had suffered. His black hair fell over his forehead, his clothes were stained and filthy, rims of dirt showed beneath his fingernails.

'I have a mind to take you by the neck and scrub you sober under the yard pump!' said Anne fiercely. 'By God, I would walk to the ends of the earth for a wicked man, but I would not waste spit on a weak one. Why did you marry Peggy Dow, Alex?'

244

'You had thought I would marry *you*?' he asked maliciously. 'Why, Miss Clarke, you are a shade too long in the tooth for my taste, and had served your turn.'

Her head prevailed over her heart, as always, and instead of striking him she leaned further forward and searched his face.

'Never mind the sottish abuse,' she said coolly. 'I was the best mistress you ever had, and your only friend, and you know it. I could show those two sluts of yours a trick or two with a man, even now. And you know that, too, or you would not be sitting here with your hand under an oyster wench's petticoat!'

He was silent, treading an obsessively turning mill that no amount of ale could render motionless.

'Patrick had everything,' he cried suddenly. 'He had my birthright, Annie. My mother loved him. Everybody loved him. Even in the Tolbooth at the end he had them dancing and singing to his blasted fiddle. Even the jailor was sorry when he died, and the hangman drank to his salvation. He went abroad, Annie, and saw the world, dressed in a scarlet uniform. Women saw him smile and listened to his nonsense and shared his bed. He wooed pretty silly Kitty away from our brother, and got a child on her, and *she* loved him too. He would have inherited the estate, if we had let him be.

'And when they hanged him, Annie, they had to keep his regiment under lock and key to stop them from cheating the gallows. And after, the crowd cried that he was a brave gentleman, and had been wrongfully convicted.'

'But we beat him,' she said, watching intently.

Alexander became boisterous.

'Yes, we took away his inheritance from him,' he cried jubilantly. 'We had him cast into prison, and set up in the Court with his Kitty as a murderer. Ah, they stretched his neck, Annie, and gave his body to Dr Munroe. I was there

245

when the doctor opened it, Annie, and that was a fine sight. And best of all, I stole his mistress, Peggy Dow, and married her. So now I have everything that was his, except his travelling. And even that I shall have, Annie, for I am going abroad. I shall see the native girls walking the shores of Malabar with their breasts bared to the sun, even as Patrick did. I shall see India and Persia, and nothing that he has known shall be strange to me.'

'Is this ale-talk, or fact?'

He looked at her with tipsy satisfaction.

'I am booked on the merchant ship *Chance*, as ship's surgeon under Captain Cheesman. And we sail for the West Indies next month.'

'And what of your wives?'

'Peggy is with child,' he said, 'and has gone down to London to live with a relative of hers, until we are settled. He is a baker in Whitechapel. As for that slut Rattray, she may do as she pleases.'

'She is in poor health,' said Anne.

'Then that is good news, for I can marry Peggy Dow in earnest, and make a decent woman of her and give a name to her bastard.'

'Are you truly infatuated with Peggy Dow, or do her charms spring from the fact that she was your brother's mistress?' Anne asked sharply.

'I tell you this, Miss Clarke,' said Alexander deliberately, 'she gives me rest and I am weary. She is young and thoughtless, and I feel older than any living thing upon this earth. She does not weigh me down with claims of love and friendship. Nor can she bind me to her with crimes that make me start awake, and cry out in the night, and jump at a shadow on the wall. You and I have been too close, Miss Clarke, and know each other too well for comfort. I shall ply my trade as ship's surgeon and make my voyages, to sip at the cup my brother snatched from me. And then I shall

246

come home to Peg and the child. And I shall be the most respectable and law-abiding citizen that any honest government could wish.'

'You are pursuing a sick fancy,' said Anne, 'and one without purpose.'

'I have my own purpose,' said Alexander wearily. 'So get you gone, Miss Clarke, and leave me to my drink and my wench.'

She rose, and smoothed her gown, looking suddenly frail and old. Some remnant of interest or conscience stirred him.

'What will *you* do, Annie?' he asked, dropping into his former way of talking to her. 'You seem to have got nothing out of this at all.'

Cheated, portionless, and yet undaunted, she replied, 'I shall survive. Good night to you, Alex.'

Anne Rattray died, and when the *Chance* docked at Tilbury Alexander married Peggy Dow, and helped to move her and their daughter from the baker's home in Whitechapel to a cottage in Middlesex. His crimes were now erased, in the eyes of the law, and he could have settled in England. But forces stronger and deeper than the law drove him. He watched the ships ride at anchor in the Thames, and brooded, and went abroad again. But before he left he made his will. He sold the East Mill estate to another James Rattray, through trustees, and banked the money. This he left, with all his worldly goods, to Margaret his wife and Margaret his daughter – with the proviso that if Peg should marry again her share would be transferred to little Peg. As executors he named Thomas Rattray, writer to the Court of Sessions in Edinburgh, and that Alexander Dow, baker, who had first offered them shelter in London. This will was signed and witnessed on 14 March 1768, before he resumed his restless voyaging.

Peggy Dow grew weary of waiting. A prettier cottage in the village of West Thurrock in Essex, between Purfleet and Tilbury, did nothing to ease her semi-widowhood; and when Alexander came home in broken health, in the summer of 1770 her impatience turned to desperation. He had sought to gain all Patrick's experiences, and had similarly contracted malaria.

He sweated and froze, shivered and tossed; and Peggy sighed and grumbled and nursed him as little as possible. As he grew worse, she grew petulant and then vindictive, and bewailed her wasted youth and Patrick's early death.

'For he was a *proper* gentleman!' she cried, slopping more water on to Alexander's shirt front than down his parched throat, 'and would not have brought me to such a pass! And I am still young and hearty.'

'Well, see me dead first, and then plight your troth elsewhere,' said Alexander, in a ghost of his old manner. 'But I wish to God you could nurse me in some comfort!'

'What would you have?' cried Peggy. 'There was six leeches laid to your chest only this morning, and your blood let yesterday, and a dose of Ipsum Salt on Monday, and a portion of chopped nettles and raw white of egg on your forehead this minute – which I made with my own hands!'

'A dram of whisky,' said Alexander, with truth, 'would serve me better.'

'Let it not be said,' cried Peggy, arms akimbo, 'that I grudged trouble or expense. The doctor's fee is five pounds, and I have bought a bottle of everything that might ease you. There is *Dr Brodum's Botanical Syrup*, and *Cornwell's Oriental Vegetable Cordial*, and *Godbold's Vegetable Balsam*, and *Daffie's Elixir*, on the table by your bed. And has not Mistress Dow herself sent over a bottle of tar-water and tincture of rhubarb?'

'Aye, you are killing me with cures,' said Alexander wryly. 'Could you not make me some beef broth? Can you

248

not get me a nurse?'

'We have no money for nurses!' said Peggy. Then she was malicious. 'But there is an old flame of yours would come if I sent for her, that has haunted me these four years. Anne Clarke keeps house for a clerical gentleman in Shoreditch.'

'Anne here?' he asked, muddled.

'Aye, she followed us to Whitechapel, though I did not know until long after. At first I was afraid she might slip me a dose, as she did your brother, and I told my cousin so. But he spoke to her one morning, as she was buying bread from his shop, and said that if any harm came to me or the child that he would see her hanged for it. And he told her to keep her distance or he would have her hounded from any employment she took. And I think she was afraid,' said Peggy lightly, 'for she did not come again, and my cousin keeps an eye on her. But then she is quite old, near forty, and must earn her living. So she is very quiet and respectable these days, and well thought of in her neighbourhood.'

He had raised his head to listen, but fell back on the pillows.

'No, do not send for her,' he said slowly. 'I have made more claims on her that I had any right to.'

But Peggy sat, hands folded, and listened to his ravings with only half an ear, for it seemed to her that she might be rid of a sick husband without further trouble. So when he fell asleep and was quiet, she called a neighbour in to watch by him, and put on her bonnet and cloak.

'I would not trouble you, Miss Roberts,' she said sweetly, 'but my poor husband has been asking for a cousin of his that lives in Shoreditch, and I am fetching her. Oh, and Miss Roberts, his mind is going. So if you hear him talk of poisonings and hangings and the like – pray take no notice. He has lived aboard ship with thieves and murderers for company, these four years past, and I think it has affected his reason as well as his health.'

The neighbour sat by him, and heard the ramblings of more wickedness than she had thought possible, either on the face of the earth or the waters of the world.

'I cannot stay for a great length of time,' said Anne, fastening her cloak with fingers that shook, 'but I can come for a few hours every day, and sit up at night, provided I am back for breakfast in the morning.'

'Oh, it is the nights that weary me, Miss Clarke,' said Peggy, deciding that casual friendship would answer her purpose better than hostility. 'And he has been asking for you.'

She was inclined to be annoyed when Anne Clarke emptied the medicines into the garden and opened the windows, but she held her tongue. In the next few days she had only to care for her daughter and herself, since Anne rolled up her sleeves and scrubbed out the cottage, and set a bowl of beer and coarse sugar to catch the beetles, as well as making Alexander comfortable. At the end of the week Peggy retreated to the baker's house in Whitechapel, taking the child with her, and begged Anne, before she went, to be sure and send if Alexander got worse.

'For he is better in your care than mine, Miss Clarke, but he is my husband. Therefore, if he is dying I will come.'

'So here I am,' said Anne gently, as he woke. 'I have spoke to my employer, who is a Christian gentleman, and he urges me to stay with you as long as I am needed. And to see you well again.'

He was silent, turning over the last betrayal and the last undeserved gift of human kindness.

'There is something sadly wrong with me, Annie,' he said at length. 'The fever should be intermittent. Patrick suffered similar bouts, but was well enough in between. And I do not know of anyone that died of it. But I am dying, Annie, so it must be some other illness plagues me. She has not poisoned me, has she?'

'No,' said Anne drily. 'She has neither the guts nor the wits to plan such a thing.'

'And the doctor has said nothing, and there is nothing in my knowledge of medicine to tell me what it is. But I lose flesh daily, Annie, and am weaker daily, and have a great pain in my bowels.'

He watched her making a bread poultice, and smiled.

'So it is just you and me in the end, Annie,' he observed. 'And yet, though Peg was a silly wench, I loved her yellow hair!'

'She would do well to wash it!' said Anne tartly.

'You were always cleanly in person, Annie. Did you see my daughter?'

Anne paused, and was tempted to say that the child's brown curly hair reminded her of Patrick. But she swallowed on temptation.

'A pretty, lively lassie,' she said charitably. 'More like an Ogilvie than a Dow.'

'So I always thought,' he cried, animated, and was pleased. 'Annie,' he said, 'will you be with me at the end – for they are waiting and I am much afraid of them?'

She was quite still, facing the shadows in the room. Then in her matter-of-fact way she turned up his nightshirt and made the poultice easy on his belly.

'I shall be here,' she said.

His head moved restlessly from side to side.

'As I grow weaker, they grow stronger,' he said, and began to mutter. 'Why, there is Patrick fiddling in the flames of Hell, and Thomas warming his hands at the fire. And my mother sits – there, Annie, do you see her? She taps on the floor with her stick and watches me suffer, and she will not relent so much as a muscle.'

'There is no one,' said Anne stoutly, but held his hand

and looked all about her.

'And Kate Campbell, that was sent off for theft, Annie, and walked those many miles. She left her bastard in the care of the miller and his wife, they say. And all she knew was that she must go back to Ireland, and the poor fool did not know where Ireland was, and thought to cross two seas to reach it. Light the candles, Annie.'

She sat by him and held his wandering hands, and closed her eyes as he dragged her roughshod through the labyrinths of their crimes, and foretasted her own death – unless God and circumstances were kinder.

Towards three o'clock in the morning he threw aside the bedclothes and, in spite of all Anne's strength, pushed her away and got unsteadily to his feet.

'Annie!' he cried in a great voice, for he did not know her. 'Don't leave me, Annie!'

'I am here,' she said. 'I am with you, Alex.'

He hid his face in her shoulder and she put her arms about him like a shield, and watched steadfastly as the long-dead came forward to claim him.

At dawn, Martha Stewart woke, hearing her mother's stick rap peremptorily on the floor. For a moment she felt herself to be a harrassed girl again, back at East Mill house under a maternal dictatorship. Then she remembered her status as Andrew's wife, and the dependence of an old woman who had no roof of her own. So she put on her shawl and found her slippers and went into the adjoining room.

'You were long enough, miss,' said Lady Eastmiln sourly, feeling it incumbent upon her to be disagreeable.

'And you are early enough, mother!' Martha commented. 'It is scarcely five of the clock. Did you want your tea so soon?'

'It is not that,' said Lady Eastmiln. 'I had something to

252

say to you, since I have no one else to say it to – though you are a good daughter,' she added, out of fairness. 'I had a letter from Miss Anne Clarke, dated the third of September, to say that Alexander was buried on that day in St Clements Parish Church, West Thurrock.'

'Well, I had thought you would tell me in your own good time,' said Martha drily. 'For Andrew and I had wondered who would write to you from London! Is that why you woke me?'

'Only in part, miss!' said Lady Eastmiln, very dignified, trying to put her woollen stockings on. 'I wished to tell you that I am not grieved.'

'Are you not?' said Martha gently.

'No, miss. He has got his deserts. Do you remember what the pamphlets said of me, when he was lying in the Tolbooth convicted of bigamy? They said that I, as the mother of the unfortunate family, was still alive, but luckily was formed by nature of too obdurate and unfeeling a disposition to be much affected by the catastrophies of my family.'

'I remember,' said Martha. 'And I thought them very wrong to say so.'

'No, miss, they were right! So be quick with my dish of tea!'

'I do not think you so unfeeling and obdurate as you would care to believe yourself,' Martha observed, going obediently to the door.

The old head was erect, the shoulders held back as well as arthritis would allow them, the old eyes fierce and full of tears.

'Then you are as big as fool as I have always taken you to be!' cried Lady Eastmiln, and stared very hard out of the window.

'That was not why you called me. Have you been lying awake all night over the letter from Miss Clarke?'

'Aye,' said Lady Eastmiln, conquered at last, 'and thinking of the time when I was young and bonnie, and married a gallant gentleman and bore him five fine sons – and now I have outlived them and my usefulness.'

She was too proud to wipe away the tears that ran down her cheeks, and Martha too kind to seem to notice them.